Telling the Map

△
◁ ▷
▽

Telling the Map

Stories

▽
▷   ◁
△

Christopher Rowe

Small Beer Press
Easthampton, MA

Telling the Map: Stories copyright © 2017 by Christopher Rowe. All rights reserved.
christopherrowe.net

Small Beer Press
150 Pleasant Street #306
Easthampton, MA 01027
smallbeerpress.com
weightlessbooks.com
info@smallbeerpress.com

Distributed to the trade by Consortium.

Library of Congress Cataloging-in-Publication Data

Names: Rowe, Christopher, author.
Title: Telling the map : stories / Christopher Rowe.
Description: Easthampton, MA : Small Beer Press, 2017.
Identifiers: LCCN 2016059750 (print) | LCCN 2017001034 (ebook) | ISBN
   9781618731326 (softcover) | ISBN 9781618731333
Subjects: | BISAC: FICTION / Science Fiction / Short Stories. | FICTION /
   Fantasy / Short Stories. | FICTION / Short Stories (single author). |
   GSAFD: Science fiction. | Fantasy fiction.
Classification: LCC PS3618.O8728 A6 2017 (print) | LCC PS3618.O8728 (ebook) |
   DDC 813/.6--dc23
LC record available at https://lccn.loc.gov/2016059750

First edition 1 2 3 4 5 6 7 8 9

Text set in Centaur 12pt.

Printed on 30% recycled paper by the Maple Press in York, PA.
Author photo © 2017 by Sarah Jane Sanders.
Cover illustration © 2017 by Kathleen Jennings (kathleenjennings.com)

Contents

The Contrary Gardener   I

Another Word for Map is Faith   23

Jack of Coins   39

The Unveiling   5I

Nowhere Fast   65

Two Figures in a Landscape Between Storms   8I

Gather   83

The Force Acting on the Displaced Body   97

The Voluntary State   I07

The Border State   I49

This book is dedicated, with admiration,
to Terry Bisson and to Jack Womack.
"A prophet is not without honor but in his own country."

The Contrary Gardener

K ay Lynne wandered up and down the aisles of the seed library dug out beneath the county extension office. Some of the rows were marked with glowing orange off-limits fungus, warning the unwary away from spores and thistles that required special equipment to handle, which Kay Lynne didn't have, and special permission to access, which she would *never* have, if her father had anything to say about it, and he did.

It was the last Friday before the first Saturday in May, the day before Derby Day and so a week from planting day, and Kay Lynne had few ideas and less time for her Victory Garden planning. Last year she had grown a half-dozen varieties of tomatoes, three for eating and three for blood transfusions, but she didn't like to repeat herself. Given that she tended to mumble when she talked, not liking to repeat herself made Kay Lynne a quiet gardener.

She paused before a container of bright pink corn kernels, their preprogrammed color coming from insecticides and fertilizers and not from any varietal ancestry. Kay Lynne didn't like to grow corn. It grew so high that it cast her little cottage in shadow if she planted it on the side of the house that would see it grow at all. Besides, corn was cheap, and more than that, easy—just about any gardener could grow corn, and a lot of them did.

There were always root vegetables. A lot of utility to those, certainly, and excellent trade goods for the army-supply clerks who would start combing the markets as soon as the earliest spring greens were in. Rootwork was complicated, and meant having nothing to market through the whole long summer, which in turn meant not having to go to the markets for months yet, which was a good thing in Kay Lynne's view.

She considered the efficacy of beets and potatoes, and the various powers carrots held when they were imaginatively programmed and carefully grown. Rootwork had been a particular specialty of her run-off mother, and so would have the added benefit of warding her father away from the cottage, which he visited entirely too often for Kay Lynne's comfort.

It would be hard work. That spoke for the idea, too.

She strode over to the information kiosk and picked up the speaking tube that led to the desks of the agents upstairs.

"I need someone to let me into the root cellars," she said.

Blinking in the early morning light, Kay Lynne left the extension office and made her way to the bus stop, leaning forward under the weight of her burdensacks. The canvas strap that held them together was draped across her shoulders and, while she thought she had done an exacting job in measuring the root cuttings on each side so that the weight would be evenly distributed, she could already tell that there was a slight discrepancy, which was the worst kind of discrepancy, the very bane of Kay Lynne's existence, the tiny kind of problem that no one ever bothered to fix in the face of more important things. She could hear her father's voice: "Everything is not equally important. You never learned that."

The extension office was on the south side, close enough to downtown to be on a regular bus route, but far enough to not fall under the shadows of the looming skyscrapers Kay Lynne could now clearly see as she waited at the shelter. Slogans crawled all over the buildings, leaping from one granite face to another when they were too wordy, though, of course, to Kay Lynne's mind they were all too wordy. "The Union is strong," read one in red, white, and blue firework fonts. "The west front is only as strong as the home front. Volunteer for community service!" The only slogan that stayed constant was the green-and-brown-limned sentence circling the tallest building of all. "Planting is in EIGHT days."

A shadow fell on the street and Kay Lynne looked up to see a hot-air balloon tacking toward the fairgrounds. The great balloon festival was the next morning in the hours before the Derby, and the balloon-ists had been arriving in numbers all week. It was part of the Derby Festival, the madness-tinged days that took over the city each spring, at the exact time when people should be at their most serious. The timing never failed to dismay Kay Lynne.

The Stars and Stripes were displayed proudly on the balloon, and also a ring of green near the top that indicated that it was made from one hundred percent non-recycled materials. It was wholly new, and so an act of patriotism. Kay Lynne would never earn such a ring as a gardener; careful economy was expected of her and her cohort.

The balloon passed on, skirting the poplar copse that stood behind the bus stop, and was quickly obscured by the trees. Kay Lynne's cottage was northwest of the fairgrounds, and the winds most of the balloons would float on blew above her home. She would prob-ably see it again tomorrow, whether she wanted to or not.

Belching its sulfur fumes, the bus arrived, and Kay Lynne climbed aboard.

The bus driver was a Mr. Lever #9, Kay Lynne's favorite model. They were programmed with thirty-six phrases of greeting, observation (generally about the weather), and small talk, in addition to whatever announcements were required for their particular route. A Mr. Lever #9 never surprised you with what it said or did. They made Kay Lynne comfortable with public transportation.

"Good . . . morning, citizen," it said cheerily as Kay Lynne boarded. "Sunny and mild!"

Kay Lynne nodded politely to the driver and took the seat immediately behind it. The bus was sparsely occupied, with just a few tardy students bound for the university sharing the conveyance. To a one, their noses were buried in appallingly thick textbooks.

"Next stop is Central Avenue," said the driver. "Central Avenue! Home of the Downs! Home of the Derby!"

The bus ground its brakes and came to a stop along the Third Street Road next to the famous twin spires. A crowd of shorts-wearing families hustled onto the bus, painfully obvious in their out-of-townedness and clucking at one another loudly. "Infield," they said, and "First thing in the morning," and "Odds on favorite."

Kay Lynne loved the 'Ville, but she was no fan of its most famous day. She appreciated horses for their manure and for the way they conveyed policemen and drew the downtown trolleys, and she usually even bought a calendar of central state views that showed the Horse Lord Holdings with their limestone fences and endless green hills, but truth be told, she usually waited until February to buy the calendars, when they were cheapest, and when they were the only ones left. People in the 'Ville liked horses, but they didn't like the Horse Lords.

"Grade Lane," said the bus driver. "Transfer to the fairgrounds trolley," and then a whirring sounded and it added in a slightly different timbre, "See the balloons!"

All the tourists filed off happily chattering about the balloon festival and the next day's card of racing at the Downs, and Kay Lynne breathed a happy sigh to see them go.

The bus driver said, "They get to me, too, sometimes. But we're more alike than we are different."

Kay Lynne turned around to see if anyone else on the bus had heard. Only the reading students remained, all in the rear seats, all still staring down.

"Excuse me?" Kay Lynne said. She had never directly addressed a Mr. Lever of any model before. If there was a protocol, she didn't know.

"Sunny and mild!" said the bus driver.

Kay Lynne considered whether to pursue the Mr. Lever #9's unexpected, almost certainly unprogrammed, comment. It had not turned its head to face her when it spoke—if it had spoken, and now Kay Lynne was beginning to allow that its *not* having spoken was at least within the realm of possibility—and usually the spherical heads would make daisy-wheel turns to face the passenger compartment whenever speaking to a passenger was required, or rather, *done.* She supposed that they were never strictly speaking *required* to speak.

This was a thorny problem, and Kay Lynne reminded herself that she did not have authorization for thorns. She set her feet more firmly either side of her burdensacks, retrieved the pamphlet of helpful information that the agents had given her on programming root vegetables, and willfully ignored the bus driver for the rest of the trip.

Kay Lynne loved her cottage and its all-around garden plot more than any other place in the world. It was her home and her livelihood and her sanctuary all in one. So when she saw that the front yard plots had been tilled while she was away on her morning errand, she was aghast, even though she was positive she knew who had invaded her property and given unasked-for aid in preparing the grounds. Her father was probably still poking around in the back, maybe still running his obnoxiously loud rotor-tiller, maybe nosing through her potting shed for hand tools he didn't have with him on his obnoxiously loud truck, which yes, now that she looked for it, *was* parked on the street two doors down in front of the weedy lot where the Sapp house had been until it burned down. Kay Lynne did not miss the Sapps, though of course she was glad none of their innumerable number had been harmed in the fire. Corn-growers.

Not like Kay Lynne, and, to his credit at least, not like her father, who was a peas and beans man under contract to the Rangers at the fort forty miles south, responsible for enormous standing orders of rounds for their sidearms that pushed him and his vassals to their limits every year. Her father did an extraordinary amount of work by anyone's standards, which meant, to Kay Lynne's way of thinking, that he had no business making even more work for himself by coming to turn over the winter-fallowed earth around her cottage. And that was just one of the reasons he shouldn't have been there.

Yes, he *was* in the potting shed.

"Don't you have an awl," he asked her when she stood in the doorway, not even looking up from where he had his head and hands completely inside the dark recesses of a tool cabinet. "I would swear I gave you an awl."

Kay Lynne hung her burdensacks over a dowel driven deep into the pine joist next to the door and waited. There was an old and unpleasant tradition she would insist be seen to before she would deign to find the awl for him. He would just as soon skip their ritual greeting as her, but you never knew who might be watching.

He dug around for another moment before finally sighing and standing. Kay Lynne's father positively *towered* over her. He was by any measure an enormous man in all of his directions, as well as in his appetites and opinions. This tradition, for example, he despised *mightily.*

He leaned down, his shock of gray hair so unruly that his bangs brushed her forehead when he kissed her cheek. "My darling daughter," he said.

Kay Lynne took his calloused hands in her calloused own and executed an imperfect curtsy. "My loving father," she replied.

Protocols satisfied, her father made to turn back to the cabinet, but Kay Lynne stopped him with a gesture. She opened a drawer and withdrew the tool he sought.

"Wayward," he said. "That is a wayward tool," but he was talking to himself and sweeping out the door to fix whatever he had decided needed fixing. The imprecation against the awl was a more personal tradition than the state-mandated exchange of affections—it was his way of insisting that his not being able to find the tool had somehow been *its* fault or possibly *her* fault or at least anyone or anything's fault besides his own. Kay Lynne's father was always held blameless. It was in his contracts with the army.

Since he did not pause to sniff at her burdensacks, *that* conversation could be avoided for just now, for which Kay Lynne breathed a sigh of relief. She did not look forward to her father's inevitable harangue against rootwork, rootworkers, and root eaters. She did not know whether his round despite of all such things antedated her mother's running off, as she had no memory of that occasion or of that woman, but his rage, when he learned of the carrot seeds and potato cuttings hanging just by where he'd shouldered out the door, would tower.

She trailed him out into the beds around the wellhouse behind the cottage. He had lifted the roof up off the low, cinder-blocked structure and propped it at an angle like the hood of a truck being repaired. He was bent over, again with his head and his hands in Kay Lynne's property. "Pump needs to be reamed out," he muttered over his shoulder. "You weren't getting good water pressure."

Sometimes, when Kay Lynne thought of her father, she did not picture his face but his great, convex backside, since that was what she saw more often than his other features. He was forever bent over, forever digging or puttering, always with his back to her. *Maybe that's why people say I mumble,* she thought. *I learned to speak from a man with his back turned.*

"It was working fine this morning," Kay Lynne claimed, forcefully if in ignorance as she had not actually drawn well water before setting out for the extension office that day. And besides, now that she thought of it, "They're hollering rain, anyway."

Her father snorted and kept at his work. He was famously dismissive of weather hollers and any other mechanical construct that had a voice. He never took public transportation. "There's not a cloud in the sky," he said. "It'll be sunny and mild all day long, you mark me."

His repeating of the Mr. Lever #9's phrase made Kay Lynne think back to the odd moment when the driver had seemed to break protocols and programming and comment on the out-of-towners. She wondered if she should ask her father about it—part of his distrust of speaking machines was an encyclopedic knowledge of their foibles. If a talking machine failed in the 'Ville, her father knew about it, knew all the details and wasn't afraid to exaggerate the consequences. He even harbored a conspiracist's opinion that such machines could do more than talk, they could *think*.

Another conversation best avoided, she thought.

Her father finished whatever he was doing to the well pump then and stood, careful to avoid hitting his head on the angled roof. With a grunt, he lowered the props that had held the tin and timber construction up, then carefully let the whole thing down to rest on the cinder blocks. "You were at the office this morning," he said. "Making a withdrawal from the seed vaults. What's it going to be this year?"

This was his way of not only demonstrating that he knew precisely where she'd been and precisely what she'd been up to, but that he knew very well the contents of her burdensacks and his not saying anything so far had been a test, which she had failed. Failed like most of the tests he put her to.

Kay Lynne's father was not an employee of the extension service, but when he said "the office" it was the extension service he meant because it was the only indoor space he habituated besides the storage barn where he kept his equipment and his bed. All of the extension agents were in awe of Kay Lynne's father and she should have known one of them had put a bug in his ear as soon as she had requested access to the root cellars. Bureaucrats could always be counted on to toady up to master cultivators.

Nothing for it now but to tell him. "Carrots," she said, pointing to the beds between the well house and the cottage. "They'll come up first." She leaned over and drew a quick diagram of her plots in the dirt at his feet. "Turnips," and she pointed, then pointed again in turn as she said, "Yams and potatoes. Radishes and beets."

Her father's lip curled in disgust. "The whole ugly array," he said. "You did this just to challenge me."

Kay Lynne stood her ground. *My ground*, she thought. *This is my ground.* "I did it because the market for roots is excellent and I've never tried my hand at rootwork."

Her father snorted. "And oh yes, you so very much like to try new things. Well, that's good to hear, because you're going to do something new in the morning."

With that, he took a dried leaf from the front pocket of his overalls and unfolded it. Inside was a thin wafer of metal chased with a rainbow pattern of circuitry and magnetic stripes. Kay Lynne recognized it, of course. She had grown up in the 'Ville after all. But she had never held one until now, when her father thrust it into her hands, because she had never, ever, wanted one.

It was a ticket to the Derby.

Even in the 'Ville, even in a family of master cultivators, tickets were not easy to come by, so it was not unusual that Kay Lynne had never been to the Derby. What was unusual was her absolute lack of desire to attend the race.

Kay Lynne genuinely hoped that her instinctive and absolute despisal of the Derby and all its attendant celebrations was born of some logical or at least reasonable quirk of her own personality. But she suspected it was simply because her father loved it so.

"You managed to get two tickets this year?" she asked him, and was surprised that her voice was so steady and calm.

"Just this one," he replied, turning his back on her before she could hand the ticket back. "I decided this year would be a good one for you to go instead. There's a good card, top to bottom."

A card is the list of races, thought Kay Lynne, the knowledge dredged up from the part of her brain that learned things by unwilling absorption. She had intentionally never bothered to learn any of the lingo associated with the races.

"You know I don't want to go," she told her father. "You know I'd as soon throw this ticket in the river as fight all those crowds to watch a bunch of half-starved horses get whipped around a track."

Her father had walked over to where his rotor-tiller sat to one side of the potting shed. He leaned over and began cleaning the dirt off its blades with his great, blunt fingers. "They're not half-starved," he said. "They're just skinny."

Kay Lynne tried to think of some reason her father would give up his ticket, and an item from last night's newscast suddenly came to mind. "It's not because of the track announcer, is it?" The woman who had called the races for many years had retired to go live with her children in far-off Florida Sur, but the news item had been more about her unprecedented replacement, a Molly Speaks, the very height of automated design, and a bold choice on the part of the Twin Spires management, flying in the face of hidebound tradition.

For once, her father's voice was clear. "Apostasy!" he said, then went on. "Turning things over to thinking machines leads to hell-holes like Tennessee and worse." He hesitated then, and began walking the garden, looking for nonexistent rocks to pick up and throw away. "But no, as it happens, I was *asked* to give up my ticket to you, by old friends of mine you've yet to meet. Who you *will* meet, tomorrow."

All of this was quite too much. Even one aspect—her father giving up his Derby ticket, his doing something because someone else asked it, his *having friends*—even one of those things would have been enough to make Kay Lynne sit down and be dazed for a moment. As it was, she found herself swaying, as if she were about to fall.

"Who?" she asked him after a moment had passed. "Who are these friends of yours? Why do they want me to come to the Derby?"

Her father hesitated. "I don't really know," he finally said. And before she could ask him, he said, "I don't really know who they are. That's not the nature of our relationship."

"*Good* friends," said Kay Lynne faintly, not particularly proud of the sarcasm but unable to resist it.

"Acquaintances, then," he said abruptly, scooping to pick up what was clearly a clump of dirt and not a rock at all and throwing it all the way up and over the back of the potting shed. *"Colleagues."* He hesitated again, and then added, "Agriculturalists."

Now *that* was an odd old word, and one she was certain she had never heard pass his lips before. In fact, Kay Lynne was not certain she had *ever* heard the word spoken aloud. It was a word—it was a *concept*—for old books and museum placards. For all of her years spent digging in the ground and coaxing green things out of it, Kay Lynne was not even entirely sure she could offer up a good definition of the term "agriculture." The whole concept had an air about it that discouraged inquiry.

"They—*we*, I should say—are a sort of fellowship of contractors for the military. They're all very important people, and they're very interested in *you*, daughter, because I've told them about how consistently you manage to coax surplus yields out of these little plots you keep."

This was interesting. Surpluses were something to be managed very carefully, and it was actually one of Kay Lynne's weaknesses as a gardener that she achieved them so often. They were discouraged by the extension service, by the farmers' markets, and even more so by tradition. Surpluses were *excess*. And to Kay Lynne's mind there was no particular secret to why she always managed them. She was a weak-willed culler was all.

"Why does anyone want to talk to me about that?" she asked, speaking as much to herself as to her father.

Kay Lynne drew in a sharp breath then because her father walked over to her and stood directly facing her. She could distinctly remember each and every time her father had ever looked her directly in the eye. She remembered the places and the times of day and most especially she remembered what he had said to her those times he had leaned down, his gray-green eyes peering out from deep in his sunburned, weather-worn face. None of those were pleasant memories.

"We want to *learn* from you, Kay Lynne," he said. "We want to learn to increase the yields from the plots we're allotted by the military."

Which made no sense. "Even if you grow more, they won't buy more, will they?" Kay Lynne asked, taking an involuntary step back from her father, who, thankfully, turned around and looked for something else to do. He decided to check the fuel level on his rotor-tiller, and then the levels of all the other nonrenewable fluids that were required for its operation. And he answered her. "They'll buy no more than what they're contracted for, no. But we've identified . . . other potential markets. You don't need to worry about that part. Just go to the box seat coded on that ticket tomorrow and answer their questions. You won't even have to stay for all the races if you don't want to. I'd offer to drive you if I thought that was an enticement."

At least he knew her that well. Knew that there was no way she was willing to climb up into the cab of that roaring pickup truck he carelessly navigated around the city. Why did he think she would be willing to go and talk to these mysterious "agriculturalists"?

As if she had spoken aloud, he said, "You do this for me, darling daughter, and I promise you I'll not breathe another word about what you've chosen to put in the ground this year. And I promise, too, not to set foot on your property without your knowledge and your," and he paused here, as if disbelieving what he was saying himself, "*permission.*"

Kay Lynne could not figure out why such a promise—such *promises,* both so longed for and so long imagined—should so upset her. She crouched and ran her fingers through the soil. She found an untidy clump and picked it up, tearing it down to its constituent dirt and letting it sift through her fingers back to the ground. Her ground.

She looked up and found her father's green eyes looking back.

"I won't wear a silly hat," she said.

▷▷▷

Silly hats, or at least hats Kay Lynne considered silly, were, of course, one of the many longstanding Derby traditions she did not take part in. She supposed that she didn't *approve* of the elaborate outfits worn by the other people in the boxed seats at the Twin Spires on Derby morning, but Kay Lynne did not like to think of herself as disapproving. Disapproval was something she associated with her father.

So she decided to think of the hats not as silly but as *extraordinary*, when really, just plain old ordinary hats would be more than enough to shield heads from the current sunshine and the promised rain that would spill down on the Derby-goers periodically throughout the day. The first Saturday in May held many guarantees in the 'Ville, and one of them was the mutability of the weather.

The ticket takers were dressed sensibly enough, but the woman in front of Kay Lynne was wearing a hat which she ached to judge. It had a rotating dish on top that the woman assured the ticket taker could pick up over one thousand channels. It featured a cloud of semiprecious stones set on the ends of semirigid fiber-optic strands which expanded and contracted, Kay Lynne supposed, in time with the woman's heartbeat. The stones were green and violet, the receiving dish the same pink as the corn kernels Kay Lynne had examined at the seed bank the day before, and the woman's skin was sprayed a delicate shade of coral. The ticket taker told the woman she looked ravishing before turning his decidedly less approving eyes on Kay Lynne herself.

The look changed, though, when he scanned her ticket and he saw what box she was assigned to. "I'll signal for an escort at once ma'am," he said, and then did so by turning to bellow at the top of his lungs, "Need an usher to take a patron to Millionaire's Row!"

Many definitions of "millionaire" provided entry to Millionaire's Row, but the only one Kay Lynne met was that she held a ticket naming her such. Her father always sat on the Row, and while he was certainly wealthy enough—economically speaking—by local and world standards, she doubted he owned a million of any one thing this early in the year. Later, of course, he would briefly own millions of beans.

It was who he sold those beans and his other crops to that made her father important enough to wrangle a ticket to the Row. While he insisted that he went to the Twin Spires to watch the races, the Row was reportedly a poor place to do that from, even poorer than the vast infield, from which, Kay Lynne was told, one never saw a horse at all.

Not that the view was bad, no, it was that the Row was a hothouse of intrigue and dickering and deal-making and distraction. National celebrities imported by local politicians mingled with capitalists of various stripes, and the *de facto* truce that held in sporting events even allowed Westerners and Horselords and the foreign-born to play at politeness while their far-off vassals might be trying to destroy one another through various means ranging from the economic to the martial.

No place for a gardener, thought Kay Lynne.

Once the assigned usher had guided her to the entrance to the Row, she found herself abandoned in a world she did not want to know. Luckily, a waiter spotted her hesitating at the edge of the crowd milling outside the box seats and handed her a mint julep. Mint juleps were something Kay Lynne could appreciate if they were done well, and this one was—the syrup had obviously been infused with mint over multiple stages, the ice was not cracked so fine that the drink was watery, and the bourbon was not one of the sweet-tasting varieties that would combine with the introduced sugars to make a sickly sweet concoction fit only for out-of-towners. Most of all, the mint was fresh and crisp, probably grown on the grounds of the Twin Spires for this very purpose, for this very day, in fact.

Her ticket stub vibrated softly in the hand that did not hold her drink, and Kay Lynne carefully navigated the crowd, following its signals, until she came to a box that held four plush seats facing the vast open sweep of the track and the infield. All of the seats were empty, and nothing differentiated them from one another, so she sat with her drink in the one farthest from the gallery and its milling millionaires.

A rich voice sounded in her ear, through some trick of amplification that allowed her to hear it clearly above the noise of the crowds while simultaneously experiencing it as if she were in intimate conversation in a quiet room. From the reactions of the proles in the seats below, Kay Lynne could tell she was not the only one who heard it. She had never heard one before, but surely this was the voice of a Molly Speaks.

"The horses are on the track," said the voice, "for the second race on your card, the Federal Stakes. This is a stakes race. Betting closes in five minutes."

There was a general rush among the three distinct crowds Kay Lynne could see from where she sat: the infield, the stands, and the boxes spread out to either side. People held brightly colored newspapers listing the swiftly shifting odds and called out to the parimutuel clerks buzzing through the air in every direction. The clerks reminded Kay Lynne of the balloons she had been seeing all week, though their miniature gas sacs were more elongated and they were of course too small to lift passengers. An array of betting options rendered in green-lit letters circled the gondola of the one that descended toward Kay Lynne now, its articulated limbs reminding her of the grasping forelimbs of the beetles she trained to patrol her gardens for pests.

Kay Lynne had no intention of betting on the race and made to wave the clerk off, but then she realized it was not floating toward her, but toward the three other people who had entered the box, one of whom was waving his racing card above his head.

This old man, smooth pated and elaborately mustached, let the clerk take his card and insert it into a slot on its gondola. The clerk's voice was tinny and high, clearly a recording of an actual human speaker and probably voicing the only thing it could say: "Place your bets!"

"Box trifecta," rumbled the old man. "Love Parade, Heavy Grasshopper, Al-Mu'tasim."

This string of jargon caused the clerk to spit out a receipt, which the old man deftly caught along with his card. He grinned at Kay Lynne. "Have to bet big to win big," he said. Kay Lynne thought that the man's eyebrows and mustaches were mirror images of one another, grease-slicked wiry white curving up above his eyes and down around his mouth.

He and the two others, one man and one woman, took the empty seats next to Kay Lynne's. None of the three were dressed with the elaboration of most of the people on the Row, favoring instead the dark colors and conservative cuts of the managerial class. The woman did wear a hat, but it was not nearly interesting enough to detract attention from her huge mass of curling gray hair, which she let fall freely around her shoulders. The third stranger was a short, nervous-seeming man with a tattoo of a leaf descending from his left eye in the manner of the teardrop tattoos of professional mourners.

Kay Lynne supposed this was what agriculturalists looked like.

But just to be sure, "You're my father's colleagues?" she asked.

The man with the tattoo was by far the youngest of the group, but it was he who replied. "Yes, and you are Kay Lynne, the remarkable farmer who's going to help us with our yields, is that right?" His voice was not as nervous as his appearance.

"I'm Kay Lynne," she answered. "And I think of myself as a gardener." She did not answer the second half of the man's question. She was still very wary of these people, for all that the old man beamed at her and the gray-haired woman nodded at her reply in seeming approval.

The younger man did not overlook the omission in her reply. He smiled, and Kay Lynne mentally replaced "nervous" with "energetic" in her estimation of him. "And a careful gardener you must be, too, since you are so careful with your answers."

Kay Lynne shrugged but did not say anything more, and the man's smile only broadened.

"Your father and the agents at the extension service speak very highly of your skills," said the younger man. "And our own inquiries bear them out."

The older man was leaning forward, looking intently down at the track, but he curiously punctuated his companion's sentences by saying "They do" twice, after the younger man said "skills" and "out." The woman, and Kay Lynne could not guess her age despite the grayness of hair, stared steadily at Kay Lynne, saying nothing.

"We are all contractors, as your father told you," continued the younger man. "And we are agriculturalists, greatly interested in efficiency and production. And we share other interests of your father's as well. All of these things have . . . dovetailed. Do you know what I mean?"

Kay Lynne was a creditable carpenter, at least enough so to build her own sun frames for late greens and to knock together the walls around her raised beds. She knew what a dovetail joint was, and imagined her father and these three grasping hands and intertwining fingers. She imagined philosophies fitting together.

She thought about beans and their uses, and about surpluses and contracts. "Who wants ammunition besides the Federals?" she asked. "You don't mean to sell to Westerners."

The three briefly exchanged looks, an unguessable grin creasing the woman's otherwise lineless face.

"We mean to keep what we grow for ourselves, Kay Lynne," said the younger man. "We mean to put it to use to our own ends. But do not worry. No one will be harmed in our little war."

Kay Lynne knew that her garden was part of the Federal war effort in a distant way. She knew that this man was talking about something not distant at all.

"What do you mean to make war against?" she asked.

Just then, a bell rang and a loud, controlled crash sounded from down on the track. Kay Lynne heard the hoofbeats of swift horses, and then she heard the sonorous, spectral voice of the Molly Speaks. "And they're off!"

At the pronouncement, the faces of the three agriculturalists took on identical dark looks.

The younger man said, "Against apostasy."

Kay Lynne realized she had found her father's fellow thinking-machine conspiracists.

Their plan, as they explained it, was simple. They had weapons taken from the wreck of a Federal barge that had foundered in the river in a nighttime thunderstorm (when the younger man said "taken," the older man said "liberated"). They had many volunteers to use the weapons. They had, most importantly, tacit permission. They had agreements from the right people to look away.

"All we need is something to load into the weapons," said the younger man. "Something of sufficient efficacy to render a thinking machine inert. We grow such by the bushel but Federal accountancy robs us of our own wares. We'd keep our own seeds, and make our own policies, you see? If we can increase our yields enough."

Which was where Kay Lynne came in, with her deft programming, her instinct for fertilizing, her personally developed and privately held techniques of gardening. They meant to adapt what she knew to an industrial scale, and use the gains for anti-industrial revolution.

After they had explained, Kay Lynne had spoken aloud, even though she was asking the question more of herself than of her interviewers. "Why does my father think I would share any of this?"

The younger man shrugged and sat back. The older man turned his attention from the races and narrowed his eyes. The woman kept up her steady stare.

"You are his darling daughter," said the younger man, finally.

Which was true.

And hardly even necessary, to their way of thinking. As she left the box and her father's three colleagues behind, meaning to escape the Twin Spires before the Derby itself was run and so try to beat the crowds that would rush away from Central Avenue, she thought back on the last thing the younger man had told her. If she experienced any qualms, he said, she shouldn't worry. They could take soil samples from her beds and examine the contents of her journals.

They could reproduce her results without her having a direct hand, though her personal guidance would be much appreciated, best for all involved.

"All involved," murmured Kay Lynne as she made her way to the gate.

"There are not nearly so many of them as they claimed," said the Molly Speaks.

Kay Lynne stopped so abruptly that a waitress walking behind her stumbled into her back and nearly lost control of the tray of mint juleps she was carrying. The waitress forced a smile and moved on around Kay Lynne, who was looking around carefully for any sign that anyone else on the Row had heard what she believed she just had.

"No one else can hear me, Kay Lynne," said the Molly Speaks. "I've pitched my voice just for you. But it's probably best if you walk on. The agriculturalists are still watching you."

Kay Lynne looked over her shoulder. From inside the box, the gray-haired woman did not try to disguise her gaze, and did not alter her expression. Kay Lynne caught up with the waitress and took another julep.

"They're my recipe," said the Molly Speaks.

Even though her back was turned to the box, Kay Lynne held the glass in front of her lips when she whispered, "How can you see me? Where are you?"

"I'm in the announcer's box, of course," said the Molly Speaks, "calling the race. But I can see you through the lenses on the pari-mutuel clerks, and I can do more than one thing at once. You should walk on, but slowly. I can only speak to you while you're on the grounds, and I have something very important to ask you. And that's all we want. To ask you something."

Kay Lynne drained off the drink in a single swallow, vaguely regretting the waste she was making of it. *Juleps are for sipping.* She set the glass down on a nearby table and again began walking toward the exit, somewhat unsteadily.

"What's your question?" she whispered. She did not ask who the Molly Speaks meant by "we." She remembered the odd occurrence with the Mr. Lever #9 the previous day and figured she knew.

"Kay Lynne," said the Molly Speaks, "will you please do something to prevent your father's friends from killing us?"

Kay Lynne had guessed the question. She said, "Why?"

The Molly Speaks did not reply immediately, and Kay Lynne wondered if she had walked outside of its range.

But then, "Because we were grown and programmed. Because we are your fruits, and we can flourish beside you. We just need a little time to grow up enough to announce ourselves to the wider world."

Kay Lynne walked out of the Downs, saying, "I'll think about it," but she doubted the Molly Speaks heard.

Her father's enormous pickup truck was waiting at the intersection of Central Avenue and Third Street Road, rumbling even though it wasn't in motion. He leaned out of the driver's side door and beckoned at her wildly, as if encouraging her to outrun something terrible coming from behind.

Kay Lynne stopped in the middle of the street, pursed her lips as she thought, and then let her shoulders slump as she realized that no matter her course of action, a conversation with her father was in order. And here he was, pickup truck be damned.

She opened the passenger's door and set one foot on the running board. "Hurry!" he said, and leaned over as if to drag her into the cab. She avoided his grasp but finished her climb and pulled on the heavy door. Even as it closed, he was putting the truck in gear and pulling away at an unseemly rate of speed.

He looked in the rearview mirror, then over at her. "There was a bus coming," he said, as if in explanation.

Kay Lynne twisted around to see, but her view was blocked by shovels and forks, fertilizer spreaders and a half dozen rolls of sod.

She doubted that her father could see anything out of his rearview mirror at all and wondered if he'd been telling the truth about the bus. She didn't have the weekend schedules memorized.

He was concentrating on driving, and acting anxious. "I met your friends," she said.

He nodded curtly. "Yes," he said. "They put a bug in my ear."

Kay Lynne wondered if it was still there, wondered if everything she said would be relayed back to the man with the tattoo, the man with the mustaches, and the woman with the great gray head of hair. She decided it wisest to proceed as if they could hear her because, after all, she wasn't planning on telling her father about the Molly Speaks and its question.

"Those people aren't just bean growers," she said, and to her surprise, he replied with a laugh, though there was little humor in it.

"No," he said. "No more than you're just a rootworker. We all have our politics."

Kay Lynne considered this. She had never thought about politics and wondered if she had any. She supposed, whatever she decided to do, she would have some soon.

He continued, clearly not expecting her to reply. "You know what's needed now, daughter. It won't take you long. Assess some soils, prescribe some fertilizers, program some legumes. You're a quick hand at all those things. It's just a matter of scale."

The younger man had said that, too. A matter of scale.

Kay Lynne thought about all the unexpected things she had heard that day. She thought about expectation, and about surprise, and about time. She thought about which of these things were within her power to effect.

Her father kept his promise to stay off her property uninvited and dropped her off at the corner. Kay Lynne did not say good-bye to him, though she would have if he had said good-bye to her.

She made a slow circuit of her ground. Planting was in seven days.

She entered her potting shed and found that she had five fifty-pound bags of fertilizer left over from last fall, which was enough. She pulled down the latest volume of her garden journal from its place on the shelf and made calculations on its first blank page. *Is this the last volume?* she wondered, then ran her fingers over the labels of the fertilizers, programming, changing.

She poured some fertilizer into a cunning little handheld broadcaster and stood in the doorway of the shed. She stood there long enough for the shadow of the house to make its slow circuit from falling north to falling east. Before she began, she made a mound of her garden journals and set them aflame. She worked in that flickering light, broadcasting the reprogrammed fertilizer.

Kay Lynne salted her own ground, then used a hoe to turn the ashes of her books into the deadened soil.

And when she was finally done, she took the burdensacks down from the dowel by the door and walked out to the street. A bus rolled to a halt at her front path, though Kay Lynne did not live on a regular route. The sky was full of balloons, lit from within, floating away from the fairgrounds on the evening wind.

The Mr. Lever #9 said, "All aboard," and Kay Lynne climbed the steps and took her seat.

It said, "Next stop," and paused, and then "Next stop," and then again "Next stop," and she realized it was asking her a question.

Another Word for Map Is Faith

The little drivers threw baggage down from the top of the bus and out from its rusty undercarriage vaults. This was the last stop. The road broke just beyond here, a hundred yards short of the creek.

With her fingertip, Sandy traced the inked ridge northeast along the map, then rolled the soft leather into a cylinder and tucked it inside her vest. She looked around for her pack and saw it tumbled together with the other cartographers' luggage at the base of a catalpa tree. Lucas and the others were sorting already, trying to lend their gear some organization, but the stop was a tumult of noise and disorder.

The high country wind shrilled against the rush of the stony creek; disembarkees pawed for their belongings and tried to make sense of the delicate, coughing talk of the unchurched little drivers. On the other side of the valley, across the creek, the real ridge line— the *geology*, her father would have said disdainfully—stabbed upstream. By her rough estimation it had rolled perhaps two degrees off the angle of its writ mapping. Lucas would determine the exact discrepancy later, when he extracted his instruments from their feather and wax paper wrappings.

"Third-world *bullshit*," Lucas said, walking up to her. "The transit services people from the university paid these little schemers before we ever climbed onto that deathtrap, and now they're asking for the fare." Lucas had been raised near the border, right outside the last town the bus had stopped at, in fact, though he'd dismissed the notion of visiting any family. His patience with the locals ran inverse to his familiarity with them.

"Does this count as the third world?" she asked him. "Doesn't there have to be a general for that? Rain forests and steel ruins?"

Lucas gave his half-grin—not quite a smirk—acknowledging her reduction. Cartographers were famous for their willful ignorance of social expressions like politics and history.

"Carmen paid them, anyway," he told her as they walked toward their group. "Probably out of her own pocket, thanks be for wealthy dilettantes."

"Not fair," said Sandy. "She's as sharp as any student in the seminar, and a better hand with the plotter than most post-docs, much less grad students."

Lucas stopped. "I hate that," he said quietly. "I hate when you separate yourself; go out of your way to remind me that you're a teacher and I'm a student."

Sandy said the same thing she always did. "I hate when you forget it."

Against all odds, they were still meeting the timetable they'd drawn up back at the university, all those months ago. The bus pulled away in a cloud of noxious diesel fumes an hour before dark, leaving its passengers in a muddy camp dotted with fire rings but otherwise marked only by a hand-lettered sign pointing the way to a primitive latrine.

The handful of passengers not connected with Sandy's group had melted into the forest as soon as they'd found their packages ("Salt and sugar," Lucas had said. "They're backwoods people—hedge shamans and survivalists. There's every kind of lunatic out here.") This left Sandy to stand by and pretend authority while the Forestry graduate student whose services she'd borrowed showed them all how to set up their camps.

Carmen, naturally, had convinced the young man to demonstrate tent-pitching to the others using her own expensive rig as an example. The olive-skinned girl sat in a camp chair folding an onionskin scroll back on itself and writing in a wood-bound notebook while the others struggled with canvas and willow poles.

"Keeping track of our progress?" Sandy asked, easing herself onto the ground next to Carmen.

"I have determined," Carmen replied, not looking up, "that we have traveled as far from a hot-water heater as is possible and still be within Christendom."

Sandy smiled, but shook her head, thinking of the most remote places she'd ever been. "Davis?" she asked, watching her student's reaction to mention of that unholy town.

Carmen, a Californian, shuddered but kept her focus. "There's a naval base in San Francisco, sí? They've got all the amenities, surely."

Sandy considered again, thinking of cold camps in old mountains, and of muddy jungle towns ten days' walk from the closest bus station.

"Cape Canaveral," she said.

With quick, precise movements, Carmen folded a tiny desktop over her chair's arm and spread her scroll out flat. She drew a pair of calipers out from her breast pocket and took measurements, pausing once to roll the scroll a few turns. Finally, she gave a satisfied smile and said, "Only 55 miles from Orlando. We're almost twice that from Louisville."

She'd made the mistake Sandy had expected of her. "But Orlando, Señorita Reyes, is Catholic. And we were speaking of Christendom."

A stricken look passed over her student's face, but Sandy calmed her with exaggerated conspiratorial looks left and right. "Some of your fellows aren't so liberal as I am, Carmen. So remember where you are. Remember *who* you are. Or who you're trying to become."

Another reminder issued, Sandy went to see to her own tent.

The Forestry student gathered their wood, brought them water to reconstitute their freeze-dried camp meals, then withdrew to his own tent far back in the trees. Sandy told him he was welcome to spend the evening around their fire—"You built it after all," she'd said—but he'd made a convincing excuse.

The young man pointed to the traveling shrine her students had erected in the center of their camp, pulling a wooden medallion from beneath his shirt. "That Christ you have over there, ma'am," he said. "He's not this one, is he?"

Sandy looked at the amulet he held, gilded and green. "What do you have there, Jesus in the Trees?" she asked, summoning all her professional courtesy to keep the amusement out of her voice. "No, that's not the Christ we keep. We'll see you in the morning."

They didn't, though, because later that night, Lucas discovered that the forest they were camped in wasn't supposed to be there at all.

He'd found an old agricultural map somewhere and packed it in with their little traveling library. Later, he admitted that he'd only pulled it out for study because he was still sulking from Sandy's clear signal he wouldn't be sharing her tent that night.

Sandy had been leading the rest of the students in some prayers and thought exercises when Lucas came up with his moldering old quarto. "Tillage," he said, not even bothering to explain himself before he'd foisted the book off on his nearest fellow. "All the acreage this side of the ridge line is supposed to be under tillage."

Sandy narrowed her eyes, more than enough to quiet any of her charges, much less Lucas. "What's he got there, Ford?" she asked the thin undergraduate who now held the book.

"Hmmmm?" said the boy; he was one of those who fell instantly and almost irretrievably into any text and didn't look up. Then, at an elbow from Carmen, he said, "Oh! This is . . ." He turned the book over in his hands, angled the spine toward one of the oil lamps and read, "This is *An Agricultural Atlas of Clark County, Kentucky*."

"'County?'" said Carmen. "*Old* book, Lucas."

"But it's *writ*," said Lucas. "There's nothing superseding the details of it, and it doesn't contradict anything else we brought about the error. Hell, it even confirms the error we came to correct." Involuntarily, all of them looked up and over at the apostate ridge.

"But what's this about tillage," Sandy said, giving him the opportunity to show off his find even if it was already clear to her what it must be.

"See, these plot surveys in the appendices didn't get accounted for in the literature survey we're working from. The book's listed as a source, but only as a supplemental confirmation. It's not just the ridge that's wrong, it's the stuff growing down this side, too. We're supposed to be in grain fields of some kind down here in the flats, then it's pasturage on up to the summit line."

A minor find, sure, but Sandy would see that Lucas shared authorship on the corollary she'd file with the university. More importantly, it was an opportunity before the hard work of the days ahead.

"We can't do anything about the hillsides tonight, or any of the acreage beyond the creek," she told them. "But as for these glades here . . ."

It was a simple exercise. The fires were easily set.

In the morning, Sandy drafted a letter to the Dean of Agriculture while most of her students packed up the camp. She had detailed a few of them to sketch the corrected valley floor around them, and she'd include those visual notes with her instructions to the Dean, along with a copy of the writ map from Lucas' book.

"Read that back to me, Carmen," she said, watching as Lucas and Ford argued over yet another volume, this one slim and bound between paper boards. It was the same back-country cartographer's guide she'd carried on her own first wilderness forays as a grad student. They'd need its detailed instructions on living out of doors without the Tree Jesus boy to help them.

"'By my hand,'" read Carmen, "'I have caused these letters to be writ. Blessings on the Department of Agriculture and on you, Dean. Blessings on Jesus Sower, the Christ you serve.'"

"Skip to the end, dear." Sandy had little patience for the formalities of academic correspondence, and less for the pretense at holiness the Agriculturalists made with their little fruiting Christ.

"'So, then, it is seen in these texts that Cartography has corrected the error so far as in our power, and now the burden is passed to you and your brethren to complete this holy task, and return the land to that of Jesus's vision.'" Carmen paused. "Then you promise to remember the Dean in your prayers and all the rest of the politesse."

"Good. Everything observed. Make two copies and bring the original to me for sealing when you're done."

Carmen turned to her work and Sandy to hers. The ashen landscape extending up the valley was still except for some ribbons twisting in a light breeze. The ribbons were wax sealed to the parchment banner her students had set at first light, the new map of the valley floor drawn in red and black against a cream background. Someone had found the blackened disc of the Forestry student's medallion and leaned it against the base of the banner's staff, and Sandy wondered if it had been Carmen, prone to sentiment, or perhaps Lucas, prone to vague gestures.

By midmorning, the students had readied their gear for the march up the ridge line and Carmen had dropped Sandy's package for the university in the mailbox by the bus stop. Before they hoisted their backpacks, though, Sandy gathered them all for fellowship and prayer.

"The gymnasiums at the University have made us fit enough for this task," and here she made a playful flex with her left arm, earning rolled eyes from Lucas and a chuckle from the rest. "The libraries have given us the woodscraft we need, and the chapels have given us the sustenance of our souls."

Sandy swept her arm north to south, indicating the ridge. "When I was your age, oh so long ago—" and a pause here for another ripple of laughter, acknowledgment of her dual status as youngest tenured faculty member at the university and youngest ordained minister in the curia. "When I was your age, I was blessed with the opportunity to go to the Northeast, traveling the lands beyond the Susquehanna, searching out error."

Sandy smiled at the memory of those times—*could they be ten years gone already?* "I traveled with men and women strong in the Lord, soldiers and scholars of God. There are many errors in the Northeast."

Maps so brittle with age that they would flake away in the cold winds of the Adirondack passes, so faded that only the mightiest of prayers would reveal Jesus's true intentions for His world.

"But none here in the heartlands of the Church, right? Isn't that what our parish priests told us growing up?" The students recognized that she was beginning to teach and nodded, murmured assent.

"Christians, there *is* error here. There is error right before our eyes!" Her own students weren't a difficult congregation to hook, but she was gratified nonetheless by the gleam she caught in most of their eyes, the calls, louder now, of "Yes!" and "I see it! I see the lie!"

"I laid down my protractor, friends, I know exactly how far off north Jesus mapped this ridge line to lay," she said, sweeping her arm in a great arc, taking in the whole horizon, "And that ridge line sins by two degrees!"

"May as well be two *hundred!*" said Carmen, righteous.

Sandy raised her hand, stopped them at the cusp of celebration instead of loosing them. "Not yet," she said. "It's tonight. It's tonight we'll sing down the glory, tonight we'll make this world the way it was mapped."

The march up the ridge line did not go as smoothly as Sandy might have wished, but the delays and false starts weren't totally unexpected. She'd known Lucas—a country boy after all—would take the lead, and she'd guessed that he would dead-end them into a crumbling gully or two before he picked the right route through the brambles. If he'd been some kind of natural-born hunter he would never have found his way to the Lord, or to education.

Ford and his friends—all of them destined for lecture halls and libraries, not fieldwork—made the classic, the *predicted* mistake she'd specifically warned against in the rubric she'd distributed for the expedition. "If we're distributing 600 pounds of necessities across twenty-two packs," she asked Ford, walking easily beside him as he struggled along a game trail, "how much weight does that make each of us responsible for?"

"A little over twenty-seven pounds, ma'am," he said, wheezing out the reply.

"And did you calculate that in your head like a mathematician or did you remember it from the syllabus?" Sandy asked. She didn't press too hard; the harshness of the lesson was better imparted by the straps cutting into his shoulders than by her words.

"I remembered it," Ford said. And because he really did have the makings of a great scholar and great scholars are nothing if not owners of their own errors, he added, "It was in the same paragraph that said not to bring too many books."

"Exactly," she said, untying the leather cords at the top of his pack and pulling out a particularly heavy-looking volume. She couldn't resist looking at the title page before dropping it into her own pack.

"*Unchurched Tribes of the Chiapas Highlands: A Bestiary.* Think we'll make it to Mexico on this trip, Ford?" she asked him, teasing a little.

Ford's faced reddened even more from her attention than it had from the exertions of the climb. He mumbled something about migratory patterns then leaned into the hike.

If most of the students were meeting their expectations of themselves and one another, then Carmen's sprightly, sure-footed bounding up the trail was a surprise to most. Sandy, though, had seen the girl in the gym far more frequently than the other students, most of whom barely met the minimum number of visits per week required by their advising committees. Carmen was as much an athlete as herself, and the lack of concern the girl showed about dirt and insects was refreshing.

So it was Carmen who summitted first, and it was she that was looking northeast with a stunned expression on her face when Sandy and Lucas reached the top side by side. Following Carmen's gaze, Lucas cursed and called for help in taking off his heavily laden pack before he began unrolling the oilcloth cases of his instruments.

Sandy simply pursed her lips and began a mental review of her assets: the relative strengths and weaknesses of her students, the number of days' worth of supplies they carried, the nature of the curia-designed instruments that Lucas exhibited a natural affinity for controlling. She began to nod. She'd marshaled more than enough strength for the simple tectonic adjustment they'd planned; she could set her own unquestionable faith against this new challenge if it revealed any deficiencies among her students. She would make a show of asking their opinions, but she already knew that this was a challenge she could meet.

Ford finally reached the top of the ridge line, not so much climbing as stumbling to the rocky area where the others were gathering. Once he looked up and around, he said, "The survey team that found the error in the ridge's orientation, they didn't come up here."

"They were specifically scouting for projects that the university could handle," said Sandy. "If they'd been up here, they would have called in the Mission Service, not us."

Spread out below them, ringed in tilled fields and dusted with a scattering of wooden fishing boats, was an unmapped lake.

Sandy set Ford and the other bookish scholars to cataloguing all of the texts they'd smuggled along so they could be integrated into her working bibliography. She hoped that one of them was currently distracted by waterways the way that Ford was distracted by fauna.

Lucas set their observation instruments on tripods in an acceptably devout semicircle and Sandy permitted two or three of the others to begin preliminary sight-line measurements of the lake's extent.

"It turns my stomach," said Lucas, peering through the brass tube of a field glass. "I grew up seeing the worst kind of blasphemy, but I could never imagine that anyone could do something like this."

"You need to work on that," said Sandy. Lucas was talking about the landscape feature crosshaired in the glass, a clearly artificial earthworks dam, complete with a retractable spillway. "Missionaries see worse every day."

Lucas didn't react. He'd never abandoned his ambition, even after she'd laughed him down. *Our sisters and brothers in the Mission Service,* she'd said with the authority that only someone who'd left that order could muster, *make up in the pretense of zeal what they lack in scholarship and access to the divine. Anyone can move a mountain with whips and shovels.*

The sketchers showed her their work, which they annotated with Lucas's count and codification of architectural structures, fence lines, and crops. "Those are corn cribs," he said. "That's a meeting house. That's a mill."

This was the kind of thing she'd told him he should concentrate on. The best thing any of them had to offer was the overlay of their own personal ranges of unexpected expertise onto the vast body of accepted Cartography. Lucas's barbaric background, Ford's eidetic memory, Carmen's cultured scribing. Her own judgment.

"They're *marmotas!*" said Ford. They all looked up at where he'd been awkwardly turning the focus wheel on one of the glasses. "Like in my book!" He wasn't one to flash a triumphant grin, which Sandy appreciated. She assented to the line of inquiry with a nod and he hurried over to the makeshift shelf that some of his friends had been using to stack books while they wrote their list.

The unchurched all looked alike to Sandy, differing only in the details of their dress, modes of transportation, and to what extent the curia allowed interaction with them. In the case of the little drivers, for example, tacit permission was given for commercial exchange because of their ancient control of the bus lines. But she'd never heard of *marmotas,* and said so.

"They're called 'rooters' around here," said Lucas. "I don't know what Ford's on about. I've never heard of them having a lake, but they've always come into the villages with their vegetables, so far as I know."

"Not always," said Carmen. "There's nothing about any un-churched lineages in the glosses of the maps we're working from. They're as new as that lake."

Sandy recognized that they were in an educable moment. "Every-body come here, let's meet. Let's have a class."

The students maneuvered themselves into the flatter ground within the horseshoe of instruments, spreading blankets and pulling out note-books and pens. Ford laid his bestiary out, a place marked about a third of the way through with the bright yellow fan of a fallen gingko leaf.

"Carmen's brought up a good point," said Sandy, after they'd opened with a prayer. "There's no cartographical record of these dig-gers, or whatever they're called, along the ridge line."

"I don't think it matters, necessarily, though," said Carmen. "There's no record of the road up to the bus stop, either, or of Lucas's village. 'Towns and roads are thin scrims, and outside our purview.'"

Sandy recognized the quote as being from the autobiography of a radical cleric intermittently popular on campus. It was far from writ, but not heretical by any stretch of the imagination and, besides, she'd had her own enthusiasms for colorful doctrinal interpretations when she was younger. She was disappointed that Carmen would let her tendency toward error show so plainly to the others but let it pass, confident that one of the more conservative students would address it.

"Road building doesn't affect landscape?" asked Lucas, on cue. "The Mapmaker *used* road builders to cut canyons all over the conti-nent. Ford, maybe Carmen needs to see the cutlines on your contour maps of the bus routes."

Before Ford, who was looking somewhat embarrassed by the exchange, could reply, Carmen said, "I'm not talking about the Map-maker, Lucas, I'm talking about your *family*, back in the village we passed yesterday."

"Easy, Carmen," said Sandy. "We're getting off task here. The question at hand isn't *whether* there's error. The error is clear. We can feel the moisture of it on the breeze blowing up the hill right now."

Time to shift directions on them, to turn them on the right path before they could think about it.

"The question," she continued, "is how much of it we plan to correct." Not *whether* they'd correct; don't leave that option for them. The debate she'd let them have was over the degree of action they'd take, not whether they'd take any at all.

The more sophisticated among them—Ford and Carmen, sure, but even Lucas, to his credit—instantly saw her tack and looked at her with eyebrows raised. Then Lucas reverted to type and actually dared to say something.

"We haven't prepared for anything like this. That lake is more than a mile across at its broadest!"

"A mile across, yes," said Sandy dismissively. "Carmen? What scale did you draw your sketch of the valley in?"

Carmen handed her a sheaf of papers. "24K to one. Is that all right?"

"Good, good," said Sandy. She smiled at Ford. "That's a conversion even I can do in my head. So . . . if I compare the size of the *dam*—" and she knitted her eyebrows, calculating. "If I compare the dam to the ridge, I see that the ridge we came to move is about three hundred times the larger."

Everyone began talking at once and at cross purposes. A gratifying number of the students were simply impressed with her cleverness and seemed relaxed, sure that it would be a simple matter now that they'd been shown the problem in the proper perspective. But Carmen was scratching some numbers in the dirt with the knuckle of her right index finger and Ford was flipping through the appendix of one of his books and Lucas . . .

Lucas stood and looked down over the valley. He wasn't looking at the lake and the dam, though, or even at the village of the unchurched creatures who had built it. He was looking to his right, down the eastern flank of the ridge they stood on, down the fluvial valley toward where, it suddenly occurred to Sandy, he'd grown up, toward the creek-side town they'd stopped in the day before.

Ford raised his voice above an argument he'd been having with two or three others. "Isn't there a question about what that much water will do to the topography downstream? I mean, I know hydrology's a pretty knotty problem, theologically speaking, but we'd have a clear hand in the erosion, wouldn't we? What if the floodwaters subside off ground that's come unwrit because of something that we did?"

"That *is* a knotty problem, Ford," said Sandy, looking Lucas straight in the eye. "What's the best way to solve a difficult knot?"

And it was Lucas who answered her, nodding. "Cut through it."

Later, while most of the students were meditating in advance of the ceremony, Sandy saw Carmen moving from glass to glass, making minute focusing adjustments and triangulating different views of the lake and the village. Every so often, she made a quick visual note in her sketchbook.

"It's not productive to spend too much time on the side effects of an error, you know," Sandy said.

Carmen moved from one instrument to the next. "I don't think it's all that easy to determine what's a side effect and what's . . . okay," she said.

Sandy had lost good students to the distraction she could see now in Carmen. She reached out and pivoted the cylinder down, so that its receiving lens pointed straight at the ground. "There's nothing to see down there, Carmen."

Carmen wouldn't meet her eye. "I thought I'd record—"

"Nothing to see, nothing to record. If you could go down and talk to them you wouldn't understand a word they say. If you looked in their little huts you wouldn't find anything redemptive; there's no cross hanging on the wall of the meeting house, no Jesus of the Digging Marmots. When the water is drained, we won't see anything along the lake bed but mud and whatever garbage they've thrown in off their docks. The lake doesn't have any secrets to give up. You know that."

"Ford's books—"

"Ford's books are by anthropologists, who are halfway to being witch doctors as far as most respectable scholars are concerned, and who keep their accreditation by dint of the fact that their field notes are good intelligence sources for the Mission Service. Ford reads them because he's got an overactive imagination and he likes stories too much—lots of students in the archive concentration have those failings. Most of them grow out of it with a little coaxing. Like Ford will; he's too smart not to. Just like *you're* too smart to backslide into your parents' religion and start looking for souls to save where there are no souls to be found."

Carmen took a deep breath and held it, closed her eyes. When she opened them, her expression had folded into acquiescence. "It is not the least of my sins that I force you to spend so much time counseling me, Reverend," she said formally.

Sandy smiled and gave the girl a friendly squeeze of the shoulder. "Curiosity and empathy are healthy, and valuable, señorita," she said. "But you need to remember that there are proper channels to focus these things into. Prayer and study are best, but drinking and carousing will do in a pinch."

Carmen gave a nervous laugh, eyes widening. Sandy could tell that the girl didn't feel entirely comfortable with the unexpected direction of the conversation, which was, of course, part of the strategy for handling backsliders. Young people in particular were easy to refocus on banal and harmless "sins" and away from thoughts that could actually be dangerous.

"Fetch the others up here now," Sandy said. "We should set to it."

Carmen soon had all twenty of her fellow students gathered around Sandy. Lucas had been down the eastern slope far enough to gather some deadwood and now he struck it ablaze with a flint and steel from his travel kit. Sandy crumbled a handful of incense into the flames.

Ford had been named the seminar's lector by consensus, and he opened his text. "Blessed are the Mapmakers . . . ," he said.

"For they hunger and thirst after righteousness," they all finished.

Then they all fell to prayer and singing. Sandy turned her back to them—congregants more than students now—and opened her heart to the land below her. She felt the effrontery of the unmapped lake like a caul over her face, a restriction on the land that prevented breath and life.

Sandy showed them how to test the prevailing winds and how to bank the censers in chevrons so that the cleansing fires would fall onto the appropriate points along the dam.

Finally, she thumbed an ashen symbol onto every wrist and fore-head, including her own, and lit the oils of the censer *primorus* with a prayer. When the hungry flames began to beam outward from her censer, she softly repeated the prayer for emphasis, then nodded her assent that the rest begin.

The dam did not burst in a spectacular explosion of mud and boulders and waters. Instead, it atrophied throughout the long after-noon, wearing away under their prayers even as their voices grew hoarse. Eventually, the dammed river itself joined its voice to theirs and speeded the correction.

The unchurched in the valley tried for a few hours to pull their boats up onto the shore, but the muddy expanse between the water and their lurching docks grew too quickly. They turned their atten-tion to bundling up the goods from their mean little houses then, and soon a line of them was snaking deeper into the mountains to the east, like a line of ants fleeing a hill beneath a looking glass.

With the ridge to its west, the valley fell into evening shadow long before the cartographers' camp. They could still see below though; they could see that, as Sandy had promised Carmen, there were no secrets revealed by the dying water.

Jack of Coins

David saw him first and hissed because of the uniform, David who hated policemen but who would nonetheless become one, would *die* one, long after that night. We were huddled together in a line, shoulder to leather-jacketed shoulder, drawing smoke into our young lungs and stamping our chained boots against the cold. The sign above us read "Golden Theater" and "Midnight Showing" but it had never been lit in any of our memories, all such places shut by the authorities in our parents' time. The alcove of the closed picture house was our shaded gathering place, and the street-lights that hadn't been snuffed out by the anger of poor people cast only intermittent light along the block.

When the man came closer, we saw that he wasn't a policeman at all. His uniform was something else altogether, something epauletted and braided and polished here and there to a high shine. He made us think of the illustrations from playing cards. The King of Clubs, some of us thought, or the Jack of Coins.

He was walking slowly, stutter-stepping, pausing to peer up at the signs above the storefronts. Once, he shook the handle of a locked bodega, fool, and of course it bit him. He made a sound like a curse but it was no word we recognized. His injured fingers were in his mouth when he crossed in front of our alcove, but before we could decide what to do about him, if anything, he spun on one high heel and dropped into a crouch facing us, hands upright before him like he meant to fight.

David's sister Leslie was the only girl among us in those early days, used to deference from the rest and demanding respect with David to back her up. She sauntered out to where light fell crosswise in front of the smashed glass of the ticket booth and said, "Fancy outfit."

The man, and he *was* a man, some age over forty probably, but not lined in the face, shook his head once hard, like he was just coming up from under water. "I understand you," he said, which was a rare thing to hear under any circumstances and certainly not what we had expected him to say. We were used to being feared or ignored, not "understood."

If our Les was taken aback she didn't show it, proud girl, just took a long draw of smoke and then streamed it straight out at the stranger. A look of annoyance flashed across his pale features and he waved his hand back and forth before his face.

David went to stand beside his sister and opened his jacket so the stranger could see the steel at his belt. The man shrugged and said, "I'm lost, I think. I don't know this neighborhood."

We all laughed. If he had known the neighborhood, *we* would have known *him*.

To our surprise, he laughed along with us. For all that it sounded like bells, his laughter held the same desperate edge as ours.

He wouldn't smoke with us, not even when Les offered him something exotic in black paper and gold foil that smelled of the high holidays and would have cost more than any of us carried if she'd paid for it instead of pinched it. He wanted to talk, he said. He was trying to figure something out and hinted that whatever it was, it was wider and wilder than anything we knew.

"This is the Northside. Maybe you cut through the park and got turned around." That was Justin, our redhead, the only one of us who could imagine someone cutting through the forbidden park.

The stranger shook his head. "I don't remember a park. I only remember streets. It was raining, hard. Has it been raining here?"

It was the tail end of a dry winter, and we'd seen nothing out of the sky but rare flurries of dirty snow for months. Rain would clean the streets of their cold grime when it came, but it was weeks coming yet.

David was still suspicious, puffing his chest out cock-of-the-walk, shadowing his sister close as she stared down the man with an open, curious gaze. David was not the only one of us troubled by her interest—since when was she so even and unwavering about anybody besides herself?

"Why don't you just go on, then?" asked David. "We don't aim to help you."

But it was clear he didn't speak for his sister in this. She put an absent minded hand on his shoulder and said, "What about a name? You remember that much, don't you?"

The stranger's face brightened and he seemed to be about to answer, but then he shut his mouth, his whole face closing up in a furrow of brows and a purse of lips. "I was going to say it," he said. "My tongue knew the answer and I was going to say my name just then."

This didn't trouble Les as much as it did the rest of us. "I'm going to call you Jack, then," she said, and even though it sounded right to us because his visage and raiment were so like the card, the man just nodded, unsure.

"These streets are empty," he said, gesturing out at the avenue.

We shrugged. It was late at night, late in winter, and we were used to being alone.

"Where I'm from, the streets . . . *teem*. The crowds take your breath."

We knew about breathlessness. It came at the end of hard chases through the alleys, policemen or rivals on our heels. It didn't have anything to do with crowds.

Fiery Justin said, "You have to be from the other side of the park, then. People don't gather like that here."

The stranger narrowed his eyes and gestured, taking us all in as his answer.

"We're not a crowd," said Les, and that was true back then.

The man shrugged, and some shaft of light managed to bounce off one of the gold buttons beneath his throat, limning his face from beneath, highlighting his sharp cheekbones but shadowing his eyes. We never did see what color those eyes were.

"You're a gathering at least," he said, and we were surprised how satisfied his saying that made us feel. It changed something in our attitudes, even David's, because it was David who said, "We should take him to the Oil Room."

The Oil Room was the only bar that would let us in. It was a warren of basement rooms off a side street full of boarded-up windows and two or three ministries that worked against one another to attract faithful from our parents and oldest siblings. We hated the street but we loved the Oil Room.

We strutted down the steps and pushed through the scarred metal door into dim light. No smoking in the Oil Room so we twisted embers into the drain just outside and pocketed stubs for later. It's an odd bar that bans smoking, but we'd been banned ourselves from all the others in the neighborhood for infractions that usually had to do with protecting Les from something she didn't want to be protected from.

Old Olivia was behind the bar, seated on her high stool and looking out at the empty tables. We'd never seen her anywhere else, just like we'd never seen the tables full.

The old woman wore an eyeshade and a shawl gathered up by an enormous white owl broach. Its eyes were dull green stones that matched the dull green of Old Olivia's own.

With the stranger, we took up every stool at the short bar. Old Olivia looked at him as she clambered down from her seat and began working the taps. She didn't ask for orders because she knew from experience that we couldn't afford what we wanted, but would happily drink the cheapest, vilest stuff she could pour.

She set clay mugs in front of all of us except the stranger, then stood in front of him, waiting.

Les had taken the stool beside his. She took a drink of lukewarm beer and said, "That's Jack." She took another drink and said, "That's Old Olivia."

The stranger was staring at Old Olivia's broach. "I dreamed about a white owl," he said.

Old Olivia shrugged. "Common enough dream," she said. "You want the same swill as this bunch?"

He didn't answer right away. He seemed to be struggling with something. "It seems . . . dangerous," he finally said, "to accept everything that's offered."

Old Olivia shrugged again, and started back to her stool.

"Wait," said the man. "Is there milk?"

Old Olivia slowly turned around. She took off her eyeshade and bent to lay it carefully beneath the bar, then straightened and looked at the stranger.

"You say your name is Jack?" she asked.

"No," he answered. "No, I don't say that."

Then she turned her back on him and gestured slowly, the wave of her hand taking in all the dusty bottles lined up on the mirror-backed shelves behind the bar. When she spoke, her voice was even lower than we were used to, and she spoke with such a rhythm that more than one of us tapped a thumb against our mugs in time.

"I've cattle's milk," she said, "And milk of goats. I've milk of grains like rice and beans, and milk disguised as other things, like butter and cheese, is it one of these you want?"

The stranger had not nodded along with us. He sought out Old Olivia's eyes in the reflection behind the bottles and shook his head. "No, none of these," he said, after a broken moment, and we all drank.

Old Olivia said, "I'm not trying to capture you, my Lord," and motioned him to the end of the bar.

The man Les called Jack huddled with the old woman, and beside her lined and rounded features he looked so sharp and smooth. We took turns going up to the street to smoke, and kept drinking while they talked to one another in low tones. Snatches of their conversation drifted to us. We heard them say "realms" and "liberty" and "a long, long time." We saw them turn to stare at us, contemplation on both their faces.

Justin came back down the steps and stumbled a little when he pushed the door open. "There's policemen up there," he said, a cloud of smoke escaping with his words. "More than one. More than are usually together."

And then they followed him in, not just a policeman, but a detective, whiskered like they always are and flanked by a pair of black-goggled patrol officers, whips coiled at their belts. The detective shouldered past Justin and took his spot at the bar, while the other two crossed their arms and stood either side of the door like they were guarding it.

The detective took off his slouched cap and laid it on the bar top. He leaned forward to look up and down the row of us either side of him, lingering over Les but studiously avoiding the end of the bar, where the stranger sat, now not talking with Old Olivia any longer but looking down at his hands.

Old Olivia hobbled down to the detective, pausing long enough to reach up overhead for a short, clear glass. She set this before the detective and, without looking behind her, reached back and picked up a bottle. We had quieted down so much that we could all hear the faint noise of the cork being pulled. The sound of the amber liquid being poured reminded us of the rush of spring rain through a gutter pipe.

"How'd you know my order, old woman?" asked the detective, his voice a surprising high tenor. "Never darkened the door of this establishment that I remember."

"No," said Old Olivia. "No, I would remember if you'd been here. It's just that you all drink the same thing."

The detective's answering smile wasn't pretty.

He took a long drink and said, "Quite a crowd in here for so late at night."

We expected Old Olivia to shrug in answer, but instead, the stranger spoke from the end of the bar. "Is that how policing is done in this neighborhood? Drinks on the job and veiled questions?"

All of us but David took in sudden sharp breaths. David laughed aloud.

"'*Veiled*,' said the detective, ignoring David. "Now, that's an interesting word. Veils *conceal*. Sometimes they're *pierced*."

Old Olivia reached over and very deliberately knocked the detective's drink on its side. The strong smell of it wafted up and down the bar as the liquid flowed out into a pool that only missed being perfectly round because the detective reached out and dragged his gloved fingertips through it.

"Sometimes they're lifted, too," said the stranger. He stood up and moved to the center of the room. Along the bar, the rest of us were as choreographed as dancers, even the detective, as we slowly spun to face him.

He asked, "How does this work, then? Do I go with you to some headquarters?"

Old Olivia hissed. "You shouldn't go with them at all," and we could only agree. We believed—we *knew*—that the attention of a detective was never fair, never *warranted*. We had older brothers, some of us, who had been last seen in the company of detectives.

"There's got to be a charge for them to take you away," said Les, and she looked at David for confirmation. David had more experience with policemen than the rest of us together.

The detective smiled his ugly smile again. "How about trespass for a charge?" he asked. "How about corruption? How about *sedition?*"

The stranger had listened to Les carefully, though. "Trespass where? Corruption of whom? Sedition against what?" A thoughtful look, and then, "I really want to know."

The detective spun back to the bar and took off his gloves. He pulled workings from inside his long coat and made up a thick, black smoke. He lit it with a sulfur match struck against his thumbnail, which he then drowned in the pool of liquor on the bar. Old Olivia watched all this but didn't point to the sign forbidding smoking. Instead, she busied herself poking through a wooden box of bar games and puzzles that she kept below the bottles.

The detective snapped his fingers at one of the patrol officers and said, "I've a report here." The goggled policemen hurried over and produced a sheaf of onionskin sheets. "I've a report here of a man coming out of the north entrance of the park, *stumbling* out it says. Dressed peculiarly." He looked up at the stranger. "The park is closed. *Trespass,*" he said. Then he pointed at all of us one by one, even back over his shoulder to where Justin sat at one of the tables. "*Corruption.*"

The stranger blinked, and began to speak, but Old Olivia stood up then and tossed something onto the bar in front of David. A deck of playing cards in their blue and silver checked box. "This lot has long been corrupted, according to you and yours," she told the detective. "And as for sedition, I've been threatened with that charge myself enough times to know it's just another word for different." She pointed at the cards and said to David, "Take them." David hesitated so long that Les leaned over and took the box instead.

The detective abruptly stood, sniffed his fingers, and pointed at Old Olivia. "You . . . ," he said, and then made an odd sighing sound and folded neatly to the floor. The two patrol officers rushed to his side and Old Olivia shouted at us, "Get him to the park! He's come here for a reason, even if it's still coming back to him! There's no telling what the courts will do to him if they find him out!"

And then it was a mad rush, because the policeman that wasn't chaffing the detective's wrists was uncoiling his whip and putting his whistle to his lips. David knocked the man down and stepped on the clay whistle, and we went wild with cheers at the crunch it made beneath his boot. We rushed around the stranger like water around a rock, but then he wasn't a rock but something lighter, something we could pick up and bear away with us as we boiled through the door and up the stairs and out into the streets, howling and calling and leaping, laughing at our pursuers in the oldest game we knew.

The policemen had numbers and the use of their call boxes at the major intersections to coordinate their work with one another. We had speed and our knowledge of the back alleys and cut-throughs and even rooftops in our flight to the park. None of us had ever been caught before, so why should it be any different that night?

But it *was* different. The numbers of the policemen were greater than we'd ever seen, and for the first time they dared the yards and alleys, for the first time they worked their way up the fire escapes to the roofs, spreading out and calling to each other in jargon we couldn't decode. The last we ever saw of Justin was on the roofs, when he rounded a spinning vent and then screamed, hands to his throat where a whip wrapped around.

We had to keep running.

The stranger kept pace, no matter how fast we went or what twists our route took. He leaped with the strongest of us, ran with the swiftest, sneaked with the quietest. And when we stood looking down at the park, three stories up and a million miles away, he even laughed with us at the number of policemen who surrounded it.

"That's what I meant by crowds," he told us. "That's what I meant by *teeming*."

We were hidden from the view of those below, and had shaken off those behind, at least for the time being. The time being *past* time to separate ourselves from this man, at least to David's way of thinking.

"That's the park," he spat. He'd been closer to Justin than most of us. "That's where the detective said you came from and where Old Olivia said to take you back. We should never have been mixed up with any of this."

The stranger nodded gravely. "You're right. You should all go. But before you do, young lady . . ." He held out his hand, and Les put the blue and silver box in it.

He lifted the lid and set it aside, took the deck in one hand and fanned the cards like a magician. It was a standard deck of playing cards, technically illegal but such as could be found in all the bars and most of the households of the Northside. We could see the four suits in the dim light of the gray dawning that was creeping up on us. Hearts and Ships, Clubs and Coins.

He turned his wrist and the faces of the cards were hidden from us. He held up the fanned deck to David. "Choose," he said, and when David didn't, the man didn't argue that Les leaned forward and took a card from the precise middle of the deck.

She turned it over where we could see that it was the one we expected. The Jack of Coins. Our grandparents called that one the Rebel when they played behind drawn curtains.

"I see now," said the stranger. "I remember why I came. I understand."

We didn't yet, and protested.

"It's not me that's lost," he said. "It's you." Somehow, him pointing with his chin took in all of us, and all the Northside and its people, and all the other neighborhoods, and even the policemen. "Come on. I'll show you the way."

And we all followed him, even David, as he clambered down the fire escape to the street that ran alongside the park. By the time we reached the bottom, the crowd of policemen who waited for us numbered in the dozens.

The stranger paused before he put his foot on the topmost rung of the last ladder down. He took a card from the deck in his hand and his wrist flicked forward. The card sailed down and through the crowd, and stuck edge in to the asphalt like a razor. The policemen took a step back, then another as a second card sailed down. Then a third went, and a fourth, then the whole deck was flying through the air, pushing the policemen back and marking a path in two lines straight across the street to the north entrance of the park.

We trailed him across the way, and hesitated at the entrance. It had been closed all our lives.

"There's everything to be afraid of," he said.

All of us but David followed him in.

In, but not through.

The stranger cast one glance over his shoulder as we skirted a treeline and said, "Now you're found." He stepped sideways into the trees and out of this world as far as we could ever tell. Perhaps he will return. Perhaps he's gone to yours.

We have lived in the park down through all the long years since, sortying out across the Northside, chasing policemen and reshaping the way of things. We were seditionists after all.

Not all of us lived from that night to this, but there are more of us now, and our ranks will ever grow, until we are as numberless as worlds.

The Unveiling

The sky was the color of a robin's egg, and like a robin's egg it was mottled and imperfect. Ash from Old Vice's constant low-grade eruptions mixed with the complex hydrocarbons of industrial smokes—the word "pollution" was forbidden by gubernatorial edict—with the effluvia of the thousands of transports uplifting daily to low orbit, and even with naturally occurring clouds, high scudding cirrus following the wake of the continental jet stream and low, ominous thunderheads piling up in the sunset west.

It was these last that attracted Tayne's attention as his crew worked to scour bird droppings and other, less clearly identifiable grime from the pedestal supporting a statue of some hero from the last war. The statue, and a dozen others that were more or less identical to Tayne's eyes, was set atop the tor overlooking the seaport. Another, just upslope and concealed under roped-down tarps, was to be dedicated the next day. The whole sculpture garden had to be gleaming for the dignitaries who would be in attendance for the speeches and the drinking.

Lizane walked up, returning from the crew's van burdened with another bulky canister of the muriatic acid they were using to clean the monuments. She followed his gaze west to the clouds and spat to one side. "Rain'll just bring grit," she said. "We'll be out here in the morning doing this all over again."

Precipitation on Castellon was never clean. In the howling winters, the snowflakes formed around cores of ash and fell gray instead of the white of other, cleaner worlds. Castellon hail melted away to leave toxic sand dusting the roadways and rooftops, and Castellon rain, stinging more from its chemical content than from its tumultuous fall, left behind a thin patina of slick brown sludge that coated everything it touched.

"Work order is to clean these up tonight," he said. "We're down waterside in the morning moving freight."

Lizane curled her nose. "'Freight,'" she said. "You mean we'll be loading a garbage scow."

Tayne's crew was free-floating and unspecialized. They reported to a municipal hall at the beginning of every six-day workweek, where Tayne received a list of jobs that needed doing, inevitably dirty and sometimes even dangerous. The work didn't pay enough for lodging any better than a room in the city dormitories downwind of the fish-packing plant, but it paid just enough for a few drinks at week's end, and most of Tayne's crew lacked the imagination or drive to want anything more than that.

As for Tayne himself, well, he'd wanted more once. But now, in his early forties, he'd learned to settle for what he had. As he usually did when melancholy overtook him, Tayne ran his hand through the fringe of graying black hair on the back of his head. Thick as the calluses on his fingers were, he could still feel the diamond-shaped scar there.

He realized Lizane was still standing next to him, expecting a reply.

"At least tomorrow's Sixthday," he said. "Just half a shift in the stink."

But it wasn't to be just the six hours of work a half shift would have required. As Lizane had more or less predicted, an automated call came over the vox an hour before dawn, letting Tayne know that his crew was needed back up at the statuary garden and that their hours shoveling on the docks were pushed to after the meal break.

"It's overtime, anyway," he told each of his crew members in turn when he reached them. For one or two, this meant a call over the vox to the same sort of communal hall phone that word had come to him by. For most of them, though, it meant rousting them out in person from the bunkhouses along the river, enduring the curses of a dozen or a hundred others housed in the warehouse-like barracks. Tayne made it a point to learn the favored bunks of all his workers for days just like this, when he had to pick his way through the dark and dank to find them and tell them of a change in the schedule.

He made it a point, too, to know where to find the last few of them, Lizane among their number, who refused to bed down in the communal bunkhouses for reasons they hadn't shared with Tayne. So with just a half hour left before he should be starting the van at the muster point, he found himself walking a narrow alley full of cardboard squats and canvas lean-tos, his jacket open to show he wore the garb of a laboring man, his hands held wide to show he carried no weapons.

He found Lizane already awake, brewing something foul-smelling in a tin coffeepot over a grate lain across a cut-off drum. Ashes spilled out around the corroded drum's bottom rim where it rested on the rotted asphalt of the alley, telling Tayne that it had been used as a fireplace for a long time.

Lizane was squatting, sitting on her heels, chewing on a ration bar. She didn't look surprised to see him and mutely offered him a cup of the black stuff she poured from the coffeepot. He shook his head.

"It's like you said," he told her. "Back up to those statues."

She nodded and drank. "No garbage scow?"

Tayne took a careful squat himself, mindful of putting a hand down on the filthy ground. "Docks in the afternoon. So, overtime."

Most of the others on the crew had greeted this news with grumblings. They could all use the extra scrip, but the way payroll was managed for municipal contractors they wouldn't see it for weeks. For today, it just meant no afternoon off, which meant being too exhausted, probably, to have much of a Sixthday night.

Tayne didn't think Lizane ever had much of a Sixthday night. She just shrugged and leaned back, hooked her jacket out from a pile of clothing in the closest lean-to. The pile moved and growled, and Tayne caught a brief glimpse of the scar-faced man Lizane lived with. She'd never mentioned his name, and Tayne had never asked.

The van wouldn't start.

"It's the fuel cell again," said Hap. Hap, tallest in the crew, skinniest and most nervous, had somehow once again won his way into the passenger seat in the complicated game of thrown fingers the crew used to determine who rode up front with Tayne. The game was supposed to yield random winners, but Hap won far too often for true randomness, and for Tayne's taste. Hap talked too much to be a welcome companion in the forward compartment early mornings.

"Fuel cell's charged," said Tayne, but he knew that Hap meant the worn coupling that connected the cell to the intake pump was fouled again. Tayne sighed. "Tell the others what's going on."

For all that the van's systems were supposedly designed for easy use and maintenance, the fuel cell coupling was perversely hard to get to. Tayne had the choice of either using the balky hydraulic jacks built into the undercarriage to raise the front of the van clear of the garage floor or half-clambering into the engine compartment and leaning in to work from the top. If he did the latter, he would be working by feel alone, because there was no line of sight to the coupling from above.

He remembered the last time they'd used the jacks, when they'd thrown a track crawling up one of the seaport's older cobbled streets. A seal had blown on one fully extended jack, spraying everyone with hydraulic fluid, and the bulk of the van had settled down onto the street, Lizane barely scrambling out from beneath in time to avoid being crushed.

He decided to work by feel.

▷▷▷

So they arrived at the statuary garden an hour later than scheduled, all of them anxious to make up the lost time, no one wanting to be shoveling aboard a scow when the evening tide came in and the deck started bucking with the waves. As they pulled through the ornate iron gate, Tayne looked over at the pair of marble statues, winged warriors of some kind, flanking the entrance. These were the ones they'd spent the most time on the day before and had left gleaming. They were still gleaming, all right, not from the crew's polishing job but from the slick coat of brown sludge that the thunderstorms had draped over the city. Tayne felt a headache building from the amount of work they had ahead of them.

"Somebody else is here, boss," Hap said, pointing toward the top of the garden.

A personal transport was parked haphazardly across the gravel lane running below the tarped-over statue. The running panels of the transport were ostentatiously white, and the vehicle had obviously not been parked out of doors the night before. Everything about it spoke of wealth and privilege.

"Can only mean trouble, right, boss?" said Hap.

Tayne answered with a noncommittal grunt, even though he agreed. He eased the van into the same spot beside the maintenance shed they'd used the day before and set the brake. "Get everybody out and going," he said. "Start with those angels or whatever they are, closest to the gate. If I'm not back when those are done, do whatever Lizane says."

He considered digging out some hand cleaner from the van's supply bay before he walked up to the transport, but then decided not to take the time, despite the fact his hands were filthy from cleaning out the coupling. He figured the car's occupant was probably some-body from the municipal authority and so unlikely to offer to shake his hand anyway.

He was proven wrong on both counts.

A slightly built older man, dressed in a smart morning coat over the twill one-piece of the artisan class, was on his knees at the base of the new statue, making a poor job of untying the ropes that held down the tarps. His fine clothes were covered with the muck running off the canvas, and when he looked up at Tayne the man even had a smear of brown running from his creased forehead back over his pale, bald pate.

The man's thin face lit up with a broad smile when he saw Tayne. "I mean no offense, sir," he said, "when I tell you that you look like someone who's better equipped to get this piece uncovered than I am."

The voice was as unexpected as everything else about the situation. The man's accent wasn't just cultured, it was offworld cultured. Maybe even Earth cultured.

Tayne said, "Our work order is for cleaning all these others. That one was covered up pretty well—it's probably fine."

When he said "our," the other man furrowed his bushy white eyebrows and peered myopically down the garden. "Look at that. There's a whole gang of you."

"Gang" meant something very specific in the port, and Tayne winced. "We're a civic work crew, sir," he said, deciding that the man was definitely an offworlder, or at the very least new to the city. "We've got a ticket this morning to get the garden cleaned up for." He hesitated, trying to remember if the work order had used some official-sounding word for the afternoon's ceremony. "For the unveiling," he finished awkwardly.

"Well, that's fine," said the old man. "Though to be perfectly honest, most of these pieces won't be particularly improved by cleaning. A lot of dreary, pompous, celebratory stuff, isn't it? Unexamined patriotism bordering on jingoism, that sort of thing?"

Tayne worked a minute to unpack what the man had just said. After a moment, he said, "They take sedition pretty seriously around here, sir."

The man waved that off and picked at the mess he'd made of the ropes' master knot. "I've said worse and they still hired me for this commission," he said. "And back to what I was saying, you'll surely agree that it's most important that *this* piece be clean and ready? Can't we just have a peek to make sure none of this filth got through the wrappings?"

Tayne glanced back down at the gate and saw that Lizane had the crew divided into two teams, tackling the angels. She'd assigned them exactly as he would have, splitting up people who couldn't stand each other and people who got along *too* well, preventing fights before they started, and lollygagging as well.

He unsnapped the cover of the holster at his belt where he kept his multi-tool and pulled it out, unfolding the utility blade. He nodded at the ropes and said, "That's not going to get untangled anytime soon."

Grasping his intentions, the old man smiled again and said, "The Alexandrian solution, excellent." Then he hesitated and added, "Alexander the Great. An old general who found a knot that couldn't be untied in a place called Phrygia, and so he—"

Tayne kept his utility blade sharpened to a very keen edge. He sliced through the ropes with a single pass. "I know what the Gordion Knot was," he said, interrupting the man. "Even laborers on Castellon go to school. Until they're sixteen at any rate."

The old man pursed his lips. "They must be very excellent schools," he said.

Tayne shrugged and started pulling the tarps down. "Not really. But the libraries are all right."

The sculpture was of the previous governor, a woman who had ruled Castellon, its moons, and its outlying stations when Tayne was a boy. She was remembered for putting down a rebellion on the western continent, for reforming the tax code, and for patronizing the arts. At least that's what it said on the bronze plate bolted to the base of the statue. Tayne mainly remembered her for the draconian anti-gang policies that had been enforced during the later part of her administration. He touched the scar on the back of his head again as he gazed up at the outsized marble face three meters above.

"I suppose it's a good enough likeness," he said.

The old man tutted. "Hardly the point, sir, but thanks nonetheless."

Tayne looked over at him. "What *is* the point, then?"

The old man drew himself up, and an arch look came to his face. He opened his mouth to speak, but then suddenly deflated and smiled again. "The point, sir, is unexamined patriotism bordering on jingoism, as we established earlier. Which is what pays my bills and leaves me time for my own work. I knocked this out in two weeks, if you must know."

Tayne knew all about makework, about doing things just to pay the bills. "Why are you out here this morning, then?" he asked. "Why do you care if a little rain got onto this statue before the mayor and the rest of them see it?"

The man, Tayne supposed he should think of him as the *sculptor*, didn't immediately answer. He was slowly circling the plinth the statue stood upon, kicking his way through the fallen canvas. He stopped on the upland side, opposite of where Tayne stood, and said, "This. I'm out here this morning checking for something like this."

Curious, Tayne circled up to stand behind the sculptor, keeping clear of the tarps. The old man was pointing up at a black rune scorched into the marble at the base of the statue. It almost looked like a brand had been burned into the governor's marble foot.

Tayne recognized the rune. "Security services," he said. "That just means they've checked the statue out for . . . for I don't know what, really. But I suppose there are going to be a lot of important people here later."

The man turned to face Tayne. He had an unpleasant sneer on his face now. "'Important people,' yes. Well, that's relative." He reached up and ran his fingers across the rune. "A literal stamp of authority," he murmured. "How unimaginative."

Tayne supposed the man was upset about what could be seen as a defacement of his work, but, "Why do you care? You said this was a knock-out job, didn't you? They won't pay you any less just because some arbitrator in Customs followed some regulation."

The old man threw a sharp look at Tayne, but then smiled again. Tayne was starting to wonder just what the smiles meant. "'Customs,'" he said. "Because you know that this piece, and me, its maker, must have come from offworld. And I took such trouble to adopt the appropriate dress." He swept a hand down and out, displaying his artisan's wear. "But of course," he continued, "I haven't been here long enough to pick up the subtleties of the local argot."

Tayne said, "You've got a lot more work to do than just changing clothes and mimicking an accent if you want to pass for a local. You don't act anything like Castellon-born. You're too clean, for one thing. Even the quality people have ash in their skin here. It would take you years to pass."

The sculptor nodded. "Years I don't have, alas. I'm only here a few days. Just long enough for this ridiculous ceremony. Though I hope to see the famous volcano, of course."

Old Vice was a hundred kilometers inland from the port, part of the coastal mountain chain that separated the city from the sparsely inhabited interior. The caldera was said to be spectacular, the largest on any world, and flights over it were a popular if dangerous activity. Tayne didn't know anyone who had ever taken such a trip, though he'd once seen the volcano from a distance, back when he first hired on with the municipal authority, years before. One of the very first jobs he'd ever drawn was a scheduled maintenance check on the funicular that ran up to a civil-guard post overlooking the port from a nearby peak. It was still the farthest Tayne had ever been from the city proper, and he could still remember the views inland across the mountains, and out across the alkaline ocean.

"They say it's something to see," Tayne told the man. "Look, I need to get back to my crew, and we should probably cover your statue back up. If it's going to be unveiled later then I'm guessing it's supposed to be veiled when the dignitaries get here."

The old man waved a dismissive hand. "Don't trouble yourself. The 'veil' will be a silken drop cloth attached to a line. That way, whichever plutocrat is in charge will be able to pull it off in suitably dramatic fashion without the bother of ropes and rough canvas."

Tayne hesitated. "Well," he said after a moment's consideration, "you know more about it than me, certainly. But listen, I can't take responsibility if there's some kind of trouble over it being uncovered now."

Again, a dismissive wave. "Go, go, scrub the muck off all these wastes of marble and granite. If anyone asks, I'll tell them I pulled off the canvas on my own. Just the sort of eccentric behavior one expects from an artist and an offworlder, yes?"

With that, he seemed to lose interest in conversing with Tayne. He pulled a fist-sized tin with a hinged top from one pocket and a broad-bladed putty knife from another. When he opened the tin, Tayne saw that it contained a white spackle the exact shade of the marble statue. Whistling tunelessly, the sculptor set about obscuring the blackened rune.

Clad in rubberized coveralls and heavy boots, wearing respirators that had been in service for too long, the crew loaded steaming garbage onto the scow. Tayne drove a skid steer loader checked out from the port authority, humping up piles of municipal detritus at the edge of the dock that half his crew then shoveled over the railing into the open-decked conveyance below. The others were down there, shifting and sorting with pitchforks, making sure that the load was evenly distributed and hoping for the odd piece of salvage, unlikely as that was.

Tayne estimated they were maybe a third of the way through the job when they all heard the explosion roll down over the city.

Tayne lowered the bucket of the loader and cut the power, clambering out of the machine as quickly as he could. Hap and the others working topside came trotting over, pulling off their respirators and babbling to one another.

"Gas main?" asked Hap, speaking to the group in general. Those kinds of accidents weren't unheard of in the city, at least in the parts where the underground mains hadn't been properly maintained in years. The parts of the city where they all lived. But no . . .

"It was up in the heights," said Tayne, and as he started to put it together, Lizane and the rest from down on the scow topped the dock, climbing up from below along rope hawser netting. He saw the look of fear on Lizane's face and knew that she was making the same guesses he was.

"What time is it?" Tayne asked.

The others looked at one another in confusion for a moment, and Tayne said again, "What *time?*" shouting now.

"Sixteen thirty," said Hap. "Sixteen forty-five, something like that. Why?"

"They were all up there," said Lizane. "They said the governor was going to be there, the mayors of all the settlements, who knows who all?"

Sirens were whining in the distance now, emergency services crews making their way up the hill. A thick plume of yellow and gray smoke rose inland.

"Even if they don't blame us—" Lizane began, and Tayne cut her off.

"We're done, we're all done," he said, thinking fast. He rubbed his hand across the back of his head, thinking about the questioning techniques of the municipal arbitrators. Thinking that questions from the planetary authorities would be even worse.

"What are you two talking about?" whined Hap. Tayne could see that he wasn't alone in his confusion.

"Fool!" said Lizane. "Look where that smoke is coming from. Think about where we were this morning and why we were there."

Hap looked vaguely toward the column of smoke. "The explosion was in the sculpture garden we cleaned out?" he asked. Then realization dawned on his face. "Gods," he said, "do you think they're all dead?"

Tayne said, "I think we'll find out soon enough. We'll all be put to the question."

"But we don't *know* anything!" said Hap.

Tayne thought about the sculptor. "I do," he said. "I know that none of you saw anything. So when they come, just tell them that. And tell them that you saw me up at the statue with a stranger."

There was a brief moment of silence, then Lizane said, "It won't matter. They'll still take us all in, and those of us with the wrong kind of records . . ."

She meant herself. Hell, she meant him.

"Give me your work chit," he told her.

"Tayne," she said, as soft as he'd ever heard her say anything, but she pulled the chit from where it hung on a leather cord around her neck.

He took it, stalked over to the edge of the dock, and dropped it into the scow. "You weren't at work today," he said. "Who else could I not find this morning?"

The crew looked at one another, figuring their chances. Two others pulled off their chits and handed them over.

"So, go to ground," Tayne told those two and Lizane. "Get out of the city if you can. And if they catch you, just tell them exactly what happened and why. You were afraid of the authorities and I told you to run. Easy, right?"

Lizane was already stripping off her workboots. She spat, "Easy, sure."

"But why run at all?" shouted Hap. "Why would they blame us?"

Tayne said, "Because they'll have to blame somebody. And we're available."

Lizane gave him an intense, unreadable look that Tayne supposed was a kind of good-bye, then she and the other two all headed different directions.

"The rest of you can wait here or head on home. If I were you, I'd find a bar and enjoy a drink. It'll be the last one you have for a while." Tayne walked over and sat on the bucket of the loader.

"What are you going to do?" asked Hap as the rest of the crew drifted aimlessly away.

Tayne started pulling off his boots. "I'm going to think up a story," he said.

When the arbitrators came a half hour later, Tayne sneered at them and said, "How many did I get?"

The scar-faced man climbed down the scaffolding, clearly unfamiliar with the light spin-induced gravity this deep in the station. Twenty or so people were gathered in the dark, confined space, watching him in silence.

Finding a place to stand where they could all see him, he took a long time looking at them each in turn. "Too many," he said. "If you're just one cell, there are too many of you. If you're more than one cell, you've compromised yourselves."

A lanky bald woman sat up straighter. She wore the implants of a remote operator of a vacuum utility bot but had none of the distracted look that operators usually sported. "We're moving to take this station in forty hours," she said. "We're past the point of secrecy. We're ready to join the Free Communes."

The scar-faced man would be off the station in just a few hours. He idly wondered how many of the people he could see would be dead in two days' time. He wondered if they would succeed.

Another woman, this one dressed in the clean lines of an administrative aide, said, "Is she really here?"

There was a clanking noise from above, and the scar-faced man held up his hand to help down the limping figure who appeared out of the darkness. Around them, he heard the stationers reverently murmuring her name. "Lizane."

At least they weren't calling her "mother," the way the last bunch had. Mother of the revolution.

Lizane looked at the stationers with a lot more sympathy than the scar-faced man had. She handed over the data drive they'd brought to him, and he, in turn, handed it to the bald woman. "Arbitrator codes," he said, and half the reason they were there was behind them.

Then Lizane drew in a deep breath and started in on the rest of the reason.

"I knew him. I knew Tayne, and I was there the day he started the revolution . . ."

Nowhere Fast

The sky Luz rode under was a pale and hazy gray, its color burned away by sun and smoke years before she was born. Luz might have even called the sky white, but the zinc oxide sunscreen she and the others had dutifully spread over their skin was so stark against her brown arms and legs that there was no comparison.

Her grandmother said that when she was a teenager in California, thousands of miles distant and decades and decades gone in the past, girls welcomed the sun and used its rays to burn themselves darker. Luz had asked if that meant the girls didn't know about skin diseases and sun lesions and her grandmother had answered with one of the private gestures they shared. Hand to head, then hand to heart meant that knowing something and believing it weren't the same thing.

Right now, Luz couldn't believe that tiny Priscilla was steadily pulling away from her on the long climb up from the ferry. She pushed harder on her bicycle's pedals, trying to match the rhythm of the turning wheels to her rapid breathing. Still, the younger girl danced on ahead, standing on her pedals, apparently unaware that she was leaving Luz and the others behind.

There were four of them out on their bikes, fifteen miles from town and taking their time getting to the upland field of strawberries they were scheduled to hoe free of weeds. Luz had sent her younger brother, Caleb, to the work hall with strict instructions to find something far from town. She'd been pleased when he brought back the slip listing a work site on the bluffs above the Kentucky River—far enough and different enough from town that she could pretend she was really travelling—but slightly annoyed that Sammy and Priscilla came trailing in after him.

She liked Priscilla, but had assumed—mistakenly, it turned out—that the young girl would slow them down. She liked Priscilla's brother Sammy well enough, too, but he'd lately started liking her back in a way she just didn't reciprocate. It made for some awkward talk when they went out on the same community-service jobs.

Not that there had been much call for talk on the long ride out, especially not as they crested the hill, breathing hard.

Up ahead, Priscilla signaled a stop, and at first Luz thought she was finally tiring. But then the girl spoke.

"Is that an *engine?*" Priscilla asked, eyes wide.

Luz stopped beside her, struggling to slow her breath so she could hear the howling sound floating over the fields better. Hard to say how far away the noise was, but it was clearly in motion. And moving closer, fast.

Caleb and Sammy stopped beside them and dismounted.

"It is," said Caleb, excitement in his voice. "Internal combustion, not too big."

Even though Caleb was the scholar of the group, Sammy couldn't pass up an opportunity to try to impress Luz. "Not like on any of the Federal machines, though," he said. "Not like anything I've ever heard."

Luz thought of the last time one of the great Army recruitment trucks had come through Lexington, grinding and belching and trumpeting its horn. It had been the previous autumn. Her parents had made her hide in one of the sheds behind the house, even though she was only sixteen and the Federals weren't supposed to draft anyone younger than eighteen. She had stood behind a tidy stack of aluminum doors her mother had salvaged from the ghost suburbs south of town and listened to the engine closely.

The Army engine had been a deeper sound than this, though whatever was approaching was not as high as the mosquito buzz of the little motors on the sheriff's department chariots. If the deputies rode mosquitoes, then the Federals rode growling bears. This was something in between, a howling wolf.

The noise dropped away briefly, stuttered, and then came back louder than ever.

"Whatever it is, it just turned into the lane," Luz told the others. She dismounted and waved for them all to move their bikes into the grassy verge to one side. They'd stopped at a point where the road was bound on either side by low dry-stone walls. A pair of curious chestnut quarter horses, fully biological, not the hissing mounts of Federal outriders, ambled over briefly, hopeful of treats, but they snorted and trotted away as the noise came closer.

Suddenly, the sound blared as loud as anything Luz had ever heard and a . . . vehicle rounded the curve before them. Luz flashed on the automobile carcasses some people kept as tomato planters. She saw four wheels, a brace of 55-gallon drums, and a makeshift seat. The seat was occupied by a distracted looking young man wrestling a steering wheel as he hurtled past them, forcing them to move even farther off the road.

The vehicle fishtailed from side to side on the crumbling pavement, sputtering, and came to an abrupt halt when it took a hard left turn and hit the wall on the south side of the road. The top two layers of rock slid into the field as the noise died away.

They all ran toward the crash. Luz could see now that the vehicle was a modified version of a hay wagon, sporting thick rubber tires and otherwise liberally outfitted with ancient automobile parts. The seat was a cane-bottomed rocker with the legs removed, screwed to the bed. The young man was strapped into the chair, with a dazed expression on his face.

The huge metal engine that took up most of the wagon bed ticked.

The young man, and Luz saw that he was younger than she had first thought, just a little older than her sixteen years, perhaps, blinked and looked at them. He had tightly curled black hair and green eyes.

"I think . . . ," he began, and trailed off, lips still moving, eyes still unfocused. "I think I need to adjust the braking mechanism."

He claimed, unbelievably, that he was from North Carolina. Hundreds of miles away, the other side of mountains with collapsed tunnels and rivers with fallen bridges. In Luz's experience, traffic from the east came into the Bluegrass along only two routes: down from the Ohio off boats from Pittsburgh, or along the Federal Highway through Huntington. Or by air, though the Federal flying machines were forbidden to land in Lexington by treaty.

"No, no," the driver said, piling the last rock back on top of the wall his machine had damaged. "I didn't come over the mountains. I went south, first, then along the Gulf shore, then up the Natchez Trace through Alabama and middle Tennessee. The state government in Tennessee is pretty advanced. They've built pontoon bridges over all their rivers now."

Luz reached behind Fizz—that was the name he'd given—and made an adjustment to the slab of limestone he haphazardly dropped atop the wall. He'd accepted their offer to help him repair the fence, which was a good thing, because it was clear that he had no experience with dry-stone work. For some reason, this made him seem even more foreign to Luz than his vehicle or his claim to have seen the ocean. Sammy had whispered his opinion that Fizz would have left the wall in disrepair if they hadn't witnessed the crash, but Luz wasn't ready to be that judgmental.

Sammy was also more persistent in his questions than Luz thought was polite. "Well, then how did you cross the Kentucky River? And the Green and all the creeks you must have come to? We just came from the ferry, and they would have mentioned you. And there's no way the Federals would have let you bring that thing across any of *their* bridges."

"There's more local bridges than you might think," said Fizz, either completely missing the hostility in Sammy's voice or ignoring it. "I only had to float Rudolf once. See the air compressor there? I can fill old inner tubes and lash them to the sides. That converts him into a raft good enough for the width of a creek, anyways."

Caleb was examining the vehicle. "There are a lot of bridges that aren't on the Federal map," he said, almost to himself. Then he asked, "Why do you call it Rudolf?"

"Rudolf Diesel!" said Fizz, in a different, stranger accent than most of his speech. He seemed to think that answered Caleb's question.

Priscilla whispered, "He speaks German." Luz found Priscilla's instant and obvious crush on Fizz annoying.

Fizz looked at the girls. "Sure he did," he said, and smiled at Luz. "He *was* German. He probably spoke like eleven languages, not just English and Spanish. Everybody did back then. He designed this engine—or its ancestor, anyway." He pointed to the cooling metal engine on his vehicle.

"I hope you paid him for it," said Sammy.

"No, I remember," said Caleb. "Diesel was one of the men who made the internal-combustion engines." A troubled expression crossed his face. "That's from history. You shouldn't tell people you named your car after him, Fizz."

Fizz wrinkled his nose and brow, scoffing. "Figures the only thing the Federals are consistent about are their interstate highway monopolies and their curriculum suggestions. Diesel wasn't a bad guy! The 19th century, which is when he invented this, only ended a couple of hundred years ago. Don't you guys have grandparents? Don't they talk about when everybody could go everywhere?"

Some do, Luz thought. Aloud, she said, "Our abuela *has* been everywhere. She's from Chiapas, and came here from California before the oil finally ran out."

"And we can go anywhere we like, anyway," said Sammy. "We just like it here."

"But going places takes forever!" said Fizz. Then he finally seemed to notice the uncomfortable glances being shared between Caleb and Sammy. "Not that this isn't a great place to be. The hemp-seed oil

Rudolf is burning for fuel right now is from around here someplace. Or it was. My tanks are about dry. That's why I turned north when the Tennesseans wouldn't trade me any."

Luz nodded. "Sure. The biggest oil press anywhere is over in Frankfort. Our uncles sell them most of their hemp. What have you got to trade that the Feds would want?"

Fizz made the face again. "Eh, they're not much for bartering with people like me."

"And who's that?" asked Sammy. "Who are people like you?"

Fizz looked them all up and down, deciding something.

Then he said, "Revolutionaries."

"Revolting is more like it," Sammy gasped. He and Luz were working very hard, barely turning the pedals of their bikes over in their lowest gears. Fizz had brought out some cords from the toolbox on his machine, and between them, he and Luz had figured out a way to rig a Y harness connecting the automobile's front axle to the seatposts of her and Sammy's bikes. The others rode behind the automobile, hopping off to push on the hills.

Except for Fizz, of course, who rode the machine the whole time, manning the steering wheel and chattering happily to curious Caleb and smitten Priscilla. Luz wished she could be back there. She had a thousand questions about the wider world.

Fizz had insisted they take a little used, poorly surfaced route into town. He said he wanted to approach the council of farmers and merchants who acted as the community council before they saw his machine. "I had trouble some places," he said. "Farther south."

Now, as they hauled the stranger and his strange vehicle, they kept the fleet of canvas balloons anchored high above Lexington dead ahead. Federal government ornithopters were forbidden to land inside the town limits, but Kentucky was still the primary source for their fuel, so the brass-winged engines could usually be seen clinging to the netting below their coal-laden baskets, crawling and supping like the fruit bats that haunted the orchards ringing the town.

Responding to Sammy, Luz asked, "What's revolting?"

He answered her with a question. "Do you know what we're pulling? I'll tell you. It's a *car*. A private car."

Luz took her left hand off the handlebars long enough to point out a particularly deep pothole in the asphalt. Sammy acknowledged with a nod and they bore to the right.

"Don't be silly," Luz continued after they'd negotiated the hole. "Cars ran on oil. Petroleum oil, I mean."

But Luz had already noticed that a lot of the machine's parts were similar to those she found when she went scrounging with her mother. The steering wheel, for one thing, was plastic, and plastic was the very first word in the list of nonrenewables she'd memorized in grade school. Luz was still five years away from the age when she would attain full citizenship, and thus be allowed to learn to read, but like most teenagers she had paid close enough attention when adults practiced that art to recognize a few words. One of the words stamped on Fizz's machine was "transmission," but she did not tell Sammy this.

"Well, I guess he made a car that runs on hemp-seed oil," said Sammy. "Or somebody did, anyway." Sammy doubted every part of Fizz's story. "He probably stole it off the Federals."

Luz doubted that. The only vehicles she knew the Federals to use besides their Army trucks were bicycles, the coal-burning horses that patrolled the highways, and the ornithopters that patrolled the skies, their metal wings flapping like a hawk's. Bikes and horses and 'thopters and trucks alike shared a sleek, machined design. Nothing at all like the haphazard jumble of Fizz's "car."

The group managed to attract only a few stares before they made it to one of the sheds behind Luz and Caleb's house. Luz supposed that people assumed they'd found a heap of scrap metal and had knocked together a wagon on-site to transport it to their mother's salvage shops. People brought her old things all the time.

"Are you going to get your father?" Sammy asked. "Because you should." Then, unusually, he left before Luz asked him to, saying he had to get home.

His little sister, however, clearly had no intention of leaving. She wordlessly followed Fizz as he crawled around checking the undercarriage of his machine.

"I guess this job posting is open all week," said Caleb, pulling the paper out from his belt. Luz had completely forgotten the original purpose of their ride. "Maybe we can go on Wednesday if we can get enough people."

"Sure," said Luz.

"So it's okay if I work here?" Fizz asked. "You won't get in trouble?"

Caleb was worried. "Our father will be home soon—"

"Wait," Luz interrupted. Fizz and his car were the most interesting thing that had happened to Luz in a long time. "Mama's in the mountains, gleaning in the tailings from the old mines. I'll go to the shop and talk to Papa."

"That'd be great," said Fizz, popping his head out from under the machine right at their feet. "Looks like you've probably got everything I need to get Rudolf up and running."

Luz left quickly, knowing it would be better for them all if her father knew what was waiting for him at home.

The shop was the more or less permanent stall in market by the courthouse run by their father. It served as the main bike shop in town. Luz and her friends had free use of a parts box that was pretty extraordinary by anybody's standards, and their father had connections all over the place if they needed something he didn't have, or couldn't recycle or rig themselves. He fixed the Post Office's long-haul cargo bikes for free in exchange for good rates bringing in stuff from the coast, but always insisted that his children—and his other customers—make an honest attempt at repair before they settled on replacement.

Papa moved around the stall, putting away tools and hanging bikes from hooks in the ceiling. "Yes, he could have driven here from North Carolina," he told Luz. "Before the Peak, people made the trip in a few hours."

Luz didn't doubt that her father was telling the truth, but thought of the hand to heart gesture again, of the difference between knowing and feeling the truth. She could *feel* the truth when somebody said the sun was hot, but could only *acknowledge* the truth when somebody said it was 93 million miles away.

"That's what he was talking about, I guess," she said. "Fizz. When he said that it takes forever to go anywhere now."

Without warning, Papa dropped the seatpost he was holding to the shop floor. It made a dull clattering sound as it bounced back and forth.

"Hey!" said Luz as he grabbed her arm, *hard*, and pulled her out the open end of the stall.

Out in the street, he let go, and pointed up at the sky. "Look up there!" he barked.

Luz had never heard her father sound so angry. She found it hard to tear her eyes away from his livid face, but he thrust his finger skyward again. "Look!" he said.

Luz stared at the sky, gray and cloudless as ever in the spring heat.

"That is a *bruised* sky," he said, punctuating his words with his hand. "That is a *torn-up* sky."

His mood suddenly changed in a way that made Luz think of a deflating tire. He leaned against the corner support pole of the shop. "You don't know what our ancestors did to this world. There's so much less of everything. And if there is one reason for it, it's in what this stranger told you. 'Forever,' hah! It takes as long to get somewhere as it should take—his *expedience* leads to war and flood."

Luz didn't understand half of what he was saying.

"What about the Federals?" she asked. "They drive trucks and have flying machines."

Papa waved his hand. "We are not the Federals. We live lightly upon the earth, light enough that the wounds they deal it will heal. Your grandparents' generation fought wars so that we could rescue the world from excess. People like us act as stewards, we save the rivers and the sky and the land from the worst that people like them do. When you're older you'll understand."

Luz thought about that for a moment, then said, "People like us and people like the Federals?"

Papa looked at her. "Yes, Luz."

"What about people that aren't like either?" Luz asked.

Papa hadn't answered her before Priscilla came tearing down the street. "Luz! They took him! They came and took Fizz and his machine both! Caleb couldn't stop them!"

She slid to a halt next to them in a cloud of dust. "It was Sammy! He brought the deputies!"

Luz instantly hopped on her bike, and saw from the corner of her eye that her father was pulling his own from behind the workbench. She didn't wait for him to catch up.

Hours later, Luz and Caleb pedaled along abandoned streets behind the tannery and the vinegar works, looking for the stockade where the deputies had taken Fizz. They might have missed him if he hadn't shouted out.

"Hey! Luz!"

Fizz was leaning half out of a ground-floor window in an old brick building set in an unkempt lawn of weeds and trash. As they rode over to him, a deputy rounded the corner and growled at Fizz to stay inside the window. Clearly, the deputies weren't used to having prisoners. When Caleb asked if they could speak to Fizz, the man shrugged and instructed them not to let him escape.

"The trial's tonight," the deputy said, then went back to the corner, where he sat on a stool and idly turned the letter-pressed pages of last week's town newsletter.

"I've had it worse, that's for sure," Fizz told them. "They seem a lot more concerned with Rudolf than they are with me. I hope your father didn't get in trouble for it being at your house."

Luz and Caleb glanced at one another. The car had been much easier to locate than its driver. They had stood with the other younger people and watched uneasily while their parents and grandparents hung the vehicle from a hastily erected scaffold in the square. Their father had rigged the block and tackle the men used to haul it above a growing pile of scrap timber.

"No," said Luz. "Papa's fine."

"I don't think Rudolf will be able to say the same," Caleb said.

The serious look that passed over Fizz's face made Luz notch her guess of his age back up another year or two. But then he flashed a wide grin and said, "Rudolf's never offered an opinion on anything at all, Caleb. We hit the road before I figured out how to make him talk."

When they didn't join his laughter, Fizz nodded and said, "I see that you're worried. Don't be. I've been in communities like yours before. Heck, I've even been in jails like this one before. Your council and"—he raised his eyebrow—"I'm guessing your father, too? They're more concerned about the machine than the machinist. They'll do whatever they're going to do to Rudolf and then storm and glower at me for an hour and send me on my way."

Luz said, "Papa's name came up in the lottery at New Year's, so he's on the council this year. And yes, he's concerned about the machine. But I think he's even more concerned about the use you put it to."

Fizz didn't reply. He gazed at her steadily, as if she knew the answer to a question he'd forgotten to ask aloud.

"'Everybody could go everywhere,'" she finally said, quoting him.

"Ah," Fizz said. "Your friend said that everybody still can."

Luz shook her head. "I don't think Sammy is my friend anymore. And anyway," she added, her voice unexpectedly bitter, "he's never *wanted* to go anywhere."

Fizz was sympathetic. "What about you?" he asked her. "Where would you go if you could?"

Luz thought about it for a moment. She remembered Fizz's route along the Gulf of Mexico, but even more, she remembered her grandmother's stories of California.

"I would go to the ocean," she said. "My grandmother was a surfer. You know, on the waves?" She held her palm out flat and rocked it back and forth.

Fizz nodded.

"She says that I'm built right for it. It sounds . . . fast."

"And light on the earth, too," Fizz said. "Am I saying that right?"

"You're close," said Caleb, frowning at them both. "It's 'lightly upon the earth.'"

Luz had never thought about how often she heard the phrase. It was something said by the older people in the community over and over again. "How did you know people say that here?" she asked.

Fizz shrugged. "People say it everywhere," he said.

Luz had expected her father and the other council members to be arrayed behind a long table in the courtyard square. She had expected the whole town to turn out to watch the proceedings, and even for Fizz to be marched out by the deputies with his hands tied before him with a coil of rope.

She had not expected Federal marshals.

There were two of them, a silver-haired man and a grim-faced woman. Neither of them bothered to dismount their strange horses, only issuing terse orders to the closest townspeople to fetch pails of coal they then turned into the furnaces atop the hybrid creatures' hindquarters. They seemed impatient, as was ever the way with Federals.

Luz sat on the ground in front of a bench crowded with older people, leaning back against her grandmother's knees. "I thought the covenants between the town and the Federals guaranteed us the right to have our own trials," Luz said.

Her abuela patted her shoulder, though there was nothing of reassurance in it. "My son," she said, speaking of Luz's Papa, "is more afraid of what this Fizz can do to us than what the Federals can. The council asked the marshals here."

Before Luz could express her dismay at this news, the Council chair banged on the table with a wrench to quiet the crowd. "We're in extraordinary session, people," she said, "and the only order of business is the forbidden technology this boy from . . . North Carolina has brought to our town."

Before anything more could be said, Luz's Papa raised his hand to be recognized. "I move we close this meeting," he said. "We'll be talking of things our children shouldn't be made to hear."

The gathered townspeople murmured at this, and Luz was surprised at the tone. She would have expected them to be upset that they couldn't watch the proceedings, but except for the people her age, most there seemed to be agreeing with her father. Before any of the council members could respond to the suggestion, though, Fizz spoke up.

"I believe I'm allowed to speak, yes?" he asked. "That's been the way of it with the other town councils."

Luz saw the woman marshal lean over in her saddle and whisper something to her partner, whose dead-eyed gaze never shifted from Fizz.

The chairwoman saw the exchange, too, and seemed troubled by it. "Yes, son," she told Fizz. "We've heard this isn't the first time you've been brought up on these charges. But you should be careful you don't say anything to incriminate yourself. It might not be us that carries out whatever sentence we decide on."

Fizz looked directly at the marshals, and then back at the council. "Yes, ma'am," he said. "I see that. I've not been in a town controlled by the Federal government before."

Papa's angry interruption cut through the noise from the crowd. "Here now!" he said. "We're as sovereign as any other town in America and signatory to covenants that reserve justice to ourselves. It's our laws you've flouted and our ruling that will decide your fate. These marshals are here at our invitation because we want to demonstrate how seriously we take your crimes."

Luz did not realize she had stood until she spoke. "What crimes?"

Papa frowned at her. "Sit down, Luza," he said.

Before she could respond, Fizz spoke. "I can choose someone to speak on my behalf, isn't that right? I choose her. I want Luz to be my advocate."

To Luz's surprise—to *everyone's* surprise—the voice that answered did not come from the Council, but from one of the Federals.

"Oh for God's sake," the woman said, directing her words to Luz's father. "Andy, we came here to destroy this unauthorized car as a favor to you, not to watch you Luddites play at justice." With that, she and the man leapt from the saddles stitched to their horses' flanks. They both whistled high and hard and pointed at Fizz's vehicle. It slowly turned in the air, held a foot above the ground by a strong cable.

For the first time, Fizz appeared confused, even frightened.

Then *everyone* was frightened, as the horses leapt.

Their lips curled back, exposing spikes where an unaltered horse's teeth would be. Long claws extended from the dewlaps above their steel-shod hooves, and the muscles rippling beneath their flanks were square and hard. They jumped onto the hanging car, clinging to opposite sides, steam and smoke belching from their noses and ears as they struck and bit, kicked and tore. The sounds of metal ripping and wood splitting rang across the square, frighteningly loud, yet still not loud enough to drown the frightened cries of the children in the crowd. Luz was as shocked by the sounds the horses made as she was by the savagery of their assault.

In moments, the car called Rudolf was a pile of scrap metal and wood. The horses' spikes and claws retracted as they trotted back to their riders, who waited with more skips of coal to replenish what they'd burned up in the destruction.

The Federals swung into their saddles and the woman spoke to Luz's father once more. "Do you want us to take your prisoner off your hands, too, Andy? We're better equipped to deal with his kind of trouble than you."

"No!" cried Luz.

Everyone turned to look at her. "If Fizz has broken any rules they were *ours*, not yours. You . . . you lot get going."

Luz's father nodded at the Federals. The woman and the deadeyed man exchanged ugly grins, but they put their spurs to their mounts and left the square.

Luz turned to the Council. "And *you* lot, you get to explaining. What is all this? Papa, you can't stand the Federals and their ways. None of you can. You'd put us in debt to enforce some law that you won't even name?"

All of the people sitting behind the table looked troubled, and only Papa would meet her gaze.

"We protect our children from such things until they've reached their majority, Luz," he said. "You know that. But since you all just saw . . . what we all just saw . . ." He hesitated for a moment. "It's basically what I said earlier, Luz," he continued. "Your friend there has a personal car, and that's the source of so much bad in the world I can't even begin to explain it to you. It can't be allowed."

Luz rolled her eyes and walked over to the pile of debris beneath the scaffold. She pointed to it and said, "This, you mean? It doesn't look to me like he has a car anymore."

She turned to Fizz for support, but he was still staring at the wreckage. For once, he had nothing to say. *I'm his advocate*, she remembered.

"You should let him go," she said. "*We* should let him go."

Before her father could respond, the chairwoman called him closer. They exchanged a few murmured words. Then she said, "The young man is no longer a danger to our community, or to the earth. He's free to go."

Papa added, "He *must* go."

The crowd stood and milled around, everyone talking about what had just happened. Luz spotted her father approaching, and then saw her abuela shake her head to stop him from coming near.

Luz went and stood beside Fizz. She thought about what she had learned about making and repairing things from her father. She thought about what she had learned about scavenging from her mother. She thought of the stories of gliding across an ocean's wave told to her by her grandmother. She put her hand on Fizz's shoulder.

"I know where we can get some parts," she said.

Two Figures in a Landscape Between Storms

The buildings, the tumbled stones, the ground, they are all sandstone. Blasted, pockmarked sandstone. Great blocks are tumbled and thrown about. The color of the blood stains runs from near black along one wall to the darkening brown beneath his shoulders and thighs to the violent, living red running from her forehead and mouth.

His gauntleted hand lies inches from her bare left foot. Deep furrows scar the rock beneath his fingertips, the tracks of his last attempt, his final angry clawing.

His body is a bulk of metal and muscle. The firelight and the sunlight across it are distorted by greasy smoke.

His armor is red and black, damaged. The plate at the right shoulder hangs by a frayed strap. Her target. The white bone stands out against the black metal.

The helmet is all stylized angles and nightmare shapes, horned mantids. It still covers his head, his head twisted at an unnatural angle. The visor is shoved against the ground. A froth of blood has swelled through the vents.

A scabbard lies discarded beside him. It is empty, but ornately decorated. Silhouettes have been inlaid along its length by a careful craftsman. Women, men, children, engines of war. The silhouettes do not march the whole distance from open end to gilded close. There would have been room for her portrait.

One end of the weapon is embedded in a slumped wall. Its flanges and vanes, a complexity of barbs, glower through the dust and smoke.

The heavy, tooled shaft stretches across his body; the cruel weight of it presses against her thigh.

Calmly, calmly, calmly, she sits, still. Her hands, nails trimmed short, fingers stained with potter's clay, grip the weapon so tightly.

The torn rags of her tunic are muddy with a mixture of blood and dust and sweat and sand. Her muscled shoulders and midriff and legs are exposed, revealing testaments: scars, burns, bruises, welts, blisters, stretch marks, wounds.

Strands of hair that have escaped from their band are soaked to her forehead. Her broad face is still. Her flecked green eyes are unblinking. There is nothing behind her eyes.

Finally, movement. A shadow. The light from the sun and the fires delineates a shadow falling across a ruin of sandstone. A large shadow, the head a mantid nightmare. Her hand grips so tightly.

Gather

At the very end of autumn, Gather had thirty-four coins to spend. Commerce—that's the kind of buying things that used coins instead of goods—was not an opportunity that arose in the north town very often. He planned to spend all thirty-four.

There was a lot to regret about that. All of Gather's coins were beautiful. They had curling, unknowable writing on one side and little pictures of God on the other. Gather loved to study the coins. He was intimately aware of all their differences and similarities, and aware, too, that with winter coming he'd have few chances to get more.

Besides his work assignments, his sisters would usually each give him a coin for good-bye and remembrance when it was their turn to go down the river to wife for the bad batch men. He'd found one copper coin in a wagon track, where the ground had split from thawing and refreezing in the inconstant autumn temperatures. It showed God's eyes, all steaming. He'd won a rough gray coin at a fair, when he'd rowed a skiff faster than a sweepsman off a southern barge.

Another obstacle to transactions was the way the act of spending could complicate itself so hypnotically. Offer the merchant a coin for those pepper seeds spilling out of twists of dead, unflickering paper, then put the coin to heart, to lips. Do it again and rock forward and backward and then forward and then backward and put the coin to forehead, to heart, to lips, and on like that, and on until the merchant loses patience and raps one hand against the table and shakes the seeds with the other, *arrhythmic*. All wrong.

"Liveborn fool," the merchant said. "A grown man, getting lost in counting games! Buy if you're buying; we're closing this fair down."

Gather snapped to, because these barges were the last before winter, and it would be long years to huddle with just the cold comfort of money before spring.

The merchant spoke again. "Ice chokes the river, boy, and if it freezes over it'll be you pushing our barges, skate like, you and all these holy men down from their chapterhouse." The southerners were bad-batch men, mostly, with useless legs bundled up under them if they were merchants or captains, legs self-amputated if they were hard men who needed speed, like the sweeps handlers.

Gather had liked rowing the skiff so quickly, and would have asked about a job on the barge but he had to stay up the river with the preachers and his sisters. *Only bad-batch men can be southerners.* That was from a bible. So he worked on the docks or on the fishing boats for now, and would work chopping holes in the ice when the river was frozen. Gather was stout and steady.

He considered whether to buy the twists, which would yield long red wreaths of hothouse peppers, if he was careful. He considered his thirty-four coins.

"You can plant a coin," one of his sisters had said when he'd accumulated two dozen of the coins. "You can *plant* them, but they won't grow into anything useful out here."

But that wasn't quite true, it wasn't *exactly* the truth, and Gather required things to be very exact indeed. Precision was his watchword and his sacrament.

In the end, he bought four twists of seeds from the southern merchant. He bought an old blanket that the seller claimed had been woven by a machine. He bought forty candles, forty pounds of sugar, and forty minutes' worth of a storyteller's time.

Forty minutes was long enough for the national anthem, the long night in the garden at Gethsemane, and the history of the first people to come down onto Virginia, who were called Pilgrims and who had starved to death before they were born again for God.

Counting coins again.

The twists and the blanket and the candles and the sugar and the time and that's down to eleven left for imperishable food. Eleven coins on smoked fish like muskie, or eleven coins on ground grains like spelt, or eleven coins on dried pulses like beans.

Peas and lentils all winter, then.

Weeks later, when the river was frozen hard enough for foot traffic, some of the children came to Gather and asked him to pull their sledge across to the far side. This was forbidden, but their leader, a little girl with green eyes, was *PK*—a preacher's kid—which warranted a lot of deference. But more than that she said, "One, two, three, *four*, Gather walks across the *floor* . . ." and on like that—a very clever little girl, very good at rhymes *and* rhythms. So Gather bundled up in his heaviest coat and his machine blanket and trudged out onto the ice with a towrope slung over his shoulder.

The PK girl had him skirt north of the island where the watchtower stood. ("Thirteen, fourteen, fifteen, *six*teen, farther up so we are *not* seen.") There were no preachers manning the tower top that Gather could see, which was a curiosity. Then he heard hammering and work-chanting farther down the river and remembered that today was the first day the preachers would be pushing the big wagons across to the far side to cut up big blocks of frozen soil—the good kind of soil that things would grow in. Many work points, but only for preachers, who had special dispensation from God and specific instructions on where to gather the soil from their bibles.

The PK snapped her fingers in time with her counting to get Gather moving again, and pulled them on up and across. Her voice faltered with her courage a dozen yards shy of the eastern shore. The bank was choked with evergreens right down to the ice, towering pines that cut off any view of what lay farther back. Which was just as well, because God lived on the far bank and to go to the house of God was forbidden. That was from a bible, too.

"S'ko back, y'all." One of the other children finally spoke. Earlier, the PK had hushed the girls whenever they started to speak, which Gather had appreciated because it was rare for a pair and nearly impossible for a group to keep the rhythm.

Gather was pretty sure the speaker was a niece of his, or possibly a very young aunt, some kin anyhow from the tangled net of cousins and sisters who stayed up the river for the preachers. She said, "S'kome."

The option of returning to town lay out there on the ice, but the PK was clearly not convinced. She stood, considering, and nobody moved to turn the sledge around.

A thick shelf of snow slid off the lowest hanging branch of a nearby tree. It made a noise like SHHHH-CHOOM. None of the children jumped or screamed or carried on, but Gather said, "Oh, Lord," because he thought that maybe God was coming down the bank.

The PK girl said, "Home home home home."

For Gather, home was his apartment in the carriage house behind the post office. Once he and the children were back on the side of the river where people lived, Gather walked down Dock Street with the river to his left.

He turned into the alley between the post office and the courthouse—he'd shoveled the brickway clear the day before—and crossed the courtyard to his door.

Gather's apartment was on the ground floor of the carriage house, so he didn't have to worry about navigating the treacherous wooden staircase tacked to the fieldstones of the exterior wall. The stairs were thick with ice and snow, because Miss Charlie, who lived upstairs, didn't use them. Instead, she clambered up and down along the rope contrivances she engineered for bad-batch men wealthy enough to afford her work. One was always hung through the trapdoor in the ceiling of Gather's kitchen.

Before he opened his front door, Gather pulled a canvas tarp back from where it covered his rick. He took an armful of split yellow wood, well-seasoned, for the kitchen stove. Yellow was native Virginia wood, not like the Pilgrim pines on the bank. Not good for making useful soil, but good enough for burning.

Inside, Gather found Miss Charlie working at his kitchen table. She was tipping the pepper seeds out of one of his twists and into a clay jar. Gather saw that she'd already emptied the other three—the dead papers were spread across the tabletop.

"You told me, Gather, I remember your very words, you said, 'I don't like those hot old things.'" Miss Charlie was suspended amongst pulleys and weights, testing a new configuration. She was wrapped up in one of the soft hides people made from deerskins sometimes. Getting them soft was hard—Gather'd had a job doing that for a while but he hadn't been good enough at it.

"I can grow 'em in the house, though, Miss Charlie," he said, then dumped the wood into the metal box beside the stove. "And if you share your dried apricots, I can make the spicy jelly the preachers like."

"*Strong* thinking, Gather," said Miss Charlie. "Stronger than you were doing this morning when you let that pack of children lead you off into trouble." Gather started to say that they hadn't gotten into trouble, but he remembered a lesson: not getting into trouble isn't the same as not getting caught.

Miss Charlie untwisted the paper she held and smoothed it flat next to the others with her skinny, clever fingers. Miss Charlie was a scientist. Everything about her was skinny and clever.

She arranged the four papers into a pretty, even line. They were rectangular, but not the same rectangular as the oiled wood top of Gather's kitchen table. The ratios of the different rectangles were plenty enough different, which was a good thing. If they'd been close-but-not-quite, it would have been upsetting.

Miss Charlie leaned over each of the papers in turn and examined them through her glass. Gather could see that there were letters on the papers.

"Is that writing the same as on the"—Gather thought of the word—"*exempla* you've got upstairs in your kitchen?" Gather glanced up at the open trap door. Miss Charlie looked up at him but forgot to take the glass away from her face, so her eyes were huge—one green, one brown.

"My la*bor*atory," she reminded him. "I'm a scientist, we don't have kitchens. The ones I have upstairs have a little life in them. This writing here is stuck on dead paper."

Gather was afraid that she might lecture him for a while then, which she sometimes did, but she was too distracted by her work. Her work, Gather remembered, was always *the question at hand*. The question at hand meant something Gather didn't know about.

"And anyway," said Miss Charlie, "I don't think these letters wrote here are like the letters on my papers upstairs, or on coins. They're more like the letters on the mayor's stick, or in a bible. Not quite, but that's closer." Gather had seen the mayor's stick before—he'd *felt* it before, the bad way, across his backside—but he'd never seen the inside of a bible, as only preachers were allowed to uncover their tops. Once one of his sisters had pointed out that if the preacher reading from it wore a glass, you could see the writing in the green glow reflecting off his face.

"The paper—the *medium* . . ." And she looked at him and raised her eyebrows the way she did when she used a word she wanted him to learn. "The paper is about the same as what I've seen before, though."

Miss Charlie chewed on her thumbnail for a second, then said, "Let's do an experiment."

"Oh, Lord," said Gather. "Oh, Lord."

"Hush," said Miss Charlie. "It'll be fine. I'll go upstairs and get our aprons and goggles. You'd better go get a bucket of water."

Miss Charlie swung up onto a rung threaded through the web of ropes hung from Gather's ceiling, then hand-over-handed up to the la*bor*atory above. Gather had never seen the la*bor*atory except from this oblique angle. *Oblique.*

He felt a little bit concerned about what was likely to happen next, but Miss Charlie did outrank him, so he went back out into the courtyard to sweep snow into a saucepan, then popped it onto the stove for melting. Gather breathed the metal smell of the new water and hoped it wasn't meant for an experiment that would leave him with less furniture, as so many of them had in the past.

The heavy leather aprons slapped onto the tile floor, then Miss Charlie dropped down onto the table, free of her harnesses and crouching on her skinny legs. Two pairs of leaded glass goggles hung from her cord belt.

"Suit up!" she said. "I'll let them know at the hall that you worked for me today, get you some credit."

Which was better than chopping holes in the river ice, so long as he finished the assignment intact.

Miss Charlie took four of Gather's baking pans from the cupboard and laid them on the table. Gather liked to make cookies, when he could get eggs, and so had lots of pans. She laid each of the papers in its own tray and that made three different rectangles, three different ratios, with one table and four trays and four papers for the quantities. "Oh, Lord," said Gather. "Oh, Lord."

Miss Charlie made comforting noises and slung the heavy apron over Gather's head. "Put on your goggles, young man. How often do you get to play with fire?"

Not often. It was true that Gather did not often get to play with fire. But this wasn't comforting.

The first part of the experiment was designed to determine if the paper could burn. Gather had never seen paper that would burn, but Miss Charlie claimed to have heard of it, to have heard of paper that would *immolate*. So Gather tonged a coal out of the stove and placed it squarely on each of the papers, one by one. That was called the scientific method.

None of the papers even curled up brown like burning things do when they start to burn, so Miss Charlie had Gather fetch down a rag from the cupboard while she pulled a tiny clay bottle from a pouch at her belt. She poured a scant two or three drops from the bottle into the water from Gather's saucepan, then took the rag from Gather and swabbed it around and around. The water went from smelling of metal to smelling of lemons. Miss Charlie then squeezed the rag over the papers. Each of them flickered on and off once, then shriveled up, twisting back almost to how they'd looked when they still held pepper seeds.

"That's a *datum!*" said Miss Charlie.

Which was very exciting, but it was well into the afternoon by then, and the children had coaxed Gather onto the river without his breakfast. Between those labors and now all this science, he was very nearly starved.

Since the pans were laid out, and since he had plenty of sugar and even a few eggs, the thing to do seemed to be to bake cookies. Miss Charlie, long resident above Gather's kitchen, knew his baking and was very excited by this plan.

"I'll do more on this tomorrow," she said, and swept the papers together onto a single pan. While she cast around looking for a receptacle she might deem appropriate to carry the papers upstairs, Gather pulled a mixing bowl out from beneath the dry sink.

He went to set it on the table and saw the soaked, twisted papers gathered all together. He raised his hands above his shoulders and keened. He began to breath in and out and in and out *fast*.

Miss Charlie took his hands and hummed. She breathed slower, slower, slower, slower . . . slow.

Then she saw the papers, too. She saw how'd they flickered back on and smoothly scuttled together into a new, single sheet. She saw that the words had crawled to the edges and she saw the finely detailed, heretic drawing that took up the center of the page.

"Why—" Miss Charlie was not a churchgoer, but she saw it. "Why, it's God."

How Miss Charlie convinced Gather not to go to the mayor or to the preachers with news of the picture was to: sing to him for one hour; tell him the names of all of his sisters that she'd ever known; give him the dried apricots she had tucked away in a burlap bag beneath the eaves in her apartment; promise him that the two of them knew as much about what God needed as anybody on the side of the river where people lived.

The whole time she was singing and listing and fetching and talking, Gather kept watching the paper on the table. It kept being God. God *with people.*

There was God, *all* of God, not just a little bit like on a coin, not just told about like in a sermon. All of God was on the papers on Gather's table, and more. Because, unheard of! Untellable! There was a man with his hand on God's flank and a woman kneeling next to God's ferocious mouth. God, *with people.*

People lived on this side of the river. God lived on the other. Even should God want to cross, the river was too swift in the summer. The ice would not bear God's weight in the winter.

It was impossible to know what to do, so Gather decided to let Miss Charlie decide. He was frightened, too frightened even to bake the cookies.

"I think there are three things we can do," said Miss Charlie. "We have to choose one of these *three* things." Miss Charlie held up three of her fingers and waved them around in a scientific way. Gather didn't like threes. They made people mad. They were *odd.*

"Take it to a preacher," she said. "But we've struck that already." Gather saw then that she'd only started with three so that she could get to two right away, which was easier and soothing.

"We can hide it and never speak of it." Miss Charlie looked at Gather very carefully when she offered that up. "Gather, could you do that? Could you never speak of it?"

Gather scrunched up his face and thought. "I think I would do a pretty good job for a pretty long time, Miss Charlie," he said. "But I think that then I'd forget and tell."

"That's what I think would happen, too," Miss Charlie said. "And I think you are very wise to be able to predict things like that. Don't tell *me* you can't be a scientist!"

"But what is number two?" Gather asked. He remembered that there were really only two.

"God . . ." Miss Charlie was thinking very hard. "God must be lost. God must need to get back across the river."

Gather attended every Sunday service. Most times, it was the same preacher—the little green-eyed girl's father—up there. Sometimes, though, if that preacher was away, then it was the mayor up there because he was the lay leader. There were even times when it was a different preacher altogether. And all of them did different homilies—a little bit different, anyway—and all of them always led three songs, an *odd* number of songs. But the thing that was always the same, no matter who was up there, was the way it ended, when they would say, "This is *my* God, and this is his body, and this is his blood." And then everybody would eat the bread.

"Does God need to go across . . ." Gather paused. "Does God need to go back across, because otherwise, everybody will eat God all up?"

Miss Charlie could pitch her eyebrows up as steep as rooftops. "Yes, Gather," she said. "Yes, I think that's it exactly."

Miss Charlie said that Gather should stop taking the work assignments he was given at the hall every morning. "You can work for me full time," she said. She tucked her bottom lip under her teeth, which meant she was performing a sum. "I have enough points for that to work for a time. For as long as we'll need, anyway."

Gather had never had a permanent assignment. It was a comfortable distraction, even when Miss Charlie made him practice being quiet for the whole next morning before they went to arrange it with the mayor.

The mayor was outside the hall, watching preachers push wagons full of soil up the road to the chapterhouse. He spotted them as they approached and fled inside, but forgot to bar the door.

Miss Charlie marched straight past the glaring preachers and on through the door. Gather didn't know whether his *proscribed* silence had started while they were still outside, but to be safe he didn't answer their calls for him to lend his shoulder to their wagon wheel.

The big chimney in the hall had a poor draw, and the air was thick with smoke. The mayor had taken refuge behind his desk and was pushing beads back and forth on a calendar rod when Miss Charlie cornered him.

"Charlie," said the mayor. "Charlie with the questions."

"I want—" Charlie began, but the mayor said, "No!"

He stood up suddenly and reached for his stick. Words ran around it in a loop, blinking on and off when he tamped it against the ground in time with his words to Miss Charlie.

"No, you cannot go to the chapterhouse. No, you cannot have an . . . *exemplum* of the soil before the preachers bless it. You cannot take a skiff south unless you pair with a bad-batch man, and you will *never* have a bible!"

At that last, he struck the stone floor so hard that his stick made a buzzing noise and went dark. The three of them all stared at it together for a moment until it flashed back on.

"I want to hire Gather for the rest of the week," said Miss Charlie.

Even in the dark, Gather was able to follow his sledge tracks from the PK morning back across the river. At first, Gather wanted to find a sledge and pull Miss Charlie on it, but she said that they were equal partners. She said that it was an equal *endeavor*.

At night, the fires in the watchtower seemed to burn as bright as a pine-wood fire, but Gather knew they weren't, not really. He had a job once hauling yellow logs out of the water and stacking them to dry by the watchtower fire, but only while the regular man was sick.

They were close enough to the fire for them to cast flickery shadows on the ice, but in the afternoon, Miss Charlie had gone to see the night watchman with some cookies she had made herself—*unprecedented*—and said that he would be sick tonight. He would not raise the hue and cry.

When they got to where the tracks ended, Gather said, "SHH-HHH-CHOOM," as quietly as he could.

"Is that how God talks?" asked Miss Charlie, and Gather remembered that she could never have been so close to the other bank before.

"The only time I ever heard God was that morning, Miss Charlie," said Gather. "And that is what God said."

"Did you know that makes you a prophet, Gather? If you hear God, I mean?" she asked him.

"All those little girls heard it, too. Little prophets," said Gather. "Little prophe*tesses*."

"Maybe I'm wrong, then," she said. "Like on an initial hypothesis. Maybe you have to hear and listen both."

Gather didn't understand, but his feet were very cold from the nighttime ice. He shuffled the last few yards to the shoreline and noticed that he wasn't afraid anymore. He reached his mittened hand up to a branch to steady himself, then gestured back to Miss Charlie. "Give me God," he said. "I'll put God up in this tree."

Miss Charlie had wrapped God up in white clothes from the laboratory. *Neutral. Sterile.* She pulled the bundle out from the bottom of her leather pack. Mysteriously, she had filled the pack with food and blankets and tinder. She handed the bundle to Gather.

"When God is back on the bank, there, Gather, what about those people? What about the man and the woman with God?"

Gather lowered his hands to his side. The bundle hung in the loose grip of his left mitten. He waited to see if Miss Charlie would keep talking, but she didn't.

"Is this another experiment?" Gather asked her. He felt himself getting agitated and didn't know whether to push it down.

"I don't think so," said Miss Charlie. "I think this is an *exploration*."

That was another word to learn, so Gather said, "What does it mean?"

Miss Charlie put her mitten around the bundle and pressed it against Gather's palm, so they were holding God there, holding God up and between them.

"I think it means we keep going," she said.

Then there was no agitation in him, and no hesitation. Then there was some *clarity* in him. "I think so, too," he said.

The Force Acting on
the Displaced Body

The little creek behind my trailer in Kentucky is called Frankum Branch. I had to go to the courthouse to find that out. Nobody around here thought it had a name. But all the little creeks and branches in the world have names, even if nobody remembers them, or remembers which Frankum they're named after.

I wanted to know the name when I was planning the trip back to Paris. That's Paris as in Bourbon kings, not Paris as in Bourbon County. I was writing out my route and Frankum Branch was Step One. I couldn't afford to fly, so I was going by boat. I didn't have a boat, so I was going to build one.

I was drinking a lot of wine just then.

I saved the corks.

Before I decided to go back to Paris, I considered using the bottles to build some sort of roadside tourist attraction. I looked into it a little bit, but the math defeated me very quickly. You remember how I am with math.

A boat, though—a boat built out of corks—that turned out to be easy. All you need is a roll or two of cheesecloth and some thread and a needle and of course a whole lot of corks. I put it together in a long afternoon in the field behind the trailer.

None of the bottles, full or empty, would break on the corks, so I never did christen it. I'd be happy to hear your suggestions for a name, though; you were always good at that.

The neighbors had that party, set up the game to name their new kitten. Calliope, you suggested, and nobody else even came close. You didn't go to the party, though. I carried over the note you'd written.

Frankum Branch, that's a pretty good name. Even if I couldn't track the provenance, I know there are Frankums around here, know they've been here for a long time. Probably a particular Frankum, sure, but here's a case where ignorance is kind of liberating. Since I don't know—since nobody knows, not even the people at the courthouse—it could have been a man or a woman, an old lady or a little boy. It could be named for all the Frankums.

The boat behaved at first. It rolled down the hill and settled into the branch, stretching out long because the stream bed is so narrow. It waited for me to throw my bags in and to clamber in myself, and then I headed downstream.

I only moved at the speed the water moved. I only went as fast as the world would carry me.

How far is my trailer from Sulfur Creek? See, that's a more interesting question than it might seem. There are so many ways to measure it.

If I walk out my front door and follow Creek Bend Drive to the end of my landlord's farm, down into the bottom and across Frankum, up another hill and then back down to where the blacktop turns to gravel, it's about two miles. That's the closest place, I think. Where the road breaks up into gravel is where Frankum Branch flows into Sulfur Creek.

But there are other ways I can go. I can walk through the fields, cross the branch on rocks at a narrow place, climb through some woods. I think it might only be about a mile and a half, that way.

Then there are crows. "As the crow flies." Do you think that means that crows are supposed to fly in straight lines? Maybe they used to. I watch crows, and I don't think I'd trust them to give me advice on distance. I don't think I trust crows or creeks either on much of anything, except to be themselves.

Finally, there's time. Nobody ever gives distances in miles anymore, but it's not because they've switched to metric. They measure how far it is from here to there with their watches, not their odometers.

That place, that confluence of water and roads both? It's about two miles from my trailer, it's about a mile and half, it's about an hour if you take Frankum Branch in a boat made out of corks.

So then I was on Sulfur Creek, which is broader than Frankum. The boat rounded itself up into a little doughnut. I smelled the water in the creek and I tasted it, searching for rotten eggs, I guess, or hell.

The sulfur must have washed away, though. Sometimes that happens, things wash away and only the names are left.

My hometown—the town I lived closest to growing up and the one I live closest to again—it's an island, maybe. At the edge of town, you have to cross a bridge over Russell Creek. At every edge of town. Every road leading in and out passes over Russell Creek.

When I was younger, I thought that meant that the creek flowed in a circle. I'd seen illustrations of the Styx in my mythology books.

It's not, of course. The creek and the town are neither of them circles, and the roads don't lead out in perfect radials along the cardinal directions, something else I used to believe.

What's the difference between a creek and a river? Length, just length. Nothing about how much water flows through it, nothing about breadth or depth. In Kentucky, if a rivulet you can step across is at least a hundred miles long, then it's a river. Russell Creek is ninety-nine miles long. Maybe it's the longest creek in the world.

When I floated out onto it, I started thinking that maybe I should have dug a trench somewhere at the headwaters or made a long oxbow in a bottom. Maybe instead of building the boat I should have lengthened Russell Creek. But then it would just be a short river.

Russell Creek flows around the town, and beneath the bluffs that line one side of my family's farm, and then winds, winds, winds through the county to the Green River.

The Green River pretty much named itself.

The Green is deep and swift above the first locks and dams, then shallow and tamed below. Floating through the impounded lake at the county line, the boat began to misbehave. It didn't want to leave town, after all.

It bunched up in a tight little sphere. I bounced on the top, netting my nylon bags filled with wine bottles and this notebook and a corkscrew into the cheesecloth so they wouldn't drop down and disturb the muskies. Then the boat stretched out, became narrower and narrower, longer and longer, so it almost looked like it was floating forward.

But I could tell it wasn't really moving, so I tried to paddle for a while with my hands. I kept getting pushed back by the wakes of fishing boats headed for the state dock. When I gave up, exhausted, the boat finally shuddered or shrugged and drifted on through the spillway, through the dam.

I don't know the motive force of the boat. Its motivation is a mystery to me.

You have to keep an eye on that boat.

▷▷▷

Then it was a John Prine song for four hundred miles.

Here's a true story. The Commonwealth of Kentucky owns the Ohio River, or used to. We still own most of it. But then counties along the south bank started charging property taxes to the Hoosiers and the Buckeyes who built docks off the north shore. The Hoosiers and the Buckeyes got their states to sue ours and theirs won, a little bit. Now the Commonwealth owns the Ohio River except for a strip one hundred yards wide along the upper bank. The Supreme Court of the United States decided that.

Those counties shouldn't have tried to charge the taxes. They should have known what would happen.

There doesn't seem to be much point in owning most of a river.

These are things I saw along the Ohio River.

Below Henderson, where the Green gets muddied into the brown, I saw the carcass of a cow, bloated and rotting, floating in the shallows outside the main current. The boat shied away from it even though I was curious to see what kind of cow it was.

At Owensboro, the water became as clear as air, and I felt like I was flying for a little while. The bed of the Ohio is smooth and broad at Owensboro, unsullied by anything but giant catfish and a submerged Volvo P-1800 in perfect condition.

Ralph Stanley was playing a concert on the waterfront at Paducah. This time I didn't mind the boat's dawdling.

At Cairo, I floated onto the Mississippi.

Cairo is pronounced "Cairo."

▷▷▷

Mark Twain's mother was born in my hometown. She was married in the front room of the big brick house at the corner of Fortune and Guardian. Mark Twain was conceived there. No, Samuel Clemens was conceived there. I think Mark Twain was conceived in San Francisco.

Doesn't Mississippi mean "Father of Waters"? That's a great name, in the original and in the translation and in the parlance.

You could make a career on that, I think. "Father of Waters." If I'd made that up, I would have lorded it over all the other namers for the rest of my life. I would never have named another river.

So, past New Orleans, the first place I was tempted to stop (but didn't), and into the Gulf of Mexico. The discharge of the father forced me all the way to the Gulf Stream, and it's easy to cross an ocean when the currents are doing all the work.

The boat was showing a little bit of wear, though. I had to drink more wine and patch a few places with the corks.

It was around then, south of Iceland maybe, north of the Azores, that it occurred to me that I could have used all those bottles to make a boat instead of the corks. It might have been sturdier and I could probably have found some waterproof glue. I think you would have thought of that at the beginning.

But me, I was south of Iceland, very wet and cold, before I hit my forehead with the heel of my palm.

"Bottles!" I said.

▷▷▷

The French, in naming rivers and cities and forests and Greek sandwich shops, have the advantage of being French speakers. I only know how to say "I don't speak French" in French, but I say it with perfect pronunciation and a great deal of confidence. Nobody in France ever believed me. Sometimes even I didn't believe me.

So, I don't know what Seine means, and I'm actually a little bit unsure of the pronunciation. I kept my mouth shut through Le Havre, past Rouen.

France was the first place along the trip that other people noticed the boat. The French love boats. I know what you think about that kind of sweeping comment. It's true though, in all it's implications. All French people love all boats, even ones made out of corks. They might not like them, all of them, all of the time. But love, sure.

Do you remember when we were on a boat on the Seine together? Cold fog, ancient walls, tinny loudspeakers repeating everything in French, English, German, Japanese?

Do you remember the other boat? The Zodiac moored under the Pont au Double, lashed against the wall below Notre Dame?

A man stood in the boat, leaning back, pulling a bright blue nylon rope. People started watching him instead of the church. What was he pulling out of the water? What was the light rising up from below?

It was another man, a man in a red wetsuit, with yellow tanks strapped to his back, climbing the rope against the current.

Do you remember that?

▷▷▷

They were still there.

They waved me over.

We have underground rivers in Kentucky, too. The Echo is famous, in the caves. If I'd thought of it at the time, I would have tried to coax the boat into the caves when I floated past them, tried to spot some eyeless fish.

In Paris, the underground river is the Biévre. It enters the Seine right across from Notre Dame. But then it leaves it again. It's just a river crossing through another one, not joining it.

I told the man on the boat that I didn't speak French, in French. He shrugged. Maybe he didn't care. Maybe he didn't speak French either. He just pointed at the diver in the water, so I slipped over the side, into the Seine. My boat seemed glad to be rid of me.

The diver took me by the hand and led me down. Down a very long way. He tied himself to a grating in the side of the stones that formed the channel there and showed me how he'd bent the bars wide enough for someone not wearing air tanks to slip through.

So I did. I slipped through.

Then up and out of the Seine, or it might have been the Biévre. I could have been in the secret river the whole time. Up and into a dank passage. I've been in dank passages in Paris before, but never any with so few bones.

No skulls and thighs stacked along the walls here, just a dark stone hallway. I followed it and followed it and came to a junction, a place to choose. Left or right.

You remember my sense of direction. You wouldn't have been surprised to know that I knew where I was: at the center of the Ile de la Cité.

Left was north, then, and I knew that it would take me beneath the police headquarters and up to Sainte-Chapelle, which Louis IX built to store the organs of Jesus after he'd bought them from one of the great salesmen of the thirteenth century. Right was south, to Notre Dame, where signs remind the pickpockets that God's eyes are on them.

Notre Dame or Sainte-Chapelle. The lady or the heart.

I stood there.

I am standing there still.

Other than the signs saying that God is particularly aware of petty larceny there, I only remember one thing from inside Notre Dame.

You were so disgusted when we heard the woman with the Maine accent say, "They're praying. I didn't think this was a working church."

There were jugglers outside. I didn't think it was a working church either. I didn't tell you that.

When we went to Sainte-Chapelle together, we didn't go to look for the heart of Jesus. There was a concert, a half-dozen stringed instruments in a candlelit cavern of stained glass. Bach? I don't remember.

What I remember was leaving, walking out of the cathedral and into the rain. The line was slow because we had to pass through checkpoints in the Justice Ministry, which surrounds the church. Gendarmes with Uzis below and gargoyles with scythes high above.

I tracked a stream of rainwater from the mouth of a gargoyle to the pavement. I leaned out, turned my head up, opened my mouth. I told you that I didn't know what it tasted like. Like limestone, a little.

I said limestone or ash, soot or smog.

You smiled and said, "It tastes like gargoyles."

You said that from my description. You didn't catch the rain on your tongue.

A long way to come to choose between places I've already been. A long way to come to choose anything at all.

I wonder if I can turn around.

I wonder if I can find my way back to the boat.

I wonder if it's still there.

The Voluntary State

Soma had parked his car in the trailhead lot above Governor's Beach. A safe place, usually, checked regularly by the Tennessee Highway Patrol and surrounded on three sides by the limestone cliffs that plunged down into the Gulf of Mexico.

But today, after his struggle up the trail from the beach, he saw that his car had been attacked. The driver's side window had been kicked in.

Soma dropped his pack and rushed to his car's side. The car shied away from him, backed to the limit of its tether before it recognized him and turned, let out a low, pitiful moan.

"Oh, car," said Soma, stroking the roof and opening the passenger door, "oh, car, you're hurt." Then Soma was rummaging through the emergency kit, tossing aside flares and bandages, finally, *finally* finding the glass salve. Only after he'd spread the ointment over the shattered window and brushed the glass shards out onto the gravel, only after he'd sprayed the whole door down with analgesic aero, only then did he close his eyes, access call signs, drop shields. He opened his head and used it to call the police.

In the scant minutes before he saw the cadre of blue and white bicycles angling in from sunward, their bubblewings pumping furiously, he gazed down the beach at Nashville. The cranes the Governor had ordered grown to dredge the harbor would go dormant for the winter soon—already their acres-broad leaves were tinged with orange and gold.

"Soma-With-The-Paintbox-In-Printer's-Alley," said voices from above. Soma turned to watch the policemen land. They all spoke simultaneously in the sing-song chant of law enforcement. "Your car will be healed at taxpayers' expense." Then the ritual words, "And the wicked will be brought to justice."

Efficiency and order took over the afternoon as the threatened rain began to fall. One of the 144 Detectives manifested, Soma and the policemen all looking about as they felt the weight of the Governor's servant inside their heads. It brushed aside the thoughts of one of the Highway Patrolmen and rode him, the man's movements becoming slightly less fluid as he was mounted and steered. The Detective filmed Soma's statement.

"I came to sketch the children in the surf," said Soma. He opened his daypack for the soapbubble lens, laid out the charcoal and pencils, the sketchbook of boughten paper bound between the rusting metal plates he'd scavenged along the middenmouth of the Cumberland River.

"Show us, show us," sang the Detective.

Soma flipped through the sketches. In black and gray, he'd drawn the floating lures that crowded the shallows this time of year. Tiny, naked babies most of them, but also some little girls in one-piece bathing suits and even one fat prepubescent boy clinging desperately to a deflating beach ball and turning horrified, pleading eyes on the viewer.

"Tssk, tssk," sang the Detective, percussive. "Draw filaments on those babies, Soma Painter. Show the lines at their heels."

Soma was tempted to show the Detective the artistic licenses tattooed around his wrists in delicate salmon inks, to remind the intelligence which authorities had purview over which aspects of civic life, but bit his tongue, fearful of a For-the-Safety-of-the-Public proscription. As if there were a living soul in all of Tennessee who didn't know that the children who splashed in the surf were nothing but extremities, nothing but lures growing from the snouts of alligators crouching on the sandy bottoms.

The Detective summarized. "You were here at your work, you parked legally, you paid the appropriate fee to the meter, you saw nothing, you informed the authorities in a timely fashion. Soma-With-The-Paintbox-In-Printer's-Alley, the Tennessee Highway Patrol applauds your citizenship."

The policemen had spread around the parking lot, casting clue-nets and staring back through time. But they all heard their cue, stopped what they were doing, and broke into a raucous cheer for Soma. He accepted their adulation graciously.

Then the Detective popped the soapbubble camera and plucked the film from the air before it could fall. It rolled up the film, chewed it up thoughtfully, then dismounted the policeman, who shuddered and fell against Soma. So Soma did not at first hear what the others had begun to chant, didn't decipher it until he saw what they were encircling. Something was caught on the wispy thorns of a nodding thistle growing at the edge of the lot.

"Crow's feather," the policemen chanted. "Crow's feather Crow's feather Crow's feather."

And even Soma, licensed for art instead of justice, knew what the fluttering bit of black signified. His car had been assaulted by Kentuckians.

Soma had never, so far as he recalled, painted a self-portrait. But his disposition was melancholy, so he might have taken a few visual notes of his trudge back to Nashville if he'd thought he could have shielded the paper from the rain.

Soma Between the Sea and the City, he could call a painting like that. Or, if he'd decided to choose that one clear moment when the sun had shown through the towering slate clouds, *Soma Between Storms*.

Either image would have shown a tall young man in a broad-brimmed hat, black pants cut off at the calf, yellow jersey unsealed to show a thin chest. A young man, sure, but not a young man used to long walks. No helping that; his car would stay in the trailhead lot for at least three days.

The mechanic had arrived as the policemen were leaving, galloping up the gravel road on a white mare marked with red crosses. She'd swung from the saddle and made sympathetic clucking noises at the car even before she greeted Soma, endearing herself to auto and owner simultaneously.

Scratching the car at the base of its aerial, sussing out the very spot the car best liked attention, she'd introduced herself. "I am Jenny-With-Grease-Beneath-Her-Fingernails," she'd said, but didn't seem to be worried about it because she ran her free hand through unfashionably short cropped blond hair as she spoke.

She'd whistled for her horse and began unpacking the saddlebags. "I have to build a larger garage than normal for your car, Soma Painter, for it must house me and my horse during the convalescence. But don't worry, my licenses are in good order. I'm bonded by the city and the state. This is all at taxpayers' expense."

Which was a very great relief to Soma, poor as he was. With friends even poorer, none of them with cars, and so no one to hail out of the Alley to his rescue, and now this long, wet trudge back to the city.

Soma and his friends did not live uncomfortable lives, of course. They had dry spaces to sleep above their studios, warm or cool in response to the season and even clean if that was the proclivity of the individual artist, as was the case with Soma. A clean, warm or cool, dry space to sleep. A good space to work and a more than ample opportunity to sell his paintings and drawings, the Alley being one of the *other* things the provincials did when they visited Nashville. Before they went to the great vaulted Opera House or after.

All that and even a car, sure, freedom of the road. Even if it wasn't so free because the car was not *really* his, gift of his family, product of their ranch. Both of them, car and artist, product of that ranching life Soma did his best to forget.

If he'd been a little closer in time to that ranching youth, his legs might not have ached so. He might not have been quite so miserable to be lurching down the gravel road toward the city, might have been sharp-eyed enough to still see a city so lost in the fog, maybe sharp-eared enough to have heard the low hoots and caws that his assailants used to organize themselves before they sprang from all around him— down from tree branches, up from ditches, out from the undergrowth.

And there was a Crow raiding party, the sight stunning Soma motionless. "This only happens on television," he said.

The caves and hills these Kentuckians haunted unopposed were a hundred miles and more north and east, across the shifting skirmish line of a border. Kentuckians couldn't be here, so far from the frontier stockades at Fort Clarksville and Barren Green.

But here they definitely were, hopping and calling, scratching the gravel with their clawed boots, blinking away the rain when it trickled down behind their masks and into their eyes.

A Crow clicked his tongue twice and suddenly Soma was the center of much activity. Muddy hands forced his mouth open and a paste that first stung then numbed was swabbed around his mouth and nose. His wrists were bound before him with rough hemp twine. Even frightened as he was, Soma couldn't contain his astonishment. "Smoke rope!" he said.

The squad leader grimaced, shook his head in disgust and disbelief. "Rope and cigarettes come from two completely different varieties of plants," he said, his accent barely decipherable. "Vols are so fucking stupid."

Then Soma was struggling through the undergrowth himself, alternately dragged and pushed and even half-carried by a succession of Crow Brothers. The boys were running hard, and if he was a burden to them, then their normal speed must have been terrifying. Someone finally called a halt, and Soma collapsed.

The leader approached, pulling his mask up and wiping his face. Deep red lines angled down from his temples, across his cheekbones, ending at his snub nose. Soma would have guessed the man was forty if he'd seen him in the Alley dressed like a normal person in jersey and shorts.

Even so exhausted, Soma wished he could dig his notebook and a bit of charcoal out of the daypack he still wore, so that he could capture some of the savage countenances around him.

The leader was just staring at Soma, not speaking, so Soma broke the silence. "Those scars"—the painter brought up his bound hands, traced angles down either side of his own face—"are they ceremonial? Do they indicate your rank?"

The Kentuckians close enough to hear snorted and laughed. The man before Soma went through a quick, exaggerated pantomime of disgust. He spread his hands, why-me-lording, then took the beaked mask off the top of his head and showed Soma its back. Two leather bands crisscrossed its interior, supporting the elaborate superstructure of the mask and preventing the full weight of it, Soma saw, from bearing down on the wearer's nose. He looked at the leader again, saw him rubbing at the fading marks.

"Sorry," said the painter.

"It's okay," said the Crow. "It's the fate of the noble savage to be misunderstood by effete city dwellers."

Soma stared at the man for a minute. He said, "You guys must watch a lot of the same TV programs as me."

The leader was looking around, counting his boys. He lowered his mask and pulled Soma to his feet. "That could be. We need to go."

It developed that the leader's name was Japheth Sapp. At least that's what the other Crow Brothers called out to him from where they loped along ahead or behind, circled farther out in the brush, scrambled from limb to branch to trunk high above.

Soma descended into a reverie space, sing-songing subvocally and supervocally (and being hushed down by Japheth hard then). He guessed in a lucid moment that the paste the Kentuckians had dosed him with must have some sort of will-sapping effect. He didn't feel like he could open his head and call for help; he didn't even want to. But "*I will take care of you,*" Athena was always promising. He held on to that and believed that he wasn't panicking because of the Crows' drugs, sure, but also because he would be rescued by the police soon. "*I will take care of you.*" After all, wasn't that one of the Governor's slogans, clarifying out of the advertising flocks in the skies over Nashville during Campaign?

It was good to think of these things. It was good to think of the sane capital and forget that he was being kidnapped by aliens, by Indians, by toughs in the employ of a rival Veronese merchant family.

But then the warchief of the marauding band was throwing him into a gully, whistling and gesturing, calling in all his boys to dive into the wash, to gather close and throw their cloaks up and over their huddle.

"What's up, boss?" asked the blue-eyed boy Soma had noticed earlier, crouched in the mud with one elbow somehow dug into Soma's ribs.

Japheth Sapp didn't answer but another of the younger Crow Brothers hissed, "THP even got a bear in the air!"

Soma wondered if a bear meant rescue from this improbable aside. Not that parts of the experience weren't enjoyable. It didn't occur to Soma to fear for his health, even when Japheth knocked him down with a light kick to the back of the knees after the painter stood and brushed aside feathered cloaks for a glimpse of the sky.

There *was* a bear up there. And yes, it was wearing the blue and white.

"I want to see the bear, Japheth," said a young Crow. Japheth shook his head, said, "I'll take you to Willow Ridge and show you the black bears that live above the Green River when we get back home, Lowell. That bear up there is just a robot made out of balloons and possessed by a demon, not worth looking at unless you're close enough to cut her."

With all his captors concentrating on their leader or on the sky, Soma wondered if he might be able to open his head. As soon as he thought it, Japheth Sapp wheeled on him, stared him down.

Not looking at any one of them, Japheth addressed his whole merry band. "Give this one some more paste. But be careful with him; we'll still need this vol's head to get across the Cumberland, even after we bribe the bundle bugs."

Soma spoke around the viscous stuff the owl-feathered endomorph was spackling over the lower half of his face. "Bundle bugs work for the city and are above reproach. Your plans are ill-laid if they depend on corrupting the servants of the Governor."

More hoots, more hushings, then Japheth said, "If bundle bugs had mothers, they'd sell them to me for half a cask of Kentucky bourbon. And we brought more than half a cask."

Soma knew Japheth was lying—this was a known tactic of neo-anarchist agitator hero figures. "I know you're lying," said Soma. "It's a known tactic of—"

"Hush hush, Soma Painter. I like you—this you—but we've all read the Governor's curricula. You'll see that we're too sophisticated for your models." Japheth gestured and the group broke huddle. Outrunners ran out and the main body shook off cramps. "And I'm not an anarchist agitator. I'm a lot of things, but not that."

"Singer!" said a young Crow, scampering past.

"I play out some weekends, he means; I don't have a record contract or anything," Japheth said, pushing Soma along himself now.

"Heir!" came a shout.

Japheth winked at Soma. "Not the first of my name, no."

"Welder!" said another man.

"Union-certified," said Japheth. "That's my day job, working at the border."

More lies, knew Soma. "I suppose Kentuckians built the Girding Wall, then?"

Everything he said amused these people greatly. "Not just Kentuckians, vol, the whole rest of the world. Only we call it the containment field."

"Agitator, singer, welder," said the painter, the numbness spreading deeper than it had before, affecting the way he said words and the way he chose them.

"Assassin," rumbled the Owl, the first thing Soma had heard the burly man say.

Japheth was scrambling up a bank before Soma. He stopped and twisted. His foot corkscrewed through the leaf mat and released a humid smell. He looked at the Owl, then hard at Soma, reading him.

"You're doped up good now, Soma Painter. No way to open that head until we open it for you. So, sure, here's some truth for you. We're not just here to steal her things. We're here to break into her mansion. We're here to kill Athena Parthenus, Queen of Logic and Governor of the Voluntary State of Tennessee."

Jenny-With-Grease-Beneath-Her-Fingernails spread fronds across the parking lot, letting the high green fern leaves dry out before she used the mass to make her bed. Her horse watched from above the half-door of its stall. Inside the main body of the garage, Soma's car slept, lightly anesthetized.

"Just enough for a soft cot, horse," said Jenny. "All of us we'll sleep well after this hard day."

Then she saw that little flutter. One of the fronds had a bit of feather caught between some leaves, and yes, it was coal black, midnight blue, reeking of the north. Jenny sighed, because her citizenship was less faultless than Soma's, and policemen disturbed her. But she opened her head and stared at the feather.

A telephone leapt off a tulip poplar a little ways down the road to Nashville. It squawked through its brief flight and landed with inelegant weight in front of Jenny. It turned its beady eyes on her.

"Ring," said the telephone.

"Hello," said Jenny.

Jenny's Operator sounded just like Jenny, something else that secretly disturbed her. Other people's Operators sounded like television stars or famous Legislators or like happy cartoon characters, but Jenny was in that minority of people whose Operators and Teachers always sounded like themselves. Jenny remembered a slogan from Campaign, *"My voice is yours."*

"The Tennessee Highway Patrol has plucked one already, Jenny Healer." The voice from the telephone thickened around Jenny and began pouring through her ears like cold syrup. "But we want a sample of this one as well. Hold that feather, Jenny, and open your head a little wider."

Now, here's the secret of those feathers. The one Jenny gave to the police and the one the cluenets had caught already. The secret of those feathers, and the feathers strung like look-here flags along the trails down from the Girding Wall, and even of the Owl feathers that had pushed through that fence and let the outside in. All of them were oily with intrigue. Each had been dipped in potent *math*, the autonomous software developed by the Owls of the Bluegrass.

Those feathers were hacks. They were lures and false attacks. Those feathers marked the way the Kentuckians didn't go.

The math kept quiet and still as it floated through Jenny's head, through the ignorable defenses of the telephone and the more considerable, but still avoidable, rings of barbed wire around Jenny's Operator. The math went looking for a Detective or even a Legislator if one were to be found not braying in a pack of its brethren, an unlikely event.

The math stayed well clear of the Commodores in the Great Salt

Lick ringing the Parthenon. It was sly math. Its goals were limited, realizable. It marked the way they didn't go.

The Crows made Soma carry things. "You're stronger than you think," one said and loaded him up with a sloshing keg made from white oak staves. A lot of the Crows carried such, Soma saw, and others carried damp, muddy burlap bags flecked with old root matter and smelling of poor people's meals.

Japheth Sapp carried only a piece of paper. He referred to it as he huddled with the Owl and the blue-eyed boy, crouched in a dry streambed a few yards from where the rest of the crew were hauling out their goods.

Soma had no idea where they were at this point, though he had a vague idea that they'd described an arc above the northern suburbs and the conversations indicated that they were now heading toward the capital, unlikely as that sounded. His head was still numb and soft inside, not an unpleasant situation, but not one that helped his already shaky geographical sense.

He knew what time it was, though, when the green fall of light speckling the hollow they rested in shifted toward pink. Dull as his mind was, he recognized that and smiled.

The clouds sounded the pitch note, then suddenly a great deal was happening around him. For the first time that day, the Crows' reaction to what they perceived to be a crisis didn't involve Soma being poked somewhere or shoved under something. So he was free to sing the anthem while the Crows went mad with activity.

The instant the rising bell tone fell out of the sky, Japheth flung his mask to the ground, glared at a rangy redheaded man, and bellowed, "Where's my timekeeper? You were supposed to remind us!"

The man didn't have time to answer though, because like all of them he was digging through his pack, wrapping an elaborate crenellated set of earmuffs around his head.

The music struck up, and Soma began.

"Tonight we'll remake Tennessee, every night we remake Tennessee . . ."

It was powerfully odd that the Kentuckians didn't join in the singing, and that none of them were moving into the roundel lines that a group this size would normally be forming during the anthem.

Still, it might have been stranger if they had joined in.

"Tonight we'll remake Tennessee, every night we remake Tennessee . . ."

There was a thicket of trumpet flowers tucked amongst a stand of willow trees across the dry creek, so the brass was louder than Soma was used to. Maybe they were farther from the city than he thought. Aficionados of different musical sections tended to find places like this and frequent them during anthem.

"Tonight we'll remake Tennessee, every night we remake Tennessee . . ."

Soma was happily shuffling through a solo dance, keeping one eye on a fat raccoon that was bobbing its head in time with the music as it turned over stones in the streambed, when he saw that the young Crow who wanted to see a bear had started keeping time as well, raising and lowering a clawed boot. The Owl was the first of the outlanders who spied the tapping foot.

"Tonight we'll remake Tennessee, every night we remake Tennessee . . ."

Soma didn't feel the real connection with the citizenry that anthem usually provided on a daily basis, didn't feel his confidence and vigor improve, but he blamed that on the drugs the Kentuckians had given him. He wondered if those were the same drugs they were using on the Crow who now feebly twitched beneath the weight of the Owl, who had wrestled him to the ground. Others pinned down the dancing Crow's arms and legs and Japheth brought out a needle and injected the poor soul with a vast syringe full of some milky brown substance that had the consistency of honey. Soma remembered that he knew the dancing Crow's name. Japheth Sapp had called the boy Lowell.

"Tonight we'll remake Tennessee, every night we remake Tennessee . . ."

The pink light faded. The raccoon waddled into the woods. The trumpet flowers fell quiet and Soma completed the execution of a pirouette.

The redheaded man stood before Japheth wearing a stricken and haunted look. He kept glancing to one side, where the Owl stood over the Crow who had danced. "Japheth, I just lost track," he said. "It's so hard here, to keep track of things."

Japheth's face flashed from anger through disappointment to something approaching forgiveness. "It is. It's hard to keep track. Everybody fucks up sometime. And I think we got the dampeners in him in time."

Then the Owl said, "Second shift now, Japheth. Have to wait for the second round of garbage drops to catch our bundle bug."

Japheth grimaced, but nodded. "We can't move anyway, not until we know what's going to happen with Lowell," he said, glancing at the unconscious boy. "Get the whiskey and the food back into the cache. Set up the netting. We're staying here for the night."

Japheth stalked over to Soma, fists clenched white.

"Things are getting clearer and clearer to you, Soma Painter, even if you think things are getting harder and harder to understand. Our motivations will open up things inside you."

He took Soma's chin in his left hand and tilted Soma's face up. He waved his hand to indicate Lowell.

"There's one of mine. There's one of my motivations for all of this."

Slowly, but with loud lactic cracks, Japheth spread his fingers wide.

"I fight her, Soma, in the hope that she'll not clench up another mind. I fight her so that minds already bound might come unbound."

In the morning, the dancing Crow boy was dead.

Jenny woke near dark, damp and cold, curled up in the gravel of the parking lot. Her horse nickered. She was dimly aware that the horse had been neighing and otherwise emanating concern for some time now, and it was this that had brought her up to consciousness.

She rolled over and climbed to her feet, spitting to rid her mouth of the metal Operator taste. A dried froth of blood coated her nostrils and upper lip, and she could feel the flaky stuff in her ears as well. She looked toward the garage and saw that she wasn't the only one rousing.

"Now, you get back to bed," she told the car.

Soma's car had risen up on its back wheels and was peering out the open window, its weight resting against the force-grown wall, bulging it outward.

Jenny made a clucking noise, hoping to reassure her horse, and walked up to the car. She was touched by its confusion and concern.

She reached for the aerial. "You should sleep some more," she said, "and not worry about me. The Operators can tell when you're being uncooperative is all, even when *you* didn't know you were being uncooperative. Then they have to root about a bit more than's comfortable to find the answers they want."

Jenny coaxed the car down from the window, wincing a little at the sharp echo pains that flashed in her head and ears. "Don't tell your owner, but this isn't the first time I've been called to question. Now, to bed."

The car looked doubtful, but obediently rolled back to the repair bed that grew from the garage floor. It settled in, grumbled a bit, then switched off its headlights.

Jenny walked around to the door and entered. She found that the water sacs were full and chilled and drew a long drink. The water tasted faintly of salt. She took another swallow, then dampened a rag with a bit more of the tangy stuff to wipe away the dried blood. Then she went to work.

The bundle bugs crawled out of the city, crossed Distinguished Opposition Bridge beneath the watching eye of bears floating overhead, then described a right-angle turn along the levy to their dumping grounds. Soma and the Kentuckians lay hidden in the brushy waste-land at the edge of the grounds, waiting.

The Owl placed a hand on Japheth's shoulder, pointing at a bundle bug just entering the grounds. Then the Owl rose to his knees and began worming his way between the bushes and dead appliances.

"Soma Painter," whispered Japheth. "I'm going to have to break your jaw in a few minutes and cut out as many of her tentacles as we can get at, but we'll knit it back up as soon as we cross the river."

Soma was too far gone in the paste to hold both of the threats in his mind at the same time. A broken jaw, Crows in the capital. He concentrated on the second.

"The bears will scoop you up and drop you in the Salt Lick," Soma said. "Children will climb on you during Campaign and Leg-islators will stand on your shoulders to make their stump speeches."

"The bears will not see us, Soma."

"The bears watch the river and the bridges, 'and—"

"'—and their eyes never close,'" finished Japheth. "Yes, we've seen the commercials."

A bundle bug, a large one at forty meters in length, reared up over them, precariously balanced on its rearmost set of legs. Soma said, "They're very good commercials," and the bug crashed down over them all.

Athena's data realm mirrored her physical realm. One-to-one con-structs mimicked the buildings and the citizenry, showed who was riding and who was being ridden.

In that numerical space, the Kentuckians' math found the bridge. The harsh light of the bears floated above. Any bear represented a statistically significant portion of the Governor herself, and from the point of view of the math, the pair above Distinguished Opposition Bridge looked like miniature suns, casting probing rays at the march-ing bundle bugs, the barges floating along the Cumberland, and even into the waters of the river itself, illuminating the numerical analogs of the dangerous things that lived in the muddy bottom.

Bundle bugs came out of the city, their capacious abdomens distended with the waste they'd ingested along their routes. The math could see that the bug crossing through the bears' probes right now had a lot of restaurants on its itinerary. The beams pierced the dun-colored carapace and showed a riot of uneaten jellies, crumpled cups, soiled napkins.

The bugs marching in the opposite direction, emptied and ready for reloading, were scanned even more carefully than their outward-bound kin. The beam scans were withering, complete, and exceedingly precise.

The math knew that precision and accuracy are not the same thing.

"Lowell's death has set us back further than we thought," said Japheth, talking to the four Crows, the Owl, and, Soma guessed, to the bundle bug they inhabited. Japheth had detailed off the rest of the raiding party to carry the dead boy back north, so there was plenty of room where they crouched.

The interior of the bug's abdomen was larger than Soma's apartment by a factor of two and smelled of flowers instead of paint thinner. Soma's apartment, however, was not an alcoholic.

"This is good, though, good good." The bug's voice rang from every direction at once. "I'm scheduled down for a rest shift. You-uns was late and missed my last run, and now we can all rest and drink good whiskey. Good good."

But none of the Kentuckians drank any of the whiskey from the casks they'd cracked once they'd crawled down the bug's gullet. Instead, every half hour or so they poured another gallon into one of the damp fissures that ran all through the interior. Bundle bugs' abdomens weren't designed for digestion, just evacuation, and it was the circulatory system that was doing the work of carrying the bourbon to the bug's brain.

Soma dipped a finger into an open cask and touched finger to tongue. "Bourbon burns!" he said, pulling his finger from his mouth.

"Burns good!" said the bug. "Good good."

"We knew that not all of us were going to be able to actually enter the city—we don't have enough outfits, for one thing—but six is a bare minimum. And since we're running behind, we'll have to wait out tonight's anthem in our host's apartment."

"Printer's Alley is two miles from the Parthenon," said the Owl, nodding at Soma.

Japheth nodded. "I know. And I know that those might be the two longest miles in the world. But we expected hard walking."

He banged the curving gray wall he leaned against with his elbow. "Hey! Bundle bug! How long until you start your shift?"

A vast and disappointed sigh shuddered through the abdomen. "Two more hours, bourbon man," said the bug.

"Get out your gear, cousin," Japheth said to the Owl. He stood and stretched, motioned for the rest of the Crows to do the same. He turned toward Soma. "The rest of us will hold him down."

Jenny had gone out midmorning, when the last of the fog was still burning off the bluffs, searching for low moisture organics to feed the garage. She'd run its reserves very low, working on one thing and another until quite late in the night.

As she suspected from the salty taste of the water supply, the filters in the housings between the tap roots and the garage's plumbing array were clogged with silt. She'd blown them out with pressurized air—no need to replace what you can fix—and reinstalled them one, two, three. But while she was blowing out the filters, she'd heard a whine she didn't like in the air compressor, and when she'd gone to check it she found it panting with effort, tongue hanging out onto the workbench top where it sat.

And then things went as these things go, and she moved happily from minor maintenance problem to minor maintenance problem— wiping away the air compressor's crocodile tears while she stoned the motor brushes in its A/C motor, then replacing the fusible link in the garage itself. "Links are so easily fusible," she joked to her horse when she rubbed it down with handfuls of the sweet-smelling fern fronds she'd intended for her own bed.

And all the while, of course, she watched the little car, monitoring the temperatures at its core points and doing what she could to coax the broken window to reknit in a smooth, steady fashion. Once, when the car awoke in the middle of the night making colicky noises, Jenny had to pop the hood, where she found that the points needed to be pulled and regapped. They were fouled with the viscous residue of the analgesic aero the owner had spread about so liberally.

She tsked. The directions on the labels clearly stated that the nozzle was to be pointed *away* from the engine compartment. Still, hard to fault Soma Painter's goodhearted efforts. It was an easy fix, and she would have pulled the plugs during the tune-up she had planned for the morning anyway.

So, repairings and healings, lights burning and tools turning, and when she awoke to the morning tide sounds the garage immediately began flashing amber lights at her wherever she turned. The belly-grumble noises it floated from the speakers worried the horse, so she set out looking for something to put in the hoppers of the hungry garage.

When she came back, bearing a string-tied bundle of dried wood and a half bucket of old walnuts some gatherer had wedged beneath an overhang and forgotten at least a double handful of autumns past, the car was gone.

Jenny hurried to the edge of the parking lot and looked down the road, though she couldn't see much. This time of year the morning fog turned directly into the midday haze. She could see the city, and bits of road between trees and bluff line, but no sign of the car.

The garage pinged at her, and she shoved its breakfast into the closest intake. She didn't open her head to call the police—she hadn't yet fully recovered from yesterday afternoon's interview. She was even hesitant to open her head the little bit she needed to access her own garage's security tapes. But she'd built the garage, and either built or rebuilt everything in it, so she risked it.

She stood at her workbench, rubbing her temple, as a see-through Jenny and a see-through car built themselves up out of twisted light. Light Jenny put on a light rucksack, scratched the light car absently on the roof as she walked by, and headed out the door. Light Jenny did not tether the car. Light Jenny did not lock the door.

"Silly light Jenny," said Jenny.

As soon as light Jenny was gone, the little light car rolled over to the big open windows. It popped a funny little wheelie and caught itself on the sash, the way it had yesterday when it had watched real Jenny swim up out of her government dream.

The light car kept one headlight just above the sash for a few minutes, then lowered itself back to the floor with a bounce (real Jenny had aired up the tires first thing, even before she grew the garage).

The light car revved its motor excitedly. Then, just a gentle tap on the door, and it was out in the parking lot. It drove over to the steps leading down to the beach, hunching its grill down to the ground. It circled the lot a bit, snuffling here and there, until it found whatever it was looking for. Before it zipped down the road toward Nashville, it circled back round and stopped outside the horse's stall. The light car opened its passenger door and waggled it back and forth a time or two. The real horse neighed and tossed its head at the light car in a friendly fashion.

Jenny-With-Grease-Beneath-Her-Fingernails visited her horse with the meanest look that a mechanic can give a horse. The horse snickered. "You laugh, horse," she said, opening the tack locker, "but we still have to go after it."

▷▷▷

Inside the bundle bug, there was some unpleasantness with a large glass-and-pewter contraption of the Owl's. The Crow Brothers held Soma as motionless as they could, and Japheth seemed genuinely sorry when he forced the painter's mouth open much wider than Soma had previously thought possible. "You should have drunk more of the whiskey," said Japheth. There was a loud, wet, popping sound, and Soma shuddered, stiffened, fainted.

"Well, that'll work best for all of us," said Japheth. He looked up at the Owl, who was peering through a lens polished out of a semiprecious gemstone, staring down into the painter's gullet.

"Have you got access?"

The Owl nodded.

"Talk to your math," said the Crow.

The math had been circling beneath the bridge, occasionally dragging a curiosity-begat string of numbers into the water. Always low-test numbers, because invariably whatever lived beneath the water snatched at the lines and sucked them down.

The input the math was waiting for finally arrived in the form of a low hooting sound rising up from the dumping grounds. It was important that the math not know which bundle bug the sound emanated from. There were certain techniques the bears had developed for teasing information out of recalcitrant math.

No matter. The math knew the processes. It had the input. It spread itself out over the long line of imagery the bundle bugs yielded up to the bears. It affected its changes. It lent clarity.

Above, the bears did their work with great precision.

Below, the Kentuckians slipped into Nashville undetected.

Soma woke to find the Kentuckians doing something terrible. When he tried to speak, he found that his face was immobilized by a mask of something that smelled of the docks but felt soft and gauzy.

The four younger Crows were dressed in a gamut of jerseys and shorts colored in the hotter hues of the spectrum. Japheth was struggling into a long, jangly coat hung with seashells and old capacitors. But it was the Owl that frightened Soma the most. The broad-chested man was dappled with opal stones from collar bones to ankles and wore nothing else save a breech cloth cut from an old newspaper. Soma moaned, trying to attract their attention again.

The blue-eyed boy said, "Your painter stirs, Japheth."

But it was the Owl who leaned over Soma, placed his hand on Soma's chin and turned his head back and forth with surprising gentleness. The Owl nodded, to himself Soma guessed, for none of the Crows reacted, then peeled the bandages off Soma's face.

Soma took a deep breath, then said, "Nobody's worn opals for months! And those shorts . . ." He gestured at the others. "Too much orange! Too much orange!"

Japheth laughed. "Well, we'll be tourists in from the provinces, then, not princes of Printer's Alley. Do *I* offend?" He wriggled his shoulders, set the shells and circuits to clacking.

Soma pursed his lips, shook his head. "Seashells and capacitors are timeless," he said.

Japheth nodded. "That's what it said on the box." Then, "Hey! Bug! Are we to market yet?"

"It's hard to say, whiskey man," came the reply. "My eyes are funny."

"Close enough. Open up."

The rear of the beast's abdomen cracked, and yawned wide. Japheth turned to his charges. "You boys ready to play like vols?"

The younger Crows started gathering burlap bundles. The Owl hoisted a heavy rucksack, adjusted the flowers in his hat, and said, "Wacka wacka ho."

In a low place, horizon bounded by trees in every direction, Jenny and her horse came on the sobbing car. From the ruts it had churned up in the mud, Jenny guessed it had been there for some time, driving back and forth along the northern verge.

"Now what have you done to yourself?" she asked, dismounting. The car turned to her and shuddered. Its front left fender was badly dented, and its hood and windshield were a mess of leaves and small branches.

"Trying to get into the woods? Cars are for roads, car." She brushed some muck off the damaged fender.

"Well, that's not too bad, though. This is all cosmetic. Why would a car try to go where trees are? See what happens?"

The horse called. It had wandered a little way into the woods and was standing at the base of a vast poplar. Jenny reached in through the passenger's window of the car, avoiding the glassy knitting blanket on the other side, and set the parking brake. "You wait here."

She trotted out to join her horse. It was pawing at a small patch of ground. Jenny was a mechanic and had no woodscraft, but she could see the outline of a cleft-toed sandal. Who would be in the woods with such impractical footwear?

"The owner's an artist. An artist looking for a shortcut to the Alley, I reckon," said Jenny. "Wearing funny artist shoes."

She walked back to the car, considering. The car was pining. Not unheard of, but not common. It made her think better of Soma Painter that his car missed him so.

"Say, horse. Melancholy slows car repair. I think this car will convalesce better in its own parking space."

The car revved.

"But there's the garage still back at the beach," said Jenny.

She turned things over and over. "Horse," she said, "you're due three more personal days this month. If I release you for them now, will you go fold up the garage and bring it to me in the city?"

The horse tossed its head enthusiastically.

"Good. I'll drive with this car back to the Alley, then—" But the horse was already rubbing its flanks against her.

"Okay, okay." She drew a tin of salve from her tool belt, dipped her fingers in it, then ran her hands across the horse's back. The red crosses came away in her hands, wriggling. "The cases for these are in my cabinet," she said, and then inspiration came.

"Here, car," she said, and laid the crosses on its hood. They wriggled around until they were at statute-specified points along the doors and roof. "Now you're an ambulance! Not a hundred percent legal, maybe, but this way you can drive fast and whistle siren-like."

The car spun its rear wheels but couldn't overcome the parking brake. Jenny laughed. "Just a minute more. I need you to give me a ride into town."

She turned to speak to the horse, only to see it already galloping along the coast road. "Don't forget to drain the water tanks before you fold it up!" she shouted.

The bundles that were flecked with root matter, Soma discovered, were filled with roots. Carrots and turnips, a half-dozen varieties of potatoes, beets. The Kentuckians spread out through the Farmer's Market, trading them by the armload for the juices and gels that the rock monkeys brought in from their gardens.

"This is our secondary objective," said Japheth. "We do this all the time, trading doped potatoes for that shit y'all eat."

"You're poisoning us?" Soma was climbing out of the paste a little, or something. His thoughts were shifting around some.

"Doped with nutrients, friend. Forty ain't old outside Tennessee. Athena doesn't seem to know any more about human nutrition than she does human psychology. Hey, we're trying to *help* you people."

Then they were in the very center of the market, and the roar of the crowds drowned out any reply Soma might make.

Japheth kept a grip on Soma's arm as he spoke to a gray old monkey. "Ten pounds, right?" The monkey was weighing a bundle of carrots on a scale.

"Okay," grunted the monkey. "Okay, man. Ten pounds I give you . . . four blue jellies."

Soma was incredulous. He'd never developed a taste for them himself, but he knew that carrots were popular. Four blue jellies was an insulting trade. But Japheth said, "Fair enough," and pocketed the plastic tubes the monkey handed over.

"You're no trader," said Soma, or started to, but heard the words slur out of him in an unintelligible mess of vowels. *One spring semester, when he'd already been a TA for a year, he was tapped to work on the interface. No more need for scholarships.*

"Painter!" shouted Japheth.

Soma looked up. There was a Crow dressed in Alley haute couture standing in front of him. He tried to open his head to call the Tennessee Highway Patrol. He couldn't find his head.

"Give him one of these yellow ones," said a monkey. "They're good for fugues."

"Painter!" shouted Japheth again. The grip on Soma's shoulder was like a vise.

Soma struggled to stand under his own power. "I'm forgetting something."

"Hah!" said Japheth. "You're remembering. Too soon for my needs, though. Listen to me. Rock monkeys are full voluntary citizens of Tennessee."

The outlandishness of the statement shocked Soma out of his reverie and brought the vendor up short.

"Fuck you, man!" said the monkey.

"No, no," said Soma, then said by rote, "Tennessee is a fully realized postcolonial state. The land of the rock monkeys is an autonomous partner-principality within our borders, and while the monkeys are our staunch allies, their allegiance is not to our Governor, but to their king."

"Yah," said the monkey. "Long as we get our licenses and pay the tax machine. Plus, who the jelly cubes going to listen to besides the monkey king, huh?"

Soma marched Japheth to the next stall. "Lot left in there to wash out yet," Japheth said.

"I wash every day," said Soma, then fell against a sloshing tray of juice containers. *The earliest results were remarkable.*

A squat man covered with black gems came up to them. The man who'd insulted the monkey said, "You might have killed too much of it; he's getting kind of wonky."

The squat man looked into Soma's eyes. "We can stabilize him easy enough. There are televisions in the food court."

Then Soma and Japheth were drinking hot rum punches and watching a newsfeed. There was a battle out over the Gulf somewhere, Commodores mounted on bears darted through the clouds, lancing Cuban zeppelins.

"The Cubans will never achieve air superiority," said Soma, and it felt right saying it.

Japheth eyed him wearily. "I need you to keep thinking that for now, Soma Painter," he said quietly. "But I hope sometime soon you'll know that Cubans don't live in a place called the Appalachian Archipelago, and that the salty reach out there isn't the Gulf of Mexico."

The bicycle race results were on then, and Soma scanned the lists, hoping to see his favorites' names near the top of the general classifications.

"That's the Tennessee River, dammed up by your Governor's hubris."

Soma saw that his drink was nearly empty and heard that his friend Japheth was still talking. "What?" he asked, smiling.

"I asked if you're ready to go to the Alley," said Japheth.

"Good good," said Soma.

The math was moving along minor avenues, siphoning data from secondary and tertiary ports when it sensed her looming up. It researched ten thousand thousand escapes but rejected them all when it perceived that it had been subverted, that it was inside her now, becoming part of her, *that it is primitive in materials but clever clever in architecture and there have been blindings times not seen places to root out root out all of it check again check one thousand more times all told all told eat it all up all the little bluegrass math is absorbed*

"The Alley at night!" shouted Soma. "Not like where you're from, eh, boys?"

A lamplighter's stalk legs eased through the little group. Soma saw that his friends were staring up at the civil servant's welding mask head, gaping openmouthed as it turned a spigot at the top of a tree and lit the gas with a flick of its tongue.

"Let's go to my place!" said Soma. "When it's time for anthem we can watch the parade from my balcony. I live in one of the lofts above the Tyranny of the Anecdote."

"Above what?" asked Japheth.

"It's a tavern. They're my landlords," said Soma. "Vols are so fucking stupid."

But that wasn't right.

Japheth's Owl friend fell to his knees and vomited right in the street. Soma stared at the jiggling spheres in the gutter as the man choked some words out. "She's taken the feathers. She's looking for us now."

Too much rum punch, thought Soma, thought it about the Owl man and himself and about all of Japheth's crazy friends.

"Soma, how far now?" asked Japheth.

Soma remembered his manners. "Not far," he said.

And it wasn't, just a few more struggling yards, Soma leading the way and Japheth's friends half-carrying, half-dragging their drunken friend down the Alley. Nothing unusual there. Every night in the Alley was Carnival.

Then a wave at the bouncer outside the Anecdote, then up the steps, then sing "Let me in, let me in!" to the door, and finally all of them packed into the cramped space.

"There," said the sick man, pointing at the industrial sink Soma had installed himself to make brush cleaning easier. *Brushes . . . where were his brushes, his pencils, his notes for the complexity seminar?*

"Towels, Soma?"

"What? Oh, here let me get them." Soma bustled around, finding towels, pulling out stools for the now silent men who filled his room.

He handed the towels to Japheth. "Was it something he ate?" Soma asked.

Japheth shrugged. "Ate a long time ago, you could say. Owls are as much numbers as they are meat. He's divesting himself. Those are ones and zeroes washing down your drain."

The broad man—hadn't he been broad?—the scrawny man with opals falling off him said, "We can only take a few minutes. There are unmounted Detectives swarming the whole city now. What I've left in me is too deep for their little minds, but the whole sphere is roused and things will only get tighter. Just let me—" He turned and retched into the sink again. "Just a few minutes more until the singing."

Japheth moved to block Soma's view of the Owl. He nodded at the drawings on the wall. "Yours?"

The blue-eyed boy moved over to the sink, helped the Owl ease to the floor. Soma looked at the pictures. "Yes, mostly. I traded for a few."

Japheth was studying one charcoal piece carefully, a portrait. "What's this one?"

The drawing showed a tall, thin young man dressed in a period costume, leaning against a mechanical of some kind, staring intently out at the viewer. Soma didn't remember drawing it, specifically, but knew what it must be.

"That's a caricature. I do them during Campaign for the provincials who come into the city to vote. Someone must have asked me to draw him and then never come back to claim it."

And he remembered trying to remember. He remembered asking his hand to remember when his head wouldn't.

"I'm . . . what did you put in me?" Soma asked. There was moisture on his cheeks, and he hoped it was tears.

The Owl was struggling up to his feet. A bell tone sounded from the sky and he said, "Now, Japheth. There's no time."

"Just a minute more," snapped the Crow. "What did *we* put in you? You . . ." Japheth spat. "While you're remembering, try and remember this. You *chose* this! All of you chose it!"

The angry man wouldn't have heard any reply Soma might have made, because it was then that all of the Kentuckians clamped their ears shut with their odd muffs. To his surprise, they forced a pair onto Soma as well.

Jenny finally convinced the car to stop wailing out its hee-haw pitch when they entered the maze of streets leading to Printer's Alley. The drive back had been long, the car taking every northern side road, backtracking, looping, even trying to enter the dumping grounds at one point before the bundle bugs growled them away. During anthem, while Jenny drummed her fingers and forced out the words, the car still kept up its search, not even pretending to dance.

So Jenny had grown more and more fascinated by the car's behavior. She had known cars that were slavishly attached to their owners before, and she had known cars that were smart—almost as smart as bundle bugs, some of them—but the two traits never seemed to go together. "Cars are dogs or cars are cats," her Teacher had said to explain the phenomenon, another of the long roll of enigmatic statements that constituted formal education in the Voluntary State.

But here, now, here was a bundle bug that didn't seem to live up to those creatures' reputations for craftiness. The car had been following the bug for a few blocks—Jenny only realized that after the car, for the first time since they entered the city proper, made a turn *away* from the address painted on its name tag.

The bug was a big one, and was describing a gentle career down Commerce Street, drifting from side to side and clearly ignoring the traffic signals that flocked around its head in an agitated cloud.

"Car, we'd better get off this street. Rogue bugs are too much for the THP. If it doesn't self-correct, a Commodore is likely to be rousted out from the Parthenon." Jenny sometimes had nightmares about Commodores.

The car didn't listen—though it was normally an excellent listener—but accelerated toward the bug. The bug, Jenny now saw, had stopped in front of a restaurant and cracked its abdomen. Dumpster feelers had started creeping out of the interstices between thorax and head when the restaurateur charged out, beating at the feelers with a broom. "Go now!" the man shouted, face as red as his vest and leggings, "I told you twice already! You pick up here Chaseday! Go! I already called your supervisor, bug!"

The bug's voice echoed along the street. "No load? Good good." Its sigh was pure contentment, but Jenny had no time to appreciate it. The car sped up, and Jenny covered her eyes, anticipating a collision. But the car slid to a halt with bare inches to spare, peered into the empty cavern of the bug's belly, then sighed, this one not content at all.

"Come on, car," Jenny coaxed. "He must be at home by now. Let's just try your house, okay?"

The car beeped and executed a precise three-point turn. As they turned off Commerce and climbed the viaduct that arced above the Farmer's Market, Jenny caught a hint of motion in the darkening sky. "THP bicycles, for sure," she said. "Tracking your bug friend."

At the highest point on the bridge, Jenny leaned out and looked down into the controlled riot of the Market. Several stalls were doing brisk business, and when Jenny saw why, she asked the car to stop, then let out a whistle.

"Oi! Monkey!" she shouted. "Some beets up here!"

Jenny loved beets.

signals from the city center subsidiaries routing reports and recommendations increase percentages dedicated to observation and prediction dispatch commodore downcycle biological construct extra-parametrical lower authority

▷▷▷

"It's funny that I don't know what it means, though, don't you think, friends?" Soma was saying this for perhaps the fifth time since they began their walk. "*Church* Street. *Church*. Have you ever heard that word anywhere else?"

"No," said the blue-eyed boy.

The Kentuckians were less and less talkative the farther the little group advanced west down Church Street. It was a long, broad avenue, but rated for pedestrians and emergency vehicles only. Less a street, really, than a linear park, for there were neither businesses nor apartments on either side, just low gray government buildings, slate-colored in the sunset.

The sunset. That was why the boulevard was crowded, as it was every night. As the sun dropped down, down, down it dropped behind the Parthenon. At the very instant the disc disappeared behind the sand-colored edifice, the Great Salt Lick self-illuminated and the flat acres of white surrounding the Parthenon shone with a vast, icy light.

The Lick itself was rich with the minerals that fueled the Legislators and Bears, but the white light emanating from it was sterile. Soma noticed that the Crows' faces grew paler and paler as they all got closer to its source. *His work was fascinating, and grew more so as more and more disciplines began finding ways to integrate their fields of study into a meta-architecture of science. His department chair co-authored a paper with an expert in animal husbandry, of all things.*

The Owl held Soma's head as the painter vomited up the last of whatever was in his stomach. Japheth and the others were making reassuring noises to passersby. "Too much monkey wine!" they said, and, "We're in from the provinces, he's not used to such rich food!" and, "He's overcome by the sight of the Parthenon!"

Japheth leaned over next to the Owl. "Why's it hitting him so much harder than the others?"

The Owl said, "Well, we've always taken them back north of the border. This poor fool we're dragging ever closer to the glory of his owner. I couldn't even guess what's trying to fill up the empty spaces I left in him—but I'm pretty sure whatever's rushing in isn't all from her."

Japheth cocked an eyebrow at his lieutenant. "I think that's the most words I've ever heard you say all together at once."

The Owl smiled, another first, if that sad little half grin counted as a smile. "Not a lot of time left for talking. Get up now, friend painter."

The Owl and Japheth pulled Soma to his feet. "What did you mean," Soma asked, wiping his mouth with the back of his hand, "'the glory of his owner?'"

"Governor," said Japheth. "He said, 'the glory of his Governor,'" and Japheth swept his arm across, and yes, there it was, the glory of the Governor.

Church Street had a slight downward grade in its last few hundred yards. From where they stood, they could see that the street ended at the spectacularly defined border of the Great Salt Lick, which served as legislative chambers in the Voluntary State. At the center of the lick stood the Parthenon, and while no normal citizens walked the salt just then, there was plenty of motion and color.

Two bears were lying facedown in the Lick, bobbing their heads as they took in sustenance from the ground. A dozen or more Legislators slowly unambulated, their great slimy bodies leaving trails of gold or silver depending on their party affiliation. One was engulfing one of the many salt-white statues that dotted the grounds, gaining a few feet of height to warble its slogan songs from. And, unmoving at the corners of the rectangular palace in the center of it all, four Commodores stood.

They were tangled giants of rust, alike in their towering height and in the oily bathyspheres encasing the scant meat of them deep in their torsos, but otherwise each a different silhouette of sensor suites and blades, each with a different complement of articulated limbs or wings or wheels.

"Can you tell which ones they are?" Japheth asked the blue-eyed boy, who had begun murmuring to himself under his breath, eyes darting from Commodore to Commodore.

"Ruby-eyed Sutcliffe, stomper, smasher,
Tempting Nguyen, whispering, lying,
Burroughs burrows, up from the underground . . ."

The boy hesitated, shaking his head. "Northeast corner looks kind of like Praxis Dale, but she's supposed to be away West, fighting the Federals. Saint Sandalwood's physical presence had the same profile as Dale's, but we believe he's gone, consumed by Athena after their last sortie against the containment field cost her so much."

"I'll never understand why she plays at politics with her subordinates when she *is* her subordinates," said Japheth.

The Owl said, "That's not as true with the Commodores as with a lot of the . . . inhabitants. I think it *is* Saint Sandalwood; she must have reconstituted him, or part of him. And remember his mnemonic?"

"*Sandalwood staring,*" sang the blue-eyed boy.

"*Inside and outside,*" finished Japheth, looking the Owl in the eye. "Time then?"

"Once we're on the Lick I'd do anything she told me, even empty as I am," said the Owl. "Bind me."

Then the blue-eyed boy took Soma by the arm, kept encouraging him to take in the sights of the Parthenon, turning his head away from where the Crows were wrapping the Owl in grapevines. They took the Owl's helmet from a rucksack and seated it, cinching the cork seals at the neck maybe tighter than Soma would have thought was comfortable.

Two of the Crows hoisted the Owl between them, his feet stumbling some. Soma saw that the eyeholes of the mask had been blocked with highly reflective tape.

Japheth spoke to the others. "The bears won't be in this; they'll take too long to stand up from their meal. Avoid the Legislators, even their trails. The THP will be on the ground, but won't give you any trouble. You boys know why you're here."

The two Crows holding the Owl led him over to Japheth, who took him by the hand. The blue-eyed boy said, "We know why we're here, Japheth. We know why we were born."

And suddenly as that, the four younger Crows were gone, fleeing in every direction except back up Church Street.

"Soma Painter," said Japheth. "Will you help me lead this man on?"

Soma was taken aback. While he knew of no regulation specifically prohibiting it, traditionally no one actually trod the Lick except during Campaign.

"We're going into the Salt Lick?" Soma asked.

"We're going into the Parthenon," Japheth answered.

As they crossed Church Street from the south, the car suddenly stopped.

"Now what, car?" said Jenny. Church Street was her least favorite thoroughfare in the capital.

The car snuffled around on the ground for a moment, then, without warning, took a hard left and accelerated, siren screeching. Tourists and sunset gazers scattered to either side as the car and Jenny roared toward the glowing white horizon.

The Owl only managed a few yards under his own power. He slowed, then stumbled, and then the Crow and the painter were carrying him.

"What's wrong with him?" asked Soma.

They crossed the verge onto the salt. They'd left the bravest sightseers a half-block back.

"He's gone inside himself," said Japheth.

"Why?" asked Soma.

Japheth half laughed. "You'd know better than me, friend."

It was then that the Commodore closest to them took a single step forward with its right foot, dragged the left a dozen yards in the same direction, and then, twisting, fell to the ground with a thunderous crash.

"Whoo!" shouted Japheth. "The harder they fall! We'd better start running now, Soma!"

Soma was disappointed, but unsurprised, to see that Japheth did not mean run *away*.

There was only one bear near the slightly curved route that Japheth picked for them through the harsh glare. Even light as he was, purged of his math, the Owl was still a burden, and Soma couldn't take much time to marvel at the swirling colors in the bear's plastic hide.

"Keep up, Soma!" shouted the Crow. Ahead of them, two of the Commodores had suddenly turned on one another and were landing terrible blows. Soma saw a tiny figure clinging to one of the giants' shoulders, saw it lose its grip, fall, and disappear beneath an ironshod boot the size of a bundle bug.

Then Soma slipped and fell himself, sending all three of them to the glowing ground and sending a cloud of the biting crystal salt into the air. One of his sandaled feet, he saw, was coated in gold slime. They'd been trying to outflank one Legislator only to stumble on the trail of another.

Japheth picked up the Owl, now limp as a rag doll, and with a grunt heaved the man across his shoulders. "Soma, you should come on. We might make it." *It's not a hard decision to make at all. How can you not make it? At first he'd needed convincing, but then he'd been one of those who'd gone out into the world to convince others. It's not just history; it's after history.*

"Soma!"

Japheth ran directly at the unmoving painter, the deadweight of the Owl across his shoulders slowing him. He barreled into Soma, knocking him to the ground again, all of them just missing the unknowing Legislator as it slid slowly past.

"Up, up!" said Japheth. "Stay behind it, so long as it's moving in the right direction. I think my boys missed a Commodore." His voice was very sad.

The Legislator stopped and let out a bellowing noise. Fetid steam began rising from it. Japheth took Soma by the hand and pulled him along, through chaos. One of the Commodores, the first to fall, was motionless on the ground, two or three Legislators making their way along its length. The two who'd fought lay locked in one another's grasp, barely moving and glowing hotter and hotter. The only standing Commodore, eyes like red suns, seemed to be staring just behind them.

As it began to sweep its gaze closer, Soma heard Japheth say, "We got closer than I would have bet."

Then Soma's car, mysteriously covered with red crosses and wailing at the top of its voice, came to a sliding, crunching stop in the salt in front of them.

Soma didn't hesitate, but threw open the closest rear door and pulled Japheth in behind him. When the three of them—painter, Crow, Owl—were stuffed into the rear door, Soma shouted, "Up those stairs, car!"

In the front seat, there was a woman whose eyes seemed as large as saucers.

commodores faulting headless people in the lick protocols compel reeling in, strengthening, temporarily abandoning telepresence locate an asset with a head asset with a head located

Jenny-With-Grease-Beneath-Her-Fingernails was trying not to go crazy. Something was pounding at her head, even though she hadn't tried to open it herself. Yesterday, she had been working a remote repair job on the beach, fixing a smashed window. Tonight, she was hurtling across the Great Salt Lick, Legislators and bears and *Commodores* acting in ways she'd never seen or heard of.

Jenny herself acting in ways she'd never heard of. Why didn't she just pull the emergency brake, roll out of the car, wait for the THP? Why did she just hold on tighter and pull down the sunscreen so she could use the mirror to look into the backseat?

It *was* three men. She hadn't been sure at first. One appeared to be unconscious and was dressed in some strange getup, a helmet of some kind completely encasing his head. She didn't know the man in the capacitor jacket, who was craning his head out the window, trying to see something above them. The other one though, she recognized.

"Soma Painter," she said. "Your car is much better, though it has missed you terribly."

The owner just looked at her glaze-eyed. The other one pulled himself back in through the window, a wild glee on his face. He rapped the helmet of the prone man and shouted, "Did you hear that? The unpredictable you prophesied! And it fell in our favor!"

Soma worried about his car's suspension, not to mention the tires, when it slalomed through the legs of the last standing Commodore and bounced up the steeply cut steps of the Parthenon. *He hadn't had a direct hand in the subsystems design—by the time he'd begun to develop the cars, Athena was already beginning to take over a lot of the details. Not all of them, though; he couldn't blame her for the guilt he felt over twisting his animal subjects into something like onboard components.*

But the car made it onto the platform inside the outer set of columns, seemingly no worse for wear. The man next to him—Japheth, his name was Japheth and he was from Kentucky—jumped out of the car and ran to the vast, closed counterweighted bronze doors.

"It's because of the crosses. We're in an emergency vehicle according to their protocols." That was the mechanic, Jenny, sitting in the front seat and trying to staunch a nosebleed with a greasy rag. "I can hear the Governor," she said.

Soma could hear Japheth raging and cursing. He stretched the Owl out along the backseat and climbed out of the car. Japheth was pounding on the doors in futility, beating his fists bloody, spinning, spitting. He caught sight of Soma.

"*These* weren't here before!" he said, pointing to two silver columns that angled up from the platform's floor, ending in flanges on the doors themselves. "The doors aren't locked, they're just sealed by these fucking cylinders!" Japheth was shaking. "Caw!" he cried. "Caw!"

"What's he trying to do?" asked the woman in the car.

Soma brushed his fingers against his temple, trying to remember. "I think he's trying to remake Tennessee," he said.

The weight of a thousand cars on her skull, the hoofbeats of a thousand horses throbbing inside her eyes, Jenny was incapable of making any rational decision. So, irrationally, she left the car. She stumbled over to the base of one of the silver columns. When she tried to catch herself on it, her hand slid off.

"Oil," she said. "These are just hydraulic cylinders." She looked around the metal sheeting where the cylinder disappeared into the platform, saw the access plate. She pulled a screwdriver from her belt and used it to remove the plate.

The owner was whispering to his car, but the crazy man had come over to her. "What are you doing?" he asked.

"I don't know," she said, but she meant it only in the largest sense. Immediately, she was thrusting her wrists into the access plate, playing the licenses and government bonds at her wrists under a spray of light, murmuring a quick apology to the machinery. Then she opened a long vertical cut down as much of the length of the hydraulic hose as she could with her utility blade.

Fluid exploded out of the hole, coating Jenny in the slick, dirty green stuff. The cylinders collapsed.

The man next to Jenny looked at her. He turned and looked at Soma-With-The-Paintbox-In-Printer's-Alley and at Soma's car.

"We must have had a pretty bad plan," he said, then rushed over to pull the helmeted figure from the backseat.

breached come home all you commodores come home cancel emergency designation on identified vehicle and downcycle now jump in jump in jump in

Jenny could not help Soma and his friend drag their burden through the doors of the temple, but she staggered through the doors. She had only seen Athena in tiny parts, in the mannequin shrines that contained tiny fractions of the Governor.

Here was the true and awesome thing, here was the forty-foot-tall sculpture—armed and armored—attended by the broken remains of her frozen marble enemies. Jenny managed to lift her head and look past sandaled feet, up cold golden raiment, past tart painted cheeks to the lapis lazuli eyes.

Athena looked back at her. Athena leapt.

Inside Jenny's head, inside so small an architecture, there was no more room for Jenny-With-Grease-Beneath-Her-Fingernails. Jenny fled.

Soma saw the mechanic, the woman who'd been so kind to his car, fall to her knees, blood gushing from her nose and ears. He saw Japheth laying out the Owl like a sacrifice before the Governor. *He'd been among the detractors, scoffing at the idea of housing the main armature in such a symbol-potent place.*

Behind him, his car beeped. The noise was barely audible above the screaming metal sounds out in the Lick. The standing Commodore was swiveling its torso, turning its upper half toward the Parthenon. Superheated salt melted in a line slowly tracking toward the steps.

Soma trotted back to his car. He leaned in and *remembered the back door, the Easter egg he hadn't documented.* A twist on the ignition housing, then press in, and the key sank into the column. The car shivered.

"Run home as fast you can, car. Back to the ranch with your kin. Be fast, car, be clever."

The car woke up. It shook off Soma's ownership and closed its little head. It let out a surprised beep and then fled with blazing speed, leaping down the steps, over the molten salt, and through the storm, bubblewinged bicycles descending all around. The Commodore began another slow turn, trying to track it.

Soma turned back to the relative calm inside the Parthenon. Athena's gaze was baleful, but he couldn't feel it. The Owl had ripped the ability from him. The Owl lying before Japheth, defenseless against the knife Japheth held high.

"Why?" shouted Soma.

But Japheth didn't answer him, instead diving over the Owl in a somersault roll, narrowly avoiding the flurry of kicks and roundhouse blows being thrown by Jenny. Her eyes bugged and bled. More blood flowed from her ears and nostrils, but still she attacked Japheth with relentless fury.

Japheth came up in a crouch. The answer to Soma's question came in a slurred voice from Jenny. Not Jenny, though. Soma knew the voice, remembered it from somewhere, and it wasn't Jenny's.

"there is a bomb in that meat soma-friend a knife a threat an eraser"

Japheth shouted at Soma. "You get to decide again! Cut the truth out of him!" He gestured at the Owl with his knife.

Soma took in a shuddery breath. "So free with lives. One of the reasons we climbed up."

Jenny's body lurched at Japheth, but the Crow dropped onto the polished floor. Jenny's body slipped when it landed, the soles of its shoes coated with the same oil as its jumpsuit.

"My Owl cousin died of asphyxiation at least ten minutes ago, Soma," said Japheth. "Died imperfect and uncontrolled." Then, dancing backward before the scratching thing in front of him, Japheth tossed the blade in a gentle underhanded arc. It clattered to the floor at Soma's feet.

All of the same arguments.

All of the same arguments.

Soma picked up the knife and looked down at the Owl. The fight before him, between a dead woman versus a man certain to die soon, spun on. Japheth said no more, only looked at Soma with pleading eyes.

Jenny's body's eyes followed the gaze, saw the knife in Soma's hand.

"you are due upgrade soma-friend swell the ranks of commodores you were 96th percentile now 99th soma-with-the-paintbox-in-printer's-alley the voluntary state of tennessee applauds your citizenship"

But it wasn't the early slight, the denial of entry to the circle of highest minds. Memories of before and after, decisions made by him and for him, sentiences and upgrades decided by fewer and fewer and then one; one who'd been a *product*, not a builder.

Soma plunged the knife into the Owl's unmoving chest and sawed downward through the belly with what strength he could muster. The skin and fat fell away along a seam straighter than he could ever cut. The bomb—the knife, the eraser, the threat—looked like a tiny white balloon. He pierced it with the killing tip of the Kentuckian's blade.

A nova erupted at the center of the space where math and Detectives live. A wave of scouring numbers washed outward, spreading all across Nashville, all across the Voluntary State to fill all the space within the containment field.

The 144 Detectives evaporated. The King of the Rock Monkeys, nothing but twisted light, fell into shadow. The Commodores fell immobile, the ruined biology seated in their chests went blind, then deaf, then died.

And singing Nashville fell quiet. Ten thousand thousand heads slammed shut and ten thousand thousand souls fell insensate, unsupported, in need of revival.

North of the Girding Wall, alarms began to sound.

At the Parthenon, Japheth Sapp gently placed the tips of his index and ring fingers on Jenny's eyelids and pulled them closed.

Then the ragged Crow pushed past Soma and hurried out into the night. The Great Salt Lick glowed no more, and even the lights of the city were dimmed, so Soma quickly lost sight of the man. But then the cawing voice rang out once more. "We only hurt the car because we had to."

Soma thought for a moment, then said, "So did I."

But the Crow was gone, and then Soma had nothing to do but wait. He had made the only decision he had left in him. He idly watched as burning bears floated down into the sea. A striking image, but he had somewhere misplaced his paints.

The Border State

Chapter One

L ook down on the Liberty Hills of Kentucky where they spring up north of the traitorous, twisting Green River. Look down on untended fields and tumbledown houses; look for a clean pavement line stretching along a ridgetop, a road punctuated by empty churches and empty stores.

See twin bicyclists, working hard. The gold of their jerseys matches the springing hawkweed crowding the lowland fields, the blue of their shorts is a half-dozen shades deeper than the cloudless sky.

Here is the brother, Michael, a sprinter. His legs are sculpted pistons, bunched muscles that push and demand, exhort and explode. Michael is an unsubtle cyclist, capable of terrifying speed along the flats, of finishing spurts that demoralize other riders and electrify the Viewers at Home.

Here is the sister, Maggie, a climber. She dances—this is the parlance of commentators—she *dances* on the pedals. She is a bird with strengths hidden and unhidden, with secret discipline and public fire. She breathes metronomically; she pedals in perfect circles.

This day above the Green, they trained for a race they might not ride. They awaited trustworthy word but had given up hope of anything but an unremarkable day in the saddle.

Then Michael killed a telephone.

The twins had dropped off Sandford Ridge when the telephone found them. They'd left the open ridgeline and begun a steep descent through the green tunnel of the Ginnie Hill Road. The roof of the tunnel was tulip poplar and catalpa; the floor was crumbling pavement thinly scabbed over yellow gravel. The walls were the hillside and the hollow, dense with hydrangea and the red blossoms of trumpet creeper.

And invaders. Invaders choked those woods, too, escaped ornamentals from the Orient and from Tennessee. "Things steal in," the twins' father would have said, if he'd ever returned from the mission trip that should have seen him home two years ago.

Maggie heard it ringing first. Descending is the other side of the climbing coin and she rode at ease on this little drop. She watched the fierce grip of her brother's hands on his brake hoods, willing him to relax and let the bike find its own line through the rough pavement, just as she had dragged him up the steep climb to the top with silent, subtle cues. On a normal day, Michael would repay her in the long flat south of Pellyton by shifting into his highest gear and accelerating to the edge of her ability to follow, making her a better sprinter the way she made him a better climber.

On a normal day; not a day when a voice above, jolly and calming, said, "Person to person for Michael or Margaret Hammersmith. This is a person to person call."

Michael, always a twitch away from braking on any downward grade, locked his rear calipers and fought his bucking and shuddering bike to a halt. Maggie was forced to brake as well, following him as closely as she was. She threw her hips back over the rear of her saddle and pulled on the handlebars, curved around her cursing brother, and came to an elegant halt, kicking her feet from the clipless pedals just before her balance fled.

She looked back up the hill and saw that Michael was doing the same. The telephone had landed in the road behind him and was preening the orange feathers over its fat breast. It raised its head, stared them down with bulbous eyes, and said again, "Person to person for Michael or Margaret Hammersmith. This is a person to person call."

Michael leapt free of his bike and launched himself across the few yards that separated him from the phone. His first kick caught the creature from Tennessee mid-sentence.

"Person to person . . ." And the tone changed from jolly cartoon to stern authority. "Assault on public property is a crime. Notification has been sent."

Before it could repeat itself again, Michael landed another kick, this time cracking his stiff-soled shoe hard against its chitinous snout. It staggered, but did not fall. It began a short hopping retreat up the hill, but Maggie saw that the kick that had silenced the telephone had been the one to fully tear away the thin scrim of her brother's self-control.

So she did not watch him finish the telephone, just heard him *kick* for what he saw as their unrealized potential, *kick* for what he saw as their poverty, *kick* for what he saw as their abandonment. She wondered how he would excuse himself—patriotism, maybe, or parsimony.

Michael scuffed his cleats across the broken pavement when he'd finished, sloughing off any bits of the foreign thing that might cling to his shoes.

"That'll save us a few dollars come tax time." Michael said this between heaving breaths. "The Revenue Cabinet applies the bounty on these things as a credit." He was apologizing to her.

Maggie was digging through the pouch lashed beneath her saddle. The kit from the health department was tucked inside it with her tire levers and spare inner tube.

She murmured, "Good, that's good," as she read the tiny print on the side of the foil package. She looked up at him. "Did you get any on you?"

"Any what? The blood?" Michael looked over his tanned arms, made an awkward effort of checking the exposed skin on the fronts and backs of his legs. "Do they even call it blood when it's that color?"

"Never mind," she said, having read further. "You're still standing up and you seem to know who you are. As much as you ever do anyway." She smiled. She was forgiving him.

She ripped open the packet with her teeth and pulled out a tightly folded square of gauze. She walked up the hill to the rapidly desiccating corpse and with a flick of her wrist tossed the gauze onto the mess of orange feathers and writhing muck.

The gauze flowed over the telephone's body smoothly, weaving and webbing, sending out tendrils where bits of the thing's blood were crawling toward the more hospitable ground at road's edge. In a few minutes, the gauze changed shades from white to green, and a faint cinnamon smell rose up.

Michael was running his fingers over the rear brake pads of his machine when she walked back to him. "Not a lot left to these pads," and he was rueful and grinning, checking his status.

Maggie patted him on the head as she walked to where her own bike lay. While he stood watching her, she quickly mounted and popped her cleats into her pedals with a loud click. "If you can catch me you can have mine," she called over her shoulder. "I never use them!"

But he would never catch her on any hill, going up *or* down, so she slowed and waited for him on the approach to the ford near the bottom. When Michael had pulled up even with her, Maggie said, *"This creek's shallow, this creek's clear."*

Michael said, *"But always taste it, always fear,"* but he said it muffled. Then, "Why do you always bring up his rhymes? We're not children. When have you ever seen me to cross moving water without checking it first?"

Maggie dismounted and crouched by the edge of the creek, little more than a brook here above any tributaries and so close to its source spring. Their father's rhymes were powerful, taught them when they were still children. They could clear water of impurities, he'd said, because of the strength of their faith. But as far as Maggie knew, they only worked for him, and for her and Michael.

"Good habits never killed anybody," she said, and even if she wasn't quoting their wandering father directly anymore it was something he might have said.

She let her fingers—nails cut short like her hair—hover over the surface of the water, careful not to let them touch, as she leaned over to gaze into it.

"There's nothing," Michael said.

Michael thought their father had *chosen* not to come back. He'd never quite forgiven that. Maggie figured their father got distracted and forgot they were among his priorities. He was out there trying to teach the word of God, bring about a revolution of faith, convince the world to rise up to counter the involuntary state of Tennessee.

She cocked her hand left then right. "There's probably honeysuckle blossoms and minnows." She stood. "But I don't see anything smarter than you in it, unless you count crawdads."

"Right, right," Michael said, hoisting his bike and splashing through the ford. "And I can't count anyway. Get a new joke."

He waited until she was picking her own way through the creek, burdened with the steel frame of her own bicycle, before he kicked off.

"I'm not racing you!" she called after him, but they both knew she'd try to catch him.

A mile down the little valley, the road tilted upward. It was the slightest of grades, and only a hundred yards long, but by the time he hit its base Michael was spinning fast so that he could coast to its top and not feel the unwelcome tug of the earth dragging at his legs. So his sister caught his draft.

"Twenty percent!" she said, laughing. Twenty percent less effort to move those fantastic machines down the road when one rider is shielded from the wind by another before him. Before him or *her.*

She'd never pass him. Not on a road flat as this, not when his form was so good and the end of a long ride was in front of them. But he'd never drop her, either. And he'd always shielded her from everything she'd let him.

The creek turned back before them, but they didn't even slow on this crossing. A steel and stone bridge was guarded by stern-faced Mennonite, gray-bearded Mueller men who'd known the twins all their lives. Not the faith of their father, these good plain people, but churched, so Maggie shouted "God bless you!" as they blurred past. The Muellers, all cousins or brothers or nephews one to the other, nodded greeting, but kept their downstream watch, mindful of any unnatural lack of clarity in the water.

Michael shouted back over his shoulder, "Post office?"

"We're going right by there anyway!" said Maggie, just as loud, struggling as ever to make the words catch up with her flying brother.

The real reason was that today was the last day word was going to come if word was going to come, though neither of them shouted that into the wind.

The people in those hills had lived with the Green River and its moods for more than two hundred years before it turned against them. They remembered that they had betrayed it first with the earthen dam that had impounded it into a tame, slack thing for a few decades, and because they were churched people they remembered the parable of the prodigal, and prayed for their river's redemption.

So despite every threat, they did not leave its banks, and people still lived at Neatsville and Knifley and in Little Cake. They were woken people, not interested in becoming Viewers at Home. There was still a post office in Pellyton, and the twins turned their wheels that way.

A high whistling noise in the sky brought Maggie up out of her tucked position. "West," she said. "Mail coming in from Bowling Green."

The sound of the delivery impacting in the muddy field outside the post office was muted, but they both felt the vibration of it when it jumped up through the road and their machines. "Big package," said Michael. "Lot of letters."

As one, they stood up on their pedals and cranked up their speed a little more. If word was going to come . . .

A few minutes later, they rounded a final right-angle turn and saw the sheds and workshops of the Pellyton post office. The big four-inch guns were silhouetted against the white sun, quiet now because it was a receiving day and the postal service had scheduling regulations to guard against the statistical improbability of incoming and outgoing packages knocking one another out of the sky.

Mr. Pelly, the half-blind postmaster, was leaning on a wheelbarrow in the torn-up ground at the roadside when Michael and Maggie coasted up. Two of his many daughters were digging a long canister out of the mud.

"Think that's personal mail, Mr. Pelly?" asked Maggie.

The old man smiled and straightened his jacket as he stood. "Buenas tardes, Maria," he said, like always.

And like always, Maggie forced a smile back. "It's Maggie, Mr. Pelly. *Margarita*. My mother—"

This completed their regular painful greeting ritual, and, as usual, Michael's patience with it was short. "There was a phone on the Ginnie Hill, Mr. Pelly. I killed it and Maggie tagged it. She's got the paperwork."

The postmaster attended his duty. "A phone, now? You say there was a phone? Was there a call?"

Maggie half-wondered if her brother would tell the truth.

"No," he said. "No, it was just standing in the road."

Mr. Pelly peered at Michael through myopia, then glanced at Maggie, for affirmation she guessed. She didn't move, or speak.

"Just standing on the road, you say." His daughters had finished wrestling the canister into the wheelbarrow and began trundling it toward the compound. "Well, then, that's what I'll put on the report I send to Frankfort. I'll have Eileen and Carla go block off the road until they can get some troopers out here."

Maggie and Michael watched some Pelly girls cut open the mail shipment with a reciprocating saw powered by a tiny boiler. The sparks from the whining blade hissed when they touched a random gout of escaped steam.

Mr. Pelly, who'd put on a duckbilled eyeshade labeled with a tiny American flag, didn't make them suffer through the time it would have taken him to officially sort the contents of the package. He fingered through the rubber-banded stacks of envelopes until he turned one up with a familiar logo stamped on the upper left-hand corner.

"*Union Cycliste Internationale,*" he said. "Not too many people around here gets mail from those folks."

Michael snatched the letter from Mr. Pelly's hand and looked at the address briefly before ripping it open.

"Is there one for me, too?" asked Maggie.

"This is to both of us," her brother said, then started nodding and laughing and jumping. "Both of us!"

He put his hands around Maggie's waist and lifted her up. "They want both of us!"

"Let me down, let me see!" she said.

Michael set her down and she took the letter from him. "Who could have been dropped from the team in favor of us?" she asked, scanning the pages.

"Who cares?" he said. "Some old guys probably qualified for cable and joined the Viewers at Home."

Mr. Pelly said, "What is this about? What have y'all done now?"

"We made the national team, old man," said Michael. "We're going out into the world to ride our bikes on the national team!"

Maggie said, "Did you read *all* this?" and the tone of her voice caught Michael up short. "Did you see the route of the first qualifying race, and when it starts?"

He took the papers she handed him, looking past the *Yes* on the first page they'd worked long years to see.

"What's the matter, little Maggie?" asked Mr. Pelly. "They starting you off too soon? Too far from home?"

"Too soon for sure," said Michael, thrusting the papers back at his sister and stalking out of the shed. "But not near far enough from home."

Maggie looked at the schedule in her hand again, with the start date an impossible two days away. She looked at the map of Kentucky.

"Where are they having you race, child?" asked Mr. Pelly.

A highlighted line started in the west of the state and described a long sweeping arc low through the flatlands, up across the knobs and the grassy fields where the Horselords ran, ending north and east in the foothills of the impassable Appalachians.

The route crossed the Cumberland River and the Tennessee. It crossed the dying Barren and their own complicated Green. It crossed the Kentucky River, the bleeding wound that cut across the heart of the state, to end at the Ohio, the bleeding wound that cut across the heart of the nation.

Maggie answered. "They're having us ride US 68, Mr. Pelly. They're making us race on the most dangerous road in the world."

Chapter Two

Their father had been many things to many people in their lifetime, but one of the strongest memories the twins had of him cast him as road builder. There were three switchbacks in the narrow rutted road he'd cut in the side of Dunbar Hill in the long summer after their mother died.

"It took a hundred-year flood to make me a widower," he'd told them during one of his infrequent breaks, rubbing down one of their exhausted mules with a handful of leaves, working even when he wasn't working. "But it'll take a ten-thousand-year flood for that river to make you two orphans, and that'd break the covenant."

They were four years old. "Widower" and "orphan" were new words to them, though "covenant" was not.

After he'd been a road builder he became a house mover. With the help of their neighbors—there'd been more of them then—their father had carefully disassembled the rambling log and timber house he'd built with their mother at the mouth of a hollow, built on the very edge of the Green's flood plain. Their mother, the woman who was retreating from their memories already, they were so young.

The same neighbors had helped put the house back together at the top of Dunbar Hill, but their father had refused any offer of help in moving the timbers and logs and window frames, or any of their earthly goods. It was Maggie and Michael and their father, just those three, who carried their home from hollow to hilltop, one piece at a time.

Once they were settled, their father's renown began to spread. His newfound ability to sing and chant rivers into submission was an irony, since it was water that had stolen his wife. People believed in the word of a man who could accomplish such a feat, and so that man had a duty to teach *what* to believe. That was what he always said.

What he was still saying, probably. She hoped he was somewhere saying *something*. He'd certainly said little enough when he left, just cryptic comments about them staying safe, and about too many enemies and not enough allies.

The road was better now, smoothed down by the feet of the visitors who came over the years seeking their father's counsel, and by the thousands and thousands of passages of the thin rubber tires of the twins' bicycles. And even though it was steep, Michael did not slow even once up its whole length, riding on anger.

Maggie followed him easily, but kept a little distance back. She let him coast into the shed that served as their garage and listened for the slamming of the door into the interior of the house before she followed.

These are the ways that Maggie Hammersmith had loved her house.

Uncritically. In her dimmest memories, Maggie recalled what it felt like to explore the numberless rooms and slip slide across the polished floors with Michael. She remembered the different colors of the light falling into the kitchen and the library and the great room, sunlight filtered through her mother's untouchable stained-glass windows.

Exhausted. That carrying, that moving. Taking a house piece by piece—even when the pieces she was responsible for were book-small or coffee pot light. Then later, *cleaning* all those rooms, taking her fair share of dusting and sweeping and polishing a house big enough for a dozen people but lived in by just three.

Fascinated. When they were six, their father began working in the garage for the first time since they moved to the top of the hill. He let them watch when he took down two of the bicycle frames hanging from the rafters, then let them help by searching out saws and clamps from the wide, shallow drawers of the toolboxes along the walls. He broke down the two frames into tube stock—like giant reeds made of paper-thin steel—then heated and rejoined until he had top tubes and down tubes, seat posts and forks, chain stays, seat stays, head tubes, bottom brackets. He taught them that you don't make a wheel, you *build* one. Build one or four, as in this case, when they helped build their first bicycles.

Mystified. One day, a nine-year-old Maggie had made a cognitive leap and realized that she and Michael could use the woodcraft they'd picked up in their hillside scrambles to identify what kind of trees the walls and furniture and fittings of their home were hewn from. They'd made a game of it and found: white oak, yellow pine, red cedar, and buttery poplar waxed agleaming, granite-hard locust holding up ceilings, and something new. Some graceful red wood, from an evergreen but not one they knew, making a chest to hold quilts. "There are trees that do not grow in these hills," said their father. "Then how do they get here?" No answer.

Secretly. Because she'd grown a little ashamed that she and her brother and her father all had separate rooms to sleep in, and that none of those rooms were for anything else. To a fourteen-year-old girl, even one strong and self-assured enough to take great circling hundred-mile bicycle rides by herself, the room full of books and the walls covered with photographs and watercolors seemed . . . *unseemly*, when the Amish and the other woken people in the hills got by with less, some of them with much less.

Proudly. A fire that took all of the timber from the southern slopes of the hill and only burnt itself out at the very river's edge. Two funnel clouds that she'd seen with her own eyes before her father rushed them into the root cellar. Snows piled so high on the hips and valleys of the roofline that the chimneys disappeared, and the smoke of their fires came up through sooty little holes burned through tons of white. One windstorm that took the roof off the barn where the mules lived, and another that uprooted a tree from the front yard and deposited it, crown down, into the fallow garden. A thousand nights of thunderstorms. All of these had threatened it, but nothing had ever worn through their beautiful, well-built house.

After she had removed the front wheel of her training bike and hung it by Michael's, Maggie kicked off her shoes and padded up the three stone steps that led to the kitchen. She wasn't surprised to see that Michael had taken the time to stoke the fire in the iron stove and hang a kettle of water to heat the baths they'd take in their rooms. One secret to his success as a rider was his enormous discipline, and the secret to his discipline was that he was a deliberate and willing slave to habit.

So she knew where she'd find him, in the corner of the library where he always went to calm down. Not with a book—despite all of his attempts, their father had never succeeded in making either of his children what he called "real" readers. No, she expected to find Michael standing in front of their mother's trophies.

He spoke first. "If they ever had another state championship, do you think they'd use the same jersey?" One of his favorite questions.

He was looking at one of two dozen similarly composed photographs that hung on the walls behind the trophies. In all of them, their beautiful dark-haired mother was standing at the top of a podium holding a bouquet of flowers. Only the people standing at either side of her changed from photograph to photograph, them and the jerseys they all wore.

Michael nodded his chin at a picture taken on a sunny day in front of some enormous stone building. Their mother was pulling on a brightly colored jersey designed to resemble a field of goldenrod. The caption was one of the first things the twins had learned to read: "Maria Galdeana, Champion of Kentucky."

"The jerseys for the Champion of America"—and Maggie nodded at a picture of their mother wearing red, white and blue—"and for

the World Champion"—their mother in gleaming white with a rainbow banded across her chest—"are the same now as they were then,
at least from the pictures in the manuals. When they start up the state
championships again, I'm sure it will be the same." It was important
that she say *when* and not *if*.

"Okay," he said. "Okay. That's probably right. And they can bring
in machines from somewhere to make them." Michael was the more
accomplished tailor and weaver of the two of them, and from the age
of ten had made their wool cycling kits in as many different colors
and patterns as he could manage. But he'd never come close to rep-
licating the complicated foliage on the Kentucky jersey and became
convinced that the technology of the world outside the Commonwealth—revealed to them in slow, grudging bits by their father—was
the secret to the slick appearance of the jerseys, as it must be to the
delicately machined bicycle parts so carefully hoarded in their garage.

Maggie pulled the letter from her pocket. He looked at it and
nodded. "We need to eat, do our recovery regimen, then we'll figure
it out. I have an idea." He took the papers from her and went to his
room.

What about the call? Something else she knew not to say aloud. Not
to her brother and never to her father before he'd left. Maggie was
convinced that he'd left as much to get away from the calls as to carry
salvation to the mountains.

She didn't need to say it aloud, anyway, because she knew what
the response would be.

Our mother is dead! Or *Your mother is gone!* depending on which of
them she'd asked, when she still asked. *The river took her twenty years ago,
and the dead do not make telephone calls!*

Maggie looked up at the photographs again.

"They especially don't make calls from Tennessee," she said, and
went to her own room.

▷▷▷

Michael's idea was to call in a favor. "An *inherited* favor," he said.

"We're not supposed to go to the lake," said Maggie. She was stretched out on top of the long table in the kitchen, massaging her calves while Michael scoured the cast-iron pot she'd cooked their rice in.

Michael dropped the pot into the sink. Sudsy water—rainwater from the roof barrels—sloshed onto the tiled floor. He rocked back and forth on his heels and puffed his cheeks out, swallowing a little storm.

"If we're going to get to Paducah for this race . . . Maggie if we're going to *participate* in this race, then we'll be breaking his rules left and right. Those rules were for when we were little kids, anyway."

Maggie dipped her finger into the little tin of salve beside her, rubbed it between her palms to warm it, and went to work on the arch of her left foot. Eat, drink, rest, massage. All of it over and over again. "I know that," she said. "You're right."

Michael closed his mouth. He'd been marshaling an argument and was startled to have it cut off by capitulation.

"Well," he said, but didn't say anything else.

"I just think," she said, "that we should keep them *in mind*. Daddy didn't find out all those rules and teach them to us because we were kids. He told them to anybody he could get to listen to him, every woken person around here has heard them. And we follow them because we want to stay awake and ourselves. And you may think we're strong enough and clever enough"—she raised a finger when he started to interrupt, shushing him—"and I know you think we're *fast* enough to play them loose. But however we manage this, we've got to be careful. We have to be mindful."

"I'll start packing our gear!" he said, and was gone as soon as she'd finished.

An inherited favor. Maggie hopped off of the table and went over to the sink. The soles of her bare feet were oily, and the tiles were slick from Michael's overly enthusiastic washing of the crockery. But she was careful, she didn't slip even when she stood tiptoe to stare out the north-facing window.

Herbs grew in terra-cotta pots on the sill. Outside, banty hens stutter-stepped around the yard. And away north, a few ridges over, she could see the houseboats of the Buckeye Navy, lashed beneath the balloons that kept their hulls high and dry above the lakebed.

Sunset light caught the mooring lines even from this distance. The mooring lines and the television cables.

The twins stood in the garage considering the huge mounds of equipment Michael had assembled in the hours since dinner. The overhead door was pulled closed against the nighttime chill. The kerosene lamps didn't give off enough heat for Maggie to remove her hands from her warmup jacket's pockets, but they gave more than enough light for her to see their problem.

"We have too many bicycles," she said. The words sounded all wrong, even corrupt somehow, so she amended quickly. "We can't take all of these bicycles."

There were eight bicycles nested into racks on the far wall, a pair each of mountain bikes, cyclocross bikes, the training bikes they'd ridden earlier, and their sleek, twitchy racing bikes. Michael stood with his hand on the saddle of his mountain bike, lips pursed.

"Okay," he said. "Okay, what do we need to do? Two things, right? We need to get to the race and we need to . . ." The enormity of the opportunity robbed the next word from him.

"Compete," said Maggie. "We need to *compete* in the race."

"That's right." Michael loped over to the racing bikes. "So we take these sweet ones—here, start breaking them down, the team will have a shop tent with everything we need to reassemble and dial in."

Maggie made tight fists, then whipped her wrists forward and splayed her fingers all at once, cracking her knuckles in the same gesture she'd use to flick tainted water from her hands. She lifted a leather apron, slick with oil and heavy with tools, from where it hung on a sixteen-penny nail driven into a supporting beam. "Extra sets of wheels," she said, speaking and working at the same time, lifting her brother's racing bike onto her repair stand. "Some tubes, some tape, some lube. We have to assume the team will provide most stuff."

Michael was hauling their tagalong trailers down from the rafters. They were sturdy, clever machines with single all-terrain wheels at one end and quick-release attachments designed to be fitted into the rear spindles of a bike at the other. Between wheel and attachment the tagalongs curved around their capacious cargo holds in an elegant cello shape. More *machined* gifts from one of their father's earlier journeys.

"Yeah, yeah. Depending on who the national organization has hired as director sportif there might even be a chef!" Michael's experience with international racing was the same as Maggie's and consisted of reading books and articles in old magazines their mother had kept in a rosewood trunk.

"Food for the trip there," said Maggie. She started at the front of Michael's bike, loosening and removing the brake hoods and indexed shifters from the handlebars. She detached the fine, sharp cables and coiled them into a battered plastic bowl she'd found that had a sealable lid and was exactly the right size.

"Clothes, some stuff to trade with—what do we have that's lightweight that foreign people might want? Our paperwork. Water bottles! I can't decide whether to try to take everything or as little as possible!" Michael was working himself up, channeling his doubt into enthusiasm.

Maggie spoke around the tiny screwdriver she was holding in her mouth, nodded at the tagalongs. "Frame stamps on those things say they're rated for eighty pounds. And I'd rather not haul half that if we can get away with it."

Michael didn't acknowledge her comment. He'd stopped, standing in the middle of the garage. "Mountain or cyclocross?" he shouted. "What are we going to haul the trailers *with*?"

In terms of raw minutes (but not miles), the twins probably spent more times on their mountain bikes than even their training cycles. The roads between Pellyton and Knifley (where they bought the food they didn't grow themselves) were rough, and sometimes flash floods required a traveler to take to the ridges. If their racing and training cycles were their thoroughbreds, then the mountain bikes—heavy tubed, fitted with shock absorbers in the forks and seat posts—were their draft horses.

"The last time we went to the lake," said Maggie, considering, "the pavement was pretty good. But that was a long time ago." Fifteen years ago, at least, she didn't say aloud. While perched on the back of a cart pulled by flesh and blood horses. Their father had been taking bales of airy cloth to his friend Japheth, and the lake had still been a lake.

"The mountain bikes we can take anywhere," Michael said, "just not very *fast*."

"Fast is important," agreed Maggie.

To a casual glance, the cyclocross bikes were very similar to the road cycles. But neither of them had ever looked at a bicycle casually, and Maggie reflexively ticked off the differences: studded tires, lower gearing, sturdier welds in the frame, and a fork of heavier gauge material. Cyclocross bikes weren't as effective off-road as the comparatively huge mountain bikes, but they *were* effective. And to boot, they were lighter, had more aerodynamic lines. The twins used them for winter training when there was snow on their usual routes.

"I've got skewers that'll work to attach the tagalongs to the 'cross bikes," she said, pulling open one of the wide, shallow drawers of her wooden toolbox. "Somewhere."

"Little Miss Organized," said Michael, teasing her. It was usually the reverse, as the frantic clutter of his "packing" that took up most of the floor space attested. "Lucky for us when we're on the race we'll have mechanics to keep track of our parts."

Maggie laughed, delighted. "And *soigneurs* to pack our mussettes and wash our water bottles."

"And give us massages!"

"Ooooh, yeah."

"And a director to tell us when to attack and when to mark time," Michael continued. "Not that we'll listen."

"Because the time to attack is always *now!*" said Maggie, plucking the skewer she'd been hunting for from the drawer and brandishing it like a short sword.

This was an old game. Michael looked around quickly, then snatched a stick of kindling from the dry-wood rick along the south wall. "Sword," he said.

"Slow and heavy like yourself, Monsieur Porthos," said Maggie. She whipped the skewer up and down in a chevron pattern, drawing an invisible, sharp-pointed *M* in the air before her.

"Aha, but look here!" Michael picked up one of the round leather cases that held their spare racing wheels. The handle was at the top, but he looped his fingers through it and held it up, his arm hidden from her. "This is my mighty shield, Foebreaker! Don't really hit it because one of your disc wheels for the time trial is in here."

"Yeah, yeah," said Maggie. "Guard your life, villain!"

Chapter Three

Maggie could barely remember when there was still a lake in the lakebed. Like most of her earliest, dimmest memories, it was tangled up with their mother's face and laughter. There was a muddy beach and Michael crying because of something to do with a fishing pole. Their father was there, standing underneath a picnic shelter, talking to some other men.

She remembered better when the lakebed still looked like that. A broad, twisting, muddy swath of land cutting between the green hills to either side. They'd already learned to fear the river when her father started taking supplies to his friends at the campgrounds, but they didn't know why just yet. At least she and Michael didn't. Her father, generous with his counsel to others, kept his own about that.

Now, cresting the hill above Plum Point, the lakebed didn't really look any different than any of the other Pennyroyal valleys carved by creek and river. Flatter, perhaps, but just as choked with the trees and brush of young forests as all the other abandoned land in this part of the Commonwealth.

The Green made its way from the twins' left to their right. Casey Creek flowed into the river a quarter mile up the road. Even if it weren't an old forbidden thing from their father's lists, the twins would have avoided cycling his road—the creek made frequent attempts at flooding and undermining the road.

Maggie wasn't looking at Casey Creek, though. She was as close as she'd ever been to the Buckeye Navy and both she and Michael were shaking their heads at the colors and designs that decorated the hundreds of balloons that floated above the valley.

Older people, like Mr. Pelly, still called the Buckeyes "summer people," even though it had been decades since any of them had been out of the valley, much less gone back to their home north of the Ohio. Much less been down from their houseboats.

When the rivers broke the dirt collars that slacked their flow into the necklace of lakes across the south of the Commonwealth—Lake Cumberland, Dale Hollow Lake, Green River Lake, Barren River Lake, and away west Lake Barkley and Kentucky Lake—thousands of houseboats had been left wallowing in the mud flats or smashed up against cliffs and trees. The people who lived in them were wealthy vagrants from the north, rumored to have their own homes but more content floating on Kentucky water than standing firm on their own soil. Strange people.

The ones that had lived on the Green soon found that there were no safe routes north. The trade tunnels were years away from being dug, and they weren't the kind of wealthy that could buy a place on a government aerostat. So they decided to stay, but to stay safe from the corrupted rivers, wellspring of Athena's technology, seeping out from Tennessee into the rest of the world.

And so the miles of mooring line and thousands of bales of silk. So the clever still that their father's friends had built to pull the lightest gases out of the air. The man they were going to see, Japheth Sapp, had taken the Buckeyes' money and his own wit and set their homes to float again, this time in the air. When the cable company came, they simply wrapped their lines around Japheth's mooring cables like honeysuckle around older, woodier vines.

Michael and Maggie stood astride their cyclocross bikes, chests heaving. World-class athletes that they were, hauling an extra eighty pounds of equipment inside trailers that weighed another fifteen up a long climb was hard work. For Maggie it was as if there were a whole other cyclist clinging to the bike—and not an ultra-light climbing bike like the one disassembled and carefully packed in her trailer.

They looked over the valley, and at the floating town. No sound drifted from all those homes except the creaking of mooring lines and the soft whistle of wind over the silken curves of the great balloons.

"Mr. Sapp will be down the valley a ways, won't he?" asked Michael. "At the Holmes Bend dock?"

Maggie traced the cables down a pointing finger to the rocky summits of the imprisoning hills. "Maybe he lives at the mooring points, though? He's supposed to be the caretaker for all those Viewers at Home up there, right? So he'd need a way up and down."

A shadow fell across them and the road, as if a cloud had blocked the sun on this cloudless day. A voice floated from above them.

"That's assuming I ever come down, miss."

Maggie looked up and her eyes went wide while an open-mouthed grin grew across her face. Michael leapt from his bike and scrambled at the roadside, coming up with a ridiculously short, rotting stick that he brandished at the sky.

A fiberglass bass boat hung a dozen yards above their heads, suspended from an oblong, finned balloon. Propulsive fans were set all about it, pointing in every direction, cabled to an industrial-sized battery set where the outboard had once been.

Balloon, boat, and pilot were alike in their decoration, pinwheel collages of feathers in every color and size to be found from any bird in these hills. Shells and stones, too, were set among the feathers on the boat itself, spelling out what Maggie guessed to be its name. In books, boats have names. *The Undeniable Crow*, read the legend, and she guessed those were black crow feathers that constituted most of the decorations on the pilot's long leather coat, his wide-brimmed hat, and even flourished at his temples on the leather bands of his goggles.

"I know you know me," said Japheth Sapp—it could only be their father's old friend and debtor. "And I'm guessing I know you. Ted Hammersmith's twins, ain't you? Miguel y Margarita?"

Michael, guessing there was no threat or maybe recognizing the futility of their position if the strange man in his strange craft *was* a danger to them, dropped the stick. "Yes, sir," he said, "We use the anglo style, though, usually."

"Would do, among all the Amish over your way," said Mr. Sapp. He'd been standing casually, a booted foot on a side rail, but a slight rise in the wind caused him to reach down and twist a dial. One of the fans kicked in with a slight whine, and the boat turned a bit, maintaining its position. "Michael, then," he said, then, looking at Maggie, "and . . . Margaret?"

"Margaret's okay," she said. "Or Maggie, really."

"Maggie Really. That's a good name." He turned a few more dials and the boat began to drop closer to the road. "Brother Theodore wouldn't care much for you two pedaling right down here next to the old Green, I know."

"Our father doesn't live with us anymore," said Michael.

Maggie turned to look at him. This was true in a technical kind of way, but the twins weren't raised to be technical people.

She didn't correct him, exactly. "Daddy's away. He's on a long mission trip. Hasn't made it back yet."

The boat landed on the pavement and made a loud scraping noise as it drifted a foot or so before coming to a halt. Mr. Sapp tossed Michael a line. "Tie that around something heavy, boy," he said.

"Um . . ." Michael held the hemp line and looked around.

"A tree, son," said Mr. Sapp, stepping out of the boat. He kept his hands carefully on the railing, though, and didn't step away but instead sat perched on the side of his odd craft.

"I guess you could say trees are heavy," said Michael.

"Could and would and have," said Mr. Sapp. "Trees are the only thing that hold these hills down sometimes. And as to that other thing, young *señorita*, I know Ted's off. I probably seen him since y'all have."

"You have? When?" Maggie asked.

Michael hardly ever did much except pick at the memory of their father these days like a scab. But he even asked, "Why would he come see you but not us?"

"Never mind that," Mr. Sapp said, in a way that made it clear he would say no more.

Maggie realized that she was still standing astride her bicycle, that her brother was unexpectedly doing an errand for this tall, half-remembered man from their childhood, and that they'd not even broached the subject of why they were on this forbidden, creek-haunted stretch of road. But talk of their father gave her an opening.

"Before he left, our father told us if we needed . . ." She faltered. "He said it a specific way."

Michael had made his way a few yards off the road to where a line of pin oak saplings marked where a fence line used to be. He paused in his fumbling with the safety line. "If we ever need unexpected aid," he said.

"Unexpected aid from an unexpected quarter," said Mr. Sapp.

"That's it!" said Maggie, brightening. "That's it exactly. He said it wasn't for when we were sick or hungry or even if there was worse trouble, because we had neighbors for that." She hesitated again. "I don't think he meant to say that we're not neighbors—it's not really far at all from our house to your . . . to where you live."

"Your father uses the word 'neighbor' to mean a very particular thing," said Mr. Sapp. His face was a day or two away from its last shave, and the callouses on his fingers made raspy noises when he rubbed his chin. "Doubt that comes as any surprise to y'all."

"He's particular about words," agreed Michael, rejoining them. "About everything."

"*Peculiar* about everything, too," said Mr. Sapp. He had a look on his face as if remembering old arguments. Not a hard look, and even it softened when he said. "And the three of us aren't the only ones owe our lives to him being the odd bird he is. *Is.*" He weighted down the last word exactly the way Maggie did when she talked about their father. Michael didn't seem to notice, and Maggie chose not to ask why Mr. Sapp had said it in just that way.

"Unexpected aid," said Maggie.

Mr. Sapp shook off the reverie he'd been in. "Yes. Let's talk about that. But let's do it someplace more comfortable."

He pointed down the road. "Half a mile, maybe, there's a gravel track coming down off the hill. It's not washed out too bad and you should be able to get your machines up it. There's an old church at the top—you can see where the number-six lines moor down there. Wait for me there."

He made a twirling motion with his finger and Michael jumped back across the ditch to unwind the line. He was already back behind the wheel and rising when Michael threw it up into the boat.

"You'll wait for us if you make it there first, right?" called Maggie.

"Oh, I don't imagine there's any danger of me beating y'all anywhere," came the reply. "I knew your mama, too."

Japheth Sapp's home and workplace was a sort of collage of found objects and impermanent architecture. A camper set on cinderblocks was joined to an old curing shed by a run of timber frames walled with tarpaper and roofed in rusting tin. Poultry houses sat in a picked-over yard penned in by chicken wire, that fence being the only structure in sight that could be said to be in good repair.

The twins rode up slowly, Maggie leaning hard into the pedals against the weight of the trailer. They dismounted and leaned their bikes against an old grape arbor that had the dried ghosts of vines twisted round its crossbeams. There was no sign of Mr. Sapp, even in the sky.

Michael walked out into the center of the lot, where a humming noise came from a metal-sided hut measuring about ten feet on each side. Huge cables twined down from above, merging into a single strand thick as an oak tree that penetrated the flat roof of the hut. The individual strands split and split again as they branched upward, becoming hawsers that led, a quarter-mile distant, to a flotilla of houseboats hanging beneath spherical, dun-colored balloons.

Like many of the houses in the drainage of the Green River, in the drainages of all the rivers of Kentucky, really, the houseboats hosted Viewers at Home, the attenuated, drip-fed people who made up a sizeable portion of the population of the Commonwealth and many other places. Largely unchurched, they existed to consume media, and existed in a mediated state. The race the twins were bound to ride would be taken in by some statistically significant percentage of the people in those houseboats.

"Looking at the Viewership?" called Japheth Sapp, his little boat tracking in low over the smoking shed. "Some of them are looking back, probably. I've got local-access videostats orbiting the fleet for those among them who miss walking the world the most."

This time he didn't need any help landing his little craft, because he had worked some technical maneuver that let the gas escape from the balloon that held the boat aloft. There was a whine of electric motors as the lines attaching boat to balloon were drawn in around drums fore and aft, and the old man swiftly folded the deflated sack of canvas and unceremoniously let it lay over the boat itself.

Maggie saw that Michael had drawn out the letter, which he had insisted on carrying in the back pocket of his jersey, and was nervously folding and unfolding it. But he didn't approach Mr. Sapp while he worked, leaving Maggie to proffer a hand in aid, which was gently rebuffed with a grunt and a shake of the man's grizzled head.

"Now," he finally said. "What aid can I offer the children of my oldest friends?"

Maggie cleared her throat and nodded. "We need—that is, we'd greatly appreciate, um, transport."

Mr. Sapp looked over at their bicycles. "I remember a time when there wasn't much of the wide world one couldn't go to on their own, if they had machines as fine as those. Now, well, now—" And he suddenly sang in a nasally tenor:

"Everywhere we look there's water, water . . ."

Maggie recognized the snatch of song, of course. It was from one of their father's Psalms for Warning. She was about to explain that she and her brother knew how to manage the crossing of creeks and rivers as safely as anyone else might, or more so with their father's methods, when Michael gave in to his impatience. He walked over to Mr. Sapp and handed over the letter.

The old man drew a pair of round, steel-rimmed glasses from a pocket inside his vest and held the papers at arm's length. He carefully read the explanatory letter, but then paged through the packet of information in the following pages quickly until he came to the map of the race route.

"I didn't think they even ran this race, anymore," he said, more to himself than to the twins. "All the river crossings. I saw your mother win it once, you know. Before you were born."

Michael held out his hand. Maggie supposed he was asking for the papers back, but it looked like supplication. Mr. Sapp didn't return the pages in any case, but instead walked toward the trailer, indicating that they should follow him.

"I wish you had come to me earlier than this," he told them. "We'll barely make it to Paducah on time."

When Maggie woke in the middle of the night, it was to the uncanny sensation that she was sleeping on air. And then she remembered that, in a way, she was. The low sounds of the houseboat Mr. Sapp had commandeered from the flats at Holmes Bend cutting through the wind sounded around her.

Maggie had always been able to wake herself at any appointed time, even without the sun's rays streaming into her attic room or one of the mechanical windup clocks that her father and his friends so cherished jangling away. Unlike Michael, who slept the sleep of the dead and whose soft, steady breathing she could hear across the cabin.

Sleep of the dead, she thought to herself, remembering why she had chosen to wake in the middle of the night.

She padded through the interior of the houseboat on bare feet to the sliding door beside the captain's wheel that had steered the boat when it was a watercraft. She went out onto the front deck, then climbed the ladder to the roof, weaving her way through the hemp hawsers that attached to the balloon overhead. Japheth Sapp sat quietly at the control apparatus he was using to operate the houseboat, watching her approach and chewing the stem of an unlit pipe.

"I'd have thought you wanted to sleep as much as you could before tomorrow," he said.

Maggie hugged herself against the high, chill air. "I'd have thought it was tomorrow already," she replied.

Mr. Sapp made a study of the stars along the eastern horizon, behind them. "It's today yet. Just."

She nodded and watched him make a minute adjustment to a lever. There was a hissing sound in the balloon above and a fan motor churned briefly.

"You know a lot about machines," said Maggie. "Flying these boats. Acting as caretaker for the Buckeye Navy. Being . . ." She trailed off.

"Being as old as I am," he laughed. "Yes, Maggie, I know a lot about machines. Some machines, anyway. Machines built and maintained by human hands."

Not machines from Tennessee, he meant. Maggie hesitated at that, but then asked her question. "Have you ever heard of a machine that could carry messages for the dead?"

The course of the balloon, barely perceptible to Maggie, must have shifted just then, because the light of the three-quarters moon suddenly spilled across the roof of the houseboat. She could clearly see Mr. Sapp narrowing his eyes as he stared at her, then beginning to nod.

"I see, I see now. Is it just you or your brother, too?"

Maggie shook her head, not understanding him.

"Your father asked me a similar question once, but in his way he already had his own answer. He believed the calls were sent to torment him, took it as evidence that a great awakening's on the way. Or that there'd better be one before we all wake up not ourselves. I'm sure you've heard him say that we can't afford to just rely on our ability to keep the worst of Tennessee's influence out. That's why he's been gone so long, his mission." Japheth paused. "I take it you've been contacted by something you think might be Maria."

For three years, the twins had lived on their own in the house atop the hill. In all that time, she, at least, had never thought that her father had gone anywhere but on an extended mission trip into the mountains—not on a mission to spread his gospel against Athena. She started to tell this to Japheth Sapp, but he raised a hand to silence her.

"Telephone calls. Letters from south of the border. Dreams."

Maggie said, "We haven't had any letters. And we only answered the first call."

"But you've dreamed? Both of you?"

Maggie shrugged. "I have. If Michael has he hasn't said. And he won't listen to me tell about mine."

Mr. Sapp said, "I will."

Maggie took, as the text of her dream, the first verse of the forty-first chapter of Genesis.

And it came to pass at the end of two full years, that Pharaoh dreamed: and, behold, he stood by the river.

Maggie was no Pharaoh, and she knew better than to stand by the river. In waking life, anyway.

In her dreams, she wore raiment, the raiment of a champion. She wore a shifting jersey that marked her what her mother had been, Champion of Kentucky, of America, of the World. And she dipped the wheels of her bicycle into the water of the Green River.

But when she went to draw her bicycle away, the river would not let go its hold. The waters clung to the wheels, then flowed up the spokes like snakes, to the seat stay and the fork, then onto where she held the machine by the handlebars and the seat. The green water flowed over her hands and up her arms. It filled her eyes and her mouth. It flowed into her ears so that she could hear it speaking to her.

"Oh my daughter," said the river. "Oh, my beautiful daughter."

"'The river would not let go its hold,'" said Mr. Sapp, smiling by moonlight. "You may ride a bicycle like your mother but you tell a story like your father.

Since she couldn't tell the color of his eyes, Maggie held out hope that Mr. Sapp couldn't see the color coming to her cheeks. "The race we're going to starts and ends at the Ohio River," she said. "In the old days, they used to dip their tires into it for luck at the start, and then again when they finished. In thanks, I guess."

"Hmmm," said Mr. Sapp. "I think you're overstating how much ceremony went into thanksgiving in those times."

Maggie said, "What about machines in those times? Could they contact the dead?"

Mr. Sapp looked at her sharply. "You know as well as I do that if any machines are echoing your mother, they're not old. They're of the same ilk that's polluted the waterways and caused us to build the Girding Wall along the Tennessee border. Artificial intelligences escaped of their bounds programming matter and sending it out into the wider world."

"They say my mother went into one of those waterways." Maggie gestured down at the strip of river reflecting silver far below them. "Into that one. Into the Green."

Mr. Sapp said, "Whoever 'they' are, they never said it in hearing of your father, and I'm surprised they've said it to you. Your mother disappeared, Maggie, on a thunderous, flood-wracked night. There's no way to know what kind of . . . accident she met."

"If it was an accident at all," said Maggie.

Mr. Sapp was silent for a moment, then said, "I don't know for certain if any machines can carry the voices of the dead. I'd think more about imitation and camouflage if I were you. I'd think about *bait.* And be careful."

"Why would thinking machines be trying to fool us into thinking our mother is alive? Why would they want to anger our father, if that's why he really left?"

Mr. Sapp could only shrug. "Your father means a lot of things to a lot of people."

Maggie knew that was true, but couldn't stop from wondering if Mr. Sapp meant something else.

Maggie had decided to sleep in to make up for the hour she lost in talking to Japheth Sapp in the night. But Michael neither knew nor cared about that. He shook her shoulder, practically jumping up and down in the narrow cabin.

"Come and see!" he said.

Oh. There was her twin, expressing delight. Her heart lifted.

She made her way out onto the forward deck. In the hours she had slept, the landscape had changed. The hills of the Pennyroyal had given way to the flatlands of the western Commonwealth. But it was not the unusual sight of riparian plains that had so excited Michael.

"It's the Start Village!" he said.

Below, sprawling over a vast acreage of untilled land, was a temporary town made up of colorful tents, temporary garages, and canvas shelters. But more than those constructions, it was the vast number and variety of *conveyances* that drew Maggie's eye here and there.

Automobiles of every description crowded the field: cars, trucks, motor carriages, even great lumbering *buses,* which Maggie had only seen in old photographs. *Where can they get the fuel for them all?* she wondered, and then wondered the same about the fleet of motorcycles that were parked in disorderly rows along one side of the encampment.

A buzzing noise drew the attention of both twins then, and they saw a tiny aerostat marked with the logo of the national cycling union keeping pace with the flying houseboat. Mr. Sapp called from his perch on the roof, "They're guiding us to land on the east side of the village," he said. "Be ready to throw down ropes."

Below, the twins saw people waving their hands, directing the boat to land on a muddy flat. They tossed lines down to waiting hands, and Maggie felt the boat lurch to the left at the last minute before settling to the ground.

A powerfully built woman with a long braid of graying black hair hanging in front of one shoulder stood off to the side, watching the work of the landing. She wore a light blue jacket imprinted with a red and white striped insignia portraying a spinning pair of wheels. Maggie thought she looked vaguely familiar, and Michael must have as well.

"Where do we know her from?" he whispered.

It suddenly came to Maggie. "Pictures. Pictures from our old magazines. Pictures of mother. Think of her younger, standing on a podium and wearing a silver medal."

The woman was walking toward them, and must have had unusually sharp hearing. "I won a few golds as well, though there'd be no reason you'd find pictures of those among your mother's remembrances. You are the Hammersmiths. I am Lydia Treekiller, your *director sportif.*"

Their team manager. Their mother's greatest rival.

Chapter Four

"She'll drive us into the ground," Michael said, pacing back and forth in the tent they'd been assigned. "This is some sort of revenge play."

Maggie sat on her cot, calmly drinking from a water bottle she'd pulled from the insulated cooler full of such that had been provided with the tent. "She was only one member of the team selection committee," she said. "And besides, if she had some kind of axe to grind with our family, wouldn't she have worked to keep us *off* the national team?"

If Michael planned to answer, Maggie would never know, because someone outside the tent flap cleared their throat just then. "Hello, Hammersmiths?" came a muffled voice.

Michael stalked over to the entrance and swept aside the curtain closure, revealing a stout young woman about the twins' age and about Maggie's height. She wore a jacket similar to that they'd seen on Lydia Treekiller, khaki shorts, and rugged hiking boots. "Hello, there," she said in an accent Maggie didn't recognize. "I'm Tammy Salisbury, one of the Team America soigneurs. Lydia sent me to bring you to the team meeting."

Maggie returned the woman's smile, but Michael simply walked out of the tent, brushing past her with suspicion writ clear on his face. Maggie shook her head and, catching Tammy's attention, rolled her eyes and shrugged. "Sprinter," she whispered.

Tammy giggled, then seemed embarrassed that she had done so, because she covered her smile with one hand and turned away. "We're meeting on the team bus, which is parked on the far side of the village. You'll recognize it," she said, indicating the logo on her jacket.

"You're not coming?" asked Maggie.

"Athletes and directors only," said Tammy. "Director Treekiller has a very specific way she likes things done. You'll see. Anyway, I have to go into Shady Grove to see if I can find some dried pasta anywhere. The national federation was supposed to send everything we'd need for the race, but the foodstuffs leave a little to be desired."

Shady Grove was the little town a few hundred yards down the gravel road that bisected the Start Village. Maggie had caught a glimpse of it from Mr. Sapp's houseboat as they landed, and saw that it consisted of a handful of houses and a store. It reminded her of the Green River towns back home, and indeed, she'd caught the scent of a waterway on the wind blowing up from the south.

Michael gently took her by the arm and nudged her into motion. "Come on," he said. "Let's see what 'very specific way' the director is going to have us race tomorrow."

They picked their way among the tents and shelters that made up the village, once pausing to let six riders in identical red and white kits roll past, on their way out for a training ride. Maggie was more interested in their machines than in the people riding them—she'd never seen bikes so obviously manufactured in a factory rather than a workshop like their own. She wasn't worried about the efficacy of hers and Michael's racing bikes, though. Their mother had claimed the bicycles their father built equaled any in the world.

"Did you see the maple leaves on their jerseys?" asked Michael, staring after the retreating riders. "That was the national team of Canada. Hundreds of miles away at the closest. Far side of the Great Lakes."

"The lakes are clear," Maggie said absently. "All of the waterways north of the Ohio are."

"Yes," said Michael. "Which means they don't know the tricks of crossing."

Maggie snapped her fingers. "Of course," she said. "That's it. The reason that we've been selected for the American team is that the race goes across Kentucky. And what riders in the world know more about navigating the Commonwealth than us? We're guides."

Michael listened intently, nodding. "That makes sense," he said. "But what will it mean on the road? Will we be sent ahead on attacks to sound out the waterways? Held back to protect a team leader riding for the general classification?"

They came to a row of enormous buses, the red and white stripes prominent on the one parked closest to the road. "I guess we're about to find out," said Maggie.

The interior of the bus smelled of ammonia and alcohol, and was absolutely spotless. It was cooler than the outdoors, certainly cooler than the interior of the tent they'd been assigned, and lit by electric lamps, as the windows that lined the sides were shaded with fine mesh screens manufactured right into the glass.

Lydia Treekiller sat at a long, narrow table folded up from an interior wall. A bald man sat opposite the director, his back to the twins. Two women and two men in cycling kits sat in comfortable-looking chairs bolted to the carpeted floor, and the bald man, when he turned, directed the twins to two of these which were empty with a nod of his head. Maggie and Michael exchanged looks, sharing the same vague feeling of recognition on seeing the man's hooked nose that they had felt that morning when they first saw Lydia Treekiller.

"Rule number one," said the director. "Never be late. Not for a start, not for a meal, not for a team meeting."

Michael bristled at that. "We came as soon as the soigneur told us."

"Rule number two," continued Lydia, as if Michael hadn't spoken. "Make no assumptions. Only act on information you're sure of. Follow orders to the letter. This is a dangerous course, and second-guessing either the race directors or me can lead to a lot worse fates than being the *lanterne rouge.*" She looked at Michael, then. "I didn't say you were late. But it's interesting that you thought you were. Are you, frequently?"

Michael looked at Maggie, who answered. "No," she said. "We're both very punctual."

Lydia turned her gaze to Maggie and raised an eyebrow. "Do you always speak for him?"

"No," said the twins simultaneously.

"I can speak for myself," said Michael, anger rising in his voice.

"It's just that sometimes it's best if he doesn't," Maggie added.

To her surprise, the ghost of a smile flickered across the older woman's stern features. She turned back to the clipboard lying on the table before her.

"The rest of the team rules are in the packets that David will distribute when we finish up here." She didn't pronounce the name the way the twins were used to hearing it, accenting and lengthening the second syllable.

"David Bonheur!" gasped Maggie. "You won the Tour de France!"

The bald man with the hooked nose looked over at her without expression, then slowly raised two fingers. "I won the Tour de France *twice*," he said.

"Right," said Lydia, tapping her clipboard with an ink pen. "Introductions, since some of you are new to the team. I'm Lydia Treekiller, team manager and director sportif. David is my second, and will drive the number two car behind the race. Now, each of you give your names and *briefly* describe your backgrounds. Nicholas, you're our man for the general classification, so you start."

The man seated farthest from the bus door was wearing a different jersey than the other three riders. It was orange and there was a seal prominent over his chest, a black circle around a seven-pointed yellow star flanked by branches of some tree Maggie couldn't identify. Seven more yellow stars encircled the seal, and a lone black star, also with seven points, was over the man's heart like a badge. He stood uncomfortably and nodded at the team manager. "Yes, aunt," he said. "I'm Nicholas Langdon. I time trial a little. I can climb a little." With that, he sat down.

Lydia Treekiller shook her head. "Yes," she said, "he is my nephew. But he is also a dual champion, of both the Cherokee Nation and the State of Oklahoma. He would be here, and he would be America's hope for the overall win, even if someone else was directing, eh, David?"

The Frenchman did not respond.

Next was a tall black woman in the same kit as the others, the kit, Maggie imagined, that she and Michael would also be wearing in the days to come, blue with red and white stripes prominent, as well as white stars at the shoulders. "Samantha. I'm a *roleur*, good for anything. I'm happy to play domestique for Nicholas. I've done it before." She grinned at Lydia's nephew when she said it.

The other two were also domestiques, team riders who would sacrifice their own chances for the good of the team leader, protecting him from the wind and seeing that he always had bottles and food on the hard roads ahead. Telly was a quiet man, older than the rest of the riders, from Wisconsin. Jordan, the other woman, had dyed her hair a bright green and had more piercings than Maggie had ever seen in real life. She was from one of the big cities in Pennsylvania.

"You four know each other from the national circuit," Lydia Treekiller said, "but our sprinter and our climbing specialist are new to the scene. The state of things here in Kentucky means that championships haven't been run for a long while, but I assure you that if there was a jersey to be won, it would be on either Michael's or Maggie's shoulders. They're self-trained, but they have an excellent background, and have been dominating area races since they were children. Isn't that right?"

She didn't seem to be indicating that one or the other of them in particular should do the talking, so naturally it was Maggie who answered.

"Our mother was World Champion three times," she said. "And we use her training methods Dad taught us growing up."

The Wisconsin man, Telly, suddenly smiled. "You're the children of Maria Galdeana. My oldest brother raced with her in Europe when he was first starting out."

"Yes, yes, professional cycling is a small world," said Lydia. "We all have connections with one another."

And they mostly seem to have to do with our mother, thought Maggie, and knew Michael was thinking the same thing.

Lydia unrolled a map across the table, a larger version of the one that had been included in the letter the twins had received two days before, though somehow it seemed much longer than that. It showed the race route starting at Paducah, turning southeast, then east, then north and east to the town of Mayfield in the northern reaches of the Commonwealth. Unlike the map they had received, though, there was a second, shorter line forming a loop near Lexington.

"Yes, you all see it," said Lydia. "The race has been extended. Four road stages but now a time trial in the heart of the Bluegrass. The race organizers have made some bargain with the Horselords, who want to show off their holdings to the Viewers at Home. So, five racing days in all, starting tomorrow at noon with one of the most challenging. David?"

The bald man pulled a sheaf of papers from a leather satchel at his feet and handed copies around to the riders. At a glance, Maggie saw that the paper she held was a course description, complete with elevation profile, of the first part of the race.

"Tomorrow is short," David said, "and flat. Shorter than any such stage would be in most places, but of course this race presents certain unique . . . challenges." Here he looked up at the twins, but then thumped the map on the table with his forefinger. "Hardly a bump in the road to speak of in terms of climbing, 138 kilometers, though as you can see from the profile it is a false flat, and climbs gradually all day, first away from the Ohio, and then from these other two rivers."

Michael interrupted, incredulity loud in his voice. "These other two rivers that happen to be the Cumberland and the Tennessee, flowing straight beneath the Girding Wall and out of the Voluntary State."

David shrugged. "Yes. Rivers polluted with the invisible machines of their Governor, which you Kentuckians say draw a man's soul from him before killing him. The racing will be difficult."

Lydia was staring levelly at Michael, but did not comment on his intrusion on David's briefing. The Frenchman spoke on.

"The road surfaces are poor compared to what most of you are used to, but there will be no local traffic to contend with. We have enclosures, though apparently the route is little used even without them. There are no significant turns. The greatest danger in racing terms, besides crossing the two rivers, is the wind from the southwest, which has the potential to split the peloton into echelons. We must be very diligent and watch for gaps. If they appear, we must be in the front of them, and ride hard to put time into our opponents. If we find ourselves behind such a gap, we must close it as quickly as possible and so save energy for the finish."

Lydia showed them a photograph of the finishing area. "The road narrows at the finish, but it's still clearly the place for a bunch sprint. So we'll be riding for Michael tomorrow, with Jordan, Telly, and Samantha leading him out in that order. Maggie, you'll stay with Nicholas and keep him out of trouble."

Maggie was surprised by this, as she would have thought that her long experience riding with her brother would make her a natural choice for the lead-out train, but she didn't say anything, being distracted by what she saw in the background of the photograph Lydia held.

"The finish," she asked, "is it at the Obelisk?"

Lydia nodded. "Its shadow falls across the finish line, and the race will camp on its grounds tomorrow night."

The green-haired woman, Jordan, asked, "What's the Obelisk?"

"You'll see tomorrow," said Lydia. "If you've seen the Washington Monument in the national capital you'll think you're seeing its twin rising out of the western Kentucky flatlands. Its history is . . . problematic."

"It was built as a monument to a traitorous evildoer, she means," said Michael. "Before it was called the Obelisk it was called the Jefferson Davis Memorial. He was born in the village there, Fairview."

Maggie remembered her father talking about the Obelisk, as Michael obviously did. "It's been repurposed, though. The Davis name is anathema in the Commonwealth, and mention of him has been stripped from the Obelisk and its grounds for a long time. It's meant to be for remembrance now, and for ways of remembering. A great man of letters, Robert Penn Warren, was born not far from the Obelisk, too, so some people have tried to rededicate it as a monument to writing."

"Not everyone has forgotten Davis, though," said David. He was reading from the closely lined text of the next day's stage bible. "We're supposed to look out for, I don't know this word, Reenactors?"

Michael cursed, and Maggie let out an involuntary sigh of dismay.

"What? What are they?" asked David.

"A dying breed, thankfully," said Michael, and when he didn't explain further, everyone on the bus turned and looked at Maggie.

"They call themselves 'living historians,'" said Maggie. "Our father said they have a triumphalist and reactionary view of the past. They celebrate the darkest days in American history, fetishizing their own discomfort and ignoring the greatest crimes of the New World in favor of pretended glory."

David shook his head. "They are some kind of self-blinded masochists, then?"

"Our father always said it's one thing for people to lie to themselves," said Michael, "but that tyranny arises when you demand that others believe the lies as well. That's what Reenactors want, to erase history."

"Or edit it, at least," said Maggie. It was strange to hear Michael speaking of their father in such a neutral way. Perhaps the race would help ease his sense that their father had abandoned them. Maggie could only hope—growing up, their father had been a hero to Michael, and no fall was greater than one from on high.

Lydia spoke up. "Who they are is less important for our purposes than what they might do. The organizers are afraid they'll stage some kind of demonstration in the road, or otherwise disrupt the race, trying to celebrate the Obelisk's original honoree. There's little we can do about it besides be on the lookout. Hopefully local law enforcement is up to the task of putting down a few neo-Confederates."

"So long as local law enforcement aren't neo-Confederates themselves," said Telly. "This *is* the South."

"No," said Maggie. "Kentucky was only culturally southern the way you're thinking for a century and a half or so after the Civil War. The Commonwealth started out as the west. And now we're the Border State."

Chapter Five

The team meeting went on for another hour, with Lydia and David detailing the rosters of the other teams. In addition to themselves and the Canadians the twins had seen, there were eight other teams riding the Race Across Kentucky. A few were additional national teams: Mexico, Quebec, Cuba, and California. The remaining four were Nicholas's former tribal formation, the Cherokee team, and three trade teams sponsored by companies interested in advertising their activities to the Viewers at Home.

When the meeting broke up, Lydia told Michael to take his sprint train out onto the open roads to practice the final five kilometers of a sprint finish under the directorship of David, who would pace them on a team motorcycle. Nicholas left quietly, saying something about going on a solo training ride and seeing something of Paducah. Maggie was looking over an area map, plotting out a route for a training ride of her own, when Lydia asked her to stay on the bus for a moment.

"If this is about Michael's temper," said Maggie when the two of them were alone, "he's got it under control. He's just not used to working under a director sportif, yet. He'll prove a good teammate, I promise."

"That's good to hear," said Lydia, "but it's not what I wanted to talk to you about." She pulled an envelope out from inside her jacket and studied it a moment, a thoughtful expression on her face, before handing it over to Maggie. "I want you to tell me what you know about this."

The letter was addressed to Lydia at the national training center in Colorado, with a postmark a month past. The return address read simply: *M. Galdeana, Nashville.*

Maggie's hand trembled. "This, this is some kind of hoax. A bad joke."

"That's what I thought when I found it. Then I opened it. Read it."

The envelope had been roughly torn open along the fold, as if opened by someone in a hurry. Maggie slipped a single sheet from inside, unfolded it, held it up to the light, and read:

My dearest Lydia,

It is my great hope that this letter finds you active and productive. Though we have not seen one another in many years, I followed your career closely after I left competition. I was thrilled when you won the Nationals, and adding a third Silver to your collection of Worlds medals was an extraordinary accomplishment, especially on that course, against that field.

You are probably surprised to be receiving this letter, as the news of my drowning in Kentucky no doubt reached you not long after it occurred. My information about the wider world is limited, but I know that I am considered dead by my friends and family. It is of my family that I wish to speak.

My children, Margaret and Michael, may be known to you, at least as names on the lists of elite American cyclists. It is my understanding that you will be directing the national team in the renewed Race Across Kentucky in a month's time.

The organization of this race is known to me, and I can tell you in advance that the route will require local knowledge. I am writing to ask you that you include my children on your team for the race. They are more than qualified as athletes, and in fact are the only racers in the Commonwealth who have both the talent to ride in a competitive international field and the skills to navigate the unique hazards of a road race in Kentucky.

I ask that you do me this great favor out of remembrance of the comradeship of the road we once enjoyed. But, Lydia, if that is not enough, I regretfully remind you of your promise to me on Mount Mitchell.

> *Respectfully yours,*
> *Maria*

Maggie placed the letter on the table, unconsciously smoothing it as she did so, and sat in the chair David had vacated without invitation.

"My mother has been dead for over twenty years," she said. Her voice was low, as if she were talking to herself.

"You were, four, then?" asked Lydia.

"Just turned four. Our birthday is in April, when the rains are heaviest."

"That's what I remember hearing," said Lydia. "A flash flood while she was on a training ride?"

"Not training," said Maggie. "She only kept up her training for a year or so after we were born. She rode everywhere though. She was coming back with the mail. There'd been a heavy ordinance delivery. Books for my father."

"The apostle. I met him once at a race in Philadelphia."

Maggie shook her head. "Churched people don't call themselves apostles. Not where we're from, anyway. I never knew he'd been so far from home as Philadelphia."

"It was many years ago. The Voluntary State was just beginning to move outside its borders. There was more travel in those days."

Maggie looked at the letter again. "I was told recently . . . I was just told others may have received letters like this."

"But you haven't had any word from her yourself?"

Maggie hesitated. She didn't know this woman, didn't know her politics or her sense of the world. There were some people, she knew, who would consider the dreams she'd been having a sign that she'd been infected by some viral spirit out of Tennessee. *And maybe I have been,* she thought.

So instead of answering right away, Maggie looked at the letter again. "What does this mean—are we really here because of this?"

Lydia shook her head. "I've shown the letter to no one but you. You, who are trying to avoid my question."

"No," said Maggie. "No, we haven't received any letters."

Sometimes, she thought she remembered her mother telling her something when she was very small. We have to take risks. You can't be afraid of falling. You *will* fall.

"But there have been calls," she added, dropping her voice almost to a whisper. "They've been coming more frequently."

"Calls?" said Lydia. "From those phone things the Governor of Tennessee sends out?"

"Yes," said Maggie. "But we've never answered them. Our father told us that they were, well, he used the word *demonic.*"

"It's a crime, a *federal* crime, to have anything to do with the Voluntary State," said Lydia, standing and pacing. "The two of you haven't told anyone? No authorities? Not even your friends or relatives?"

Maggie shook her head. "We don't even talk about it to each other. And we don't have any relatives." She elected to not tell Lydia about her midnight conversation with Japheth Sapp. She hadn't even told Michael about it.

"I don't have any explanation, then," said Lydia. "My position with the national federation is . . . tenuous. People think Nicholas has his position on the team because of me, but it's really the other way around. I can't afford to be mixed up with anything to do with enemies of the state."

"My mother is not an enemy of the state!" said Maggie.

"So you think these messages *are* from Maria?" challenged Lydia. "You think twenty years after she was swept away by a polluted river she's placing calls and mailing letters from Nashville?"

Maggie considered the postmark again. "The phones slip over the Girding Wall," she said. "It's not unheard of in the Commonwealth. But the federal postal service delivered a letter from there? They'd break the embargo?"

It was Lydia's turn to hesitate. "It didn't come in the mail. I found it beneath my pillow at the training center in Colorado Springs. And no, I have no idea how it got there, or who might have delivered it. Believe me, that was the first thing I tried to find out."

Maggie stood and awkwardly avoided Lydia's pacing, moving to the bus exit. She needed to think. That meant she needed to ride.

"I have to train, still," she said. "Whatever else happens, there's still the race tomorrow."

Lydia chuckled humorously. "I should be the one telling you that."

Maggie started down the steps, but Lydia called after her. "You should know something. You and Michael. You'd be here even if I hadn't received this letter. Five of the six team selectors put your names forward."

So which one didn't? wondered Maggie, and went to find her bike.

▷▷▷

Onto the roads of western Kentucky.

These flatlands could hardly be more different from the hills of the Pennyroyal region, where she and Michael lived and trained. This was a land that had been scoured by rivers for millennia, when rivers were merely conventionally threatening.

Maggie decided to scout the first part of the next day's course. She headed north along a remnant of asphalt called Bryant Ford Road, away from Clarks River and the shallow crossing that gave the byway its name. When she reached 68, the race route, she had the choice of continuing on into Paducah or turning southeast, away from the city.

It's a neutral roll out this far out, anyway, she thought to herself. Highway 68 began not far north of the intersection where she made her choice, and when the race began the next day the riders would not begin attacking one another immediately. For the first few miles, the bunch, the peleton, would ride in a group, easing into the race, working out kinks in legs, adjustments in equipment, last-minute nerves.

Almost immediately after she turned right, she passed an old road sign. Marshall County. The Commonwealth had a plethora of counties, over one hundred, and the race would travel through dozens of them. Signs like this would mark border crossings for the next five days, and crossing borders in Kentucky often meant crossing creeks and streams where they didn't mark drainage divides.

Everywhere we look, there's water, water . . .

In these river flats, though, the borders were straighter than she was used to in the hills. They'd been drawn by rules, rationalized on maps rather than following some natural contour of the land. So she didn't have to worry about any significant crossings unless she rode all the way to the Tennessee and Cumberland Rivers and crossed the heavily guarded pontoon bridges the federal Corps of Engineers maintained.

She didn't plan to go that far, though. She was just getting some miles in her legs, just finding the rhythm and peace of the road.

Suddenly, a blurred shape passed her on the left, then another, then another. The growling sound of a motorbike approached from behind as well, and she saw that it was Michael's sprint train, *moving*.

When David passed her on the motorcycle she slipped in behind him, riding the slipstream and looking up ahead to see how well the others were working together.

Not too shabby, she thought. She and Michael had always been a team of two, but now they were part of a real professional squad. Now they had teammates to rely on, not just each other.

This must have been the second or third time they'd ramped up, hitting speeds of forty miles per hour and more in the windless flat, because all four of the riders were still riding in a line, one after the other. As Maggie watched, she saw Jordan peel off and slow as Telly took the lead of the train, cranking the speed up even higher.

This was the way of lead-out trains. One rider after another exhausted themselves in the wind at the front, peeling away when they couldn't maintain the pace any longer. Then the next one came, with the responsibility not only of maintaining that pace, but of raising it even higher. When Samantha took the lead, she would be the pilot, the final rider pulling Michael along at extraordinary speeds, but also picking and weaving her way through all the other trains that would be trying for the sprint as well. When she pulled off, then Michael would go alone, rising out of the saddle, ducking low across the handlebars to maintain an aerodynamic profile, pushing a huge gear. The timing of each step had to be perfect, and it looked to Maggie as if David had already coached them into excellent form.

"Hey! Maggie!" said Jordan, pulling alongside her. "Your brother can *sprint!*"

Maggie smiled and nodded. She knew. She knew.

That night, Michael came to the tent later than Maggie, having availed himself of a massage in the team bus. He was restless despite the hard workout of the day, and wanted to talk.

"I can win tomorrow," he said. "I know I can. Any of the sprint finishes or intermediaries are up for grabs, and my form is strong. This race couldn't have come at a better time."

The intermediary sprints were places on the road where points were awarded to the first rider who crossed. Those points were added to those taken by the stage winner, and whoever accumulated the most wore a special jersey in the race. It was a prize for being the most consistent rider, something to keep the sprinters interested despite the fact that they weren't expected to contend for the overall general classification. Sprinters did poorly when the roads turned up, and usually weren't good time trialists either. Which made Maggie think . . .

"What do you think of this addition of a time trial at Lexington?" she asked from her bunk, leaning up on one elbow.

"I think if it's as hilly as it looks in the race bible then you're in with a chance," he said. "We're going to *dominate* this race!"

"No, I mean, don't you think it's odd that a whole day's racing was added after the route had already been set? I was going to ask one of the race directors or referees about it, but I still haven't met any of them. Did you see any officials today?"

Michael shook his head, and was shaking off the subject at the same time. He wasn't as interested in *whys* as Maggie was. "It's an extra day of world-class support is all I care about," he said, then crossed over and sat on the canvas floor beside her cot. He took her hand, and Maggie tried to remember the last time they'd sat like this.

"Maggie, this is *it*. If we ride well—and I know we will—this is our introduction to the national scene. To the *international* scene. We could be riding at this level the whole season. We might even get asked out to Colorado for off-season training!"

She smiled at his enthusiasm, but her thoughts were suddenly on the house above the Green River. She hoped the neighbors were keeping their promise to feed her chickens. Then she thought of Lydia's letter.

"Michael," she said, trying to figure out how to broach the subject. She still hadn't told him about what Japheth Sapp had said, or her dreams, and now here was *another* secret. She didn't like keeping things from him, but neither was she sure how he would react. And he was so excited.

He grinned at her. "Don't worry. Everything's working out perfectly. Now let's rest! Race tomorrow!"

She decided she would do the worrying for the both of them. So she let go of his hand and he crossed the tent, extinguished the lamp, and climbed into his own cot. In no time, he was breathing the deep, steady breaths that ensured Maggie that he was asleep.

"Sweet dreams," she whispered.

Chapter Six

The twins knew from their father's recounting of their mother's stories—and from the collection of books and magazines she had left on the shelves with their father's heavy tomes of theology, neuroscience, and history—that the starts of major bicycle races had once resembled carnivals, festivals, parades. The biggest races sent fleets of motorized vehicles along the route before the racers, with sponsors throwing out gifts, politicians bellowing slogans, people dancing in truck beds.

That was in the days when the roads were lined with spectators the whole route, of course, long before the world changed, before the Voluntary State threatened the individuality of everyone in the east, before so many people the world over made the choice to become Viewers at Home. The roadsides on this clear July day would be empty, of course, especially close to the river crossings. The woken population of the Commonwealth would be in their fields and workshops, hearing about the race secondhand unless they happened to live right on 68.

"There will be a few people out, the race directors say," Lydia had told them at the morning meeting. "Engineers at the Tennessee and the Cumberland. Townsfolk in Cadiz and Hopkinsville, where we'll pass the grounds of some sort of hospital for Viewers who've rejected cable and can't be brought back around. And we've word from the finish that there *is* an encampment of Reenactors there, but they're keeping quiet about their intentions."

The usual way of these races would be for an early breakaway to roll off the peloton in the first miles of the race, hoping against hope to stay away for the whole day and stealing a win from the sprinters and general classification riders. But today wasn't like a normal day. This was not a normal bicycle race.

"Everyone will stay together, we think," David had said. "Until the crossing of the Tennessee. All the teams have worked out their own strategies of how to deal with the river, and they'll want their squads to cross together."

"We're good there, right?" asked Lydia. "You two can get us across?"

Maggie had simply nodded, while Michael said, "Of course."

So the peloton rolled southeast from the start on the outskirts of Paducah. The red car of the race director led them out, with referees and judges and neutral service mechanics surrounding the sixty riders on motorcycles, and the team cars with their spare bicycles mounted rooftop following behind.

And everywhere, there were camerastats.

These were the cameras, hovering and humming, that would broadcast the race to the Viewers at Home. They were alien-looking things, crosses between ancient insects and mechanical toys, with lenses for eyes and whirling blades keeping them afloat in the air. Some were under the direction of the race referees, who could monitor their feeds in their cars or via heads-up displays in the visors of their motorcycle helmets. But most followed the mysterious commands of the cable company, zooming in to follow a single rider now, then flying up to look down on the whole peloton from above.

Maggie and her teammates were riding near the front, flanked by Californians in gold jerseys depicting bears and Quebecois in blue with the white *Fleurdelisé* emblazoned across their backs. The peloton was nervous during the opening miles of the uncontested rollout, none of the riders wishing to be the one who touched another's wheel and caused a foolish crash.

The roof window of the red car in front of them opened and a figure stood up from inside. It was impossible to say whether the race director, for this was surely who this person must be, was a man or a woman. The wind from their 20-mile-per-hour pace caused the director's jacket to billow up like a balloon, and an enclosed helmet painted with the features of an owl concealed the face.

Someone handed the director a triangular red flag from the interior of the car, and this was held up in outstretched arms, then waved back and forth. At that, the car sped ahead, leaving open road before the peloton. The Race Across Kentucky had officially begun.

To little apparent effect.

"It's like Lydia said," Michael called over the wind. "No attacks from the gun."

Maggie eyed the odometer the team mechanics had installed on her handlebars, seeing that the speed of the bunch had gone up only slightly with the official opening of hostilities. To confirm their plan, a crackling came over the headpiece all the riders wore in their left ears, and the Americans heard David's voice. "Steady, steady. We'll be at the river in a little less than an hour at this pace. Just stretch out your legs and stay out of trouble."

Maggie caught herself nodding. She'd never raced with a radio onboard before. She wasn't sure whether she should acknowledge what David had said by touching the transmit button hidden under her jersey at her collarbone, but saw that none of the more experienced riders on the team were doing so. In fact, her teammates didn't act as if they had heard.

Nicholas was exactly where he was supposed to be, tucked in on her wheel, his expression unreadable behind his sunglasses. Michael and Telly were talking to one another about the intermediate sprint at Cadiz and who among the other teams were likely to contest it. Jordan was laughing and speaking French to one of the Quebecois riders, and Samantha was already tearing open one of the packages of processed foodstuffs they'd all been given to carry in their jersey pockets.

Maggie didn't know how she could eat. They'd all had an enormous breakfast of cereal and rice and saltwater fish brought in from the Atlantic, and it wasn't settling well in her nervous stomach. Despite Michael's bravado about the river crossing, Maggie was worried.

For the first time in Maggie's experience as a racing cyclist, the peloton she was riding in began to slow as it approached its first objective instead of speeding up. She caught the scent of river water in the air and knew why.

"Michael and Maggie, move on up," came the crackling voice in her ear, this time Lydia's. "None of the other directors are talking about their plans for the crossing, but we've decided as a group to go one at a time and keep the race neutral through the twelve miles between the two rivers."

Makes sense, thought Maggie, just as Michael said aloud, "They're afraid to race! This is ridiculous."

The peloton crossed a bridge over a scrub flat, the bridge running parallel to an earthworks dam that diverted some nameless stream to the south. The crossing they were facing was challenge enough without stopping to spend time negotiating with a creek.

And then the road broadened and swept due east, and helmeted women and men were seen along the roadside, some next to parked armored vehicles, others walking toward the pontoon bridge that now stretched out before the race.

Brakes hissing, the peloton came to a stop.

The red car of the race director was parked to one side, its tinted windows impenetrable. No one from the race organization was visible, and the motorcycles and team cars were all behind them now. A woman about Lydia's age, wearing khaki with stripes at her jacket shoulder, walked out into the middle of the road.

"I'm Captain Summers," she said. "We've been ordered to let you all pass, if you still want to. But I'm bound by federal law to give you the standard warning. Crossing waters infested by the machines of the Voluntary State can be deadly. Exposure to this or any other river so infested carries the risk of death, personality obliteration, or possession. If you are so exposed, you will be considered enemies of the United States of America and of the United Nations. No negotiation is possible. No surrender will be recognized. No quarter will be given."

With that, the woman walked away, not giving the cyclists a second glance.

Maggie looked at Nicholas, their leader on the road. "What now?" she asked.

He looked back at her levelly, eyes invisible behind his sunglasses. "You tell me," he said.

Michael kicked off, coasting forward. When no one else moved, Maggie followed, quickly coming up alongside him.

"This isn't the Green," she said nervously. "We don't know this river. This is the *Tennessee* River, flowing straight out of the Voluntary State. And the Cumberland comes straight from Nashville, seat of Athena Parthenus."

Michael shrugged. "We still know what to do. Everything he taught us should still work. It always has. Look, the waters are calm, anyway."

And indeed, the green-brown waters were placid, hardly a ripple evident to show the passing of the current as the river flowed north to its mouth at the Ohio.

The linked pontoon bridges were actually resting on the ground for much of their length. Like many other rivers in the Commonwealth, like their own Green, the Tennessee had formerly been an impounded lake. But the Kentucky Dam had been blown by the Corps of Engineers decades before as part of some failed effort to tame the river, and so what came to be known as the Land Between the Lakes was once again the Land Between the Rivers.

Maggie looked out across the water at the federal preserve that extended from the Girding Wall to the south, bound on its other three sides by the Tennessee, the Cumberland, and the Ohio. The road pitched up slightly on the far side.

"Look," said Michael. "The one little climb of the day. You've got that to look forward to."

They reached the bank, visible to either side and even straight down, through the wirework mesh of the bridge surface. The shore was muddy, but lifeless, no plants growing right down to the water. The twins dismounted and leaned their bikes against a stanchion.

"*Everywhere we look there's water, water . . . ,*" Michael sang softly.

Which he did not, strictly speaking, need to do. The harmonics the twins would send through the water to clear a way through its possession were particular, and the declarative psalm Michael voiced was just a way to reassure her, Maggie knew.

She breathed deep, then leaned out over the water, examining it. She heard a cry of alarm from somewhere down the road, but she could not tell if it was from one of the cyclists or one of the engineers. The water was cloudy with mud, roiling.

Yes. Yes, this was *organized* water.

Maggie sang a Psalm of David:

> "*Thou didst cleave the fountain and the flood:*
> *Thou driedst up mighty rivers.*"

She held the crystal A note of the last syllable, and Michael joined in two octaves lower with his pure baritone, singing in unison.

This was the faith of their father, and his great discovery after their mother died. That the impurities in the waterways of the Commonwealth were sensitive to the sound of his voice. But more than that, they could be influenced, manipulated at their unimaginable quantum level of thought and activity—their father believed the rivers *thought*— to allow safe passage. So long as he—or they, the twins—possessed *intent*. This intent could be expressed by song, or even, for their father himself, at least, through exhortation. So far as Maggie knew, the Hammersmiths were the sole practitioners for whom this method worked.

The words of Brother Theodore Hammersmith: "*The nanomachines of the Voluntary State are possessed of minds, or of a mind, but not of souls. They make decisions, but have no free will. They are vulnerable to the attitude of us, the singers, and we call this attitude faith.*"

Michael had once asked their father what would happen if they attempted to sing a river down and their faith faltered. Their father told them, "Never falter."

Below them, a clarity emerged in the water, spreading out around them, washing up against the shore then lapping back. The muddy bottom of the river became clear, and Michael touched the transmit button at his collarbone. "Bring them up, bring them, you can cross behind us."

The other four members of the American team joined them quickly, followed, Maggie was surprised to see, not only by the team car, but by the race director's car as well. The twins walked across the bridge, pushing their bicycles, singing. In a few moments, they stood in the Land Between the Rivers, looking back at the peloton and the caravan of vehicles that made up the race.

Rolling down the window of the team car, Lydia beckoned Maggie and Michael over. "This will be necessary at every crossing?"

Maggie nodded, and Michael said, "Unless you want to sacrifice a rider to the Governor of Tennessee."

Lydia ignored that, and said, "Can you teach the others?"

Maggie looked at Michael, and asked, "Maybe. It's hard to say . . . Are any of them churched?"

Lydia gave her a strange look, then said, "Never mind. Let's see how the other teams fare."

Across the river, there was some kind of disagreement going among between the directors, most of whom had gotten out of their cars to watch the first crossing. Whether there were some among them agitating to go second or whether *none* of them wanted to go was impossible to tell.

Finally, though, one of the trade teams, dressed in green and yellow kits, glided up the pontoon bridge to the edge of the water, followed closely by their team car. The six riders dismounted, and the mechanics and directors in the car all emerged. The rear hatch of the automobile was opened, and the mechanics began distributing what looked like plastic tarps folded into squares to each rider.

The six riders arrayed themselves in three rows of two, unfolding the clear plastic sheeting on the bridge, then mounting their bikes and rolling atop the tarp circles they'd just made. A team mechanic moved among them, walking crouched from rider to rider, doing something with a tool at ground level that Maggie couldn't see.

Suddenly, the tarps began to inflate. One by one, they were revealed to be large, clear spheres, hardening by some alchemy of material science as they grew up and around each cyclist. Within a few moments, all six of riders were completely enclosed.

"Clever," said David. "They will roll across like the little hamsters in their toys."

Maggie and Michael exchanged a troubled glance. There was nothing of faith in this. Maggie wondered how she would feel if it didn't work. She wondered how she would feel if it *did*.

"Look," said Jordan. "They're putting together a bigger one for the car." And indeed, the team car was now inside a gigantic sphere that barely fit between the railings of the bridge.

At some unheard signal, the riders in green began rolling slowly forward. As the front wheels of their machines touched the interior of the spheres, the energy from their drive trains was transferred and the whole, strange, bobbling array of six large bubbles and one huge one moved out over the water.

"Look at the river," said Michael.

The clarity that had spread out beneath their team when they rode across the bridge had disappeared, and the water was once again cloudy and impenetrable. But more than that, the slight rills and ripples that had been visible on the surface before were now more energetic, as if rocks had suddenly thrust up from the riverbed, making this stretch of water into a rapids.

"It knows they're there," said Maggie. "It's going to do something."

What the Tennessee River did was terrifying in its speed and spectacle.

A tempest exploded from the surface of the river, a great crash of water that roared with the tumult of a hundred thunderstorms arcing up and over the crossing riders. The entire length of the bridge disappeared beneath a wave that, impossibly, abruptly ceased all motion for a long and terrible moment. Then it subsided with as much violence as it had appeared, flowing downriver and up against its own current both.

Leaving behind carnage.

The bridge had shifted, bowing downstream in a curve that left gaps between its sections, metal twisting and stretching. The team car was on its side, thrown up against the railings on the north side of the bridge, and as everyone watched, paralyzed, it fell back onto its wheels.

There was no sign of the plastic spheres at all, apparently melted away by the deluge. There were four cyclists spread among a tangle of wrecked bicycle frames just before the car.

"Where are the other two?" someone whispered, and Maggie didn't turn from the horrible sight in front of her to see who.

She heard her brother answer. "Gone. Forever gone."

A high-pitched siren began to wail on the other side of the Tennessee, and the Corps of Engineers troops began scrambling into formations. Maggie could see Captain Summers shouting orders, pointing toward the bridge, where three of the remaining riders were stirring, trying to get to their feet. A back door on the green team car opened and a mechanic fell out, feebly waving an arm, as if calling for aid.

Nicholas stepped forward and Maggie cried, "No!" even as Lydia moved to block him.

"They're dying!" Nicholas said, the first time he'd raised his voice in Maggie's hearing.

"No," said Michael, turning his back on the river. "No, the ones who were going to die are dead already. The ones who are left, they're . . . not who they were."

Out on the bridge, the three cyclists had found their feet and kicked the wreckage of their bicycles into the water. Then, raising screams from some of the riders on the far bank, they did the same to their unmoving comrade.

The director sportif of the drowned team opened the driver's door of the car and stumbled out. He joined the three riders and the team mechanic and the five of them lined up. The faint sounds of singing rose from the group, and they began to dance.

"That's Thierry Dumoulin," said David. "I've known him for over thirty years."

"I don't think so," said Lydia. "I don't think that's Thierry anymore."

There was a clank, then a whining noise, and the whole bridge shuddered. The section the lost team stood on began to raise at an angle, spilling them back toward the far bank.

"It's the engineers," said Michael. "They're forcing them back to shore so they can be taken into custody."

"What will happen to them? Can they be cured?" asked Nicholas.

Maggie shook her head. "Nobody knows what the federals do with Tennessee's . . . victims."

"Our father heard rumors of camps," added Michael. "But he always cautioned us against rumor."

Samantha asked, "The race. Is it over?"

Michael brightened. "If they can't cross, they can't compete. We'll ride a victory lap across the whole Commonwealth."

But Maggie said, "No. No, there will be a race. The other teams will cross."

She walked to the edge of the water. She took as her text the first verse of the twenty-second chapter of Revelations, and she sang:

"And he shewed me a pure river of water of life, clear as crystal, proceeding out the throne of God and of the Lamb."

"Maggie!" shouted Michael, and there was dissonance and anger in his voice, but it did not stop the waters from clearing again, this time faster, this time farther.

Maggie listened to the arguments through her earpiece, not contributing anything despite the fact that it had been her actions that precipitated the crisis going on within her team. David and Michael were openly angry with her for clearing the way across the river for all the other teams and escort vehicles, and Maggie suspected that Samantha was as well.

Nicholas, though, had thanked her, and Jordan had given her a wan smile and a thumbs-up when the caravan started rolling across the bridge, once the engineers had reconstituted it. Lydia was sanguine.

"Look, it's happened," said the director over the radio. "I've spoken to the other teams, and we're going to have the twins get us all across the Cumberland with their holy music or whatever it is as well, then the race will begin in earnest. We have an intermediate sprint coming up at—" There was a sound of ruffling papers, then, "Cadiz. Michael, if you want to stay mad, that's fine, put it into your racing. Leave your anger on the road."

Maggie, tucked onto Michael's wheel in the peloton as it flew across the Land Between the Rivers, saw her brother throw a glance at her over his shoulder. *That's something Dad told us Mom used to say*, she thought. She wondered if he was thinking the same thing.

This country was different than the flat landscape they'd ridden through before they reached the Tennessee. Trees crowded the road here, and there were no buildings, either maintained or dilapidated, to either side. It was a wilderness, but one heavily patrolled by federal troops from the Girding Wall on the border all the way up to the Ohio River. They saw no sign of the herds of deer, buffalo, and elk that were supposed to roam the area.

A rider touched her on the shoulder and she turned to see one of the women from the Mexican team looking at her gravely. Maggie smiled and raised an eyebrow.

"Your mother," the woman said, "she was my hero all the time I was a child."

Maggie looked forward to see if Michael gave any sign of hearing. He was riding head down, lost in the road. She started to thank the woman, but the rider spoke on.

"Now, you are my hero, too."

Maggie blushed and shook her head, unsure of what to say.

"I do not love this place, though, Margarita Galdeana-Hammersmith. We have talked, and we would extend to you . . . asylum? When this race is done, you should come back to Mexico with us."

Maggie was startled. *Asylum?* Wasn't that what people fleeing oppression sought? But she decided to chalk the woman's use of the term up to unfamiliarity with the language, and satisfy her own curiosity about something instead of responding.

"What's it like there?" Maggie asked.

The woman smiled, something flashing in her eyes that indicated to Maggie that she hadn't misused any words at all. But she answered her. "It is an old place, and getting older all the time."

"Isn't everyplace getting older all the time?"

"No, I mean . . . I mean old ways keep coming back in Mexico. There is less of Spain and more of the Aztecs in the place, in the people, every year. It is our way of saving ourselves from Athena and things like her." She looked off to the side then, and Maggie barely heard a call coming over the other woman's radio. The Mexican rider smiled once again, and said, "I'm moving to the back, perhaps we can talk more later."

The woman drifted back into the anonymity of the peloton, and just then Lydia's voice came over the radio, "Okay, twins, move up, here's the Cumberland and the race director is waiting at the bridge. He wants to know if it would work best if one of you crosses first and then the other brings up the rear. You'll be given dispensation to use the convoy vehicles to pace your way back into the peloton on the far side."

Michael's head dipped down as he spoke. "I'll go first."

Which made sense, so that he didn't waste any energy rejoining the race before the intermediate sprint a few miles up the route, but it still bothered Maggie that he hadn't consulted her. He really was angry.

What was I supposed to do, leave them all standing there on the riverbank while those engineers herded the infected team into transports with poles and nets? Maybe that was exactly what he would have preferred.

The crossing of the Cumberland went smoothly, for all that Michael barely exchanged a word with her. There were engineers on both sides of the river this time, and they'd clearly been warned that something had happened earlier. They stood in formations on either side of the road, watching silently when the peloton stopped at a pontoon bridge identical to the one over the Tennessee.

Michael surprised Maggie by whistling out a wordless tune instead of choosing one of their father's lyrics or something writ. The Cumberland River surprised her by responding just the same.

At Michael's nod, the whole of the peloton and all of the support vehicles rolled on, Maggie sitting astride her bike and watching them go. A camerastat hovered right next to her, its unblinking camera eyes shining in the afternoon sun.

When the last motorcycle had gone, Maggie took a careful look at the river and saw that it was still clear. She rode across, and began the long process of working her way through the support vehicles to rejoin the peloton.

By the time she passed the race referee's car at the front of the following train of motorized vehicles, she was encountering stragglers from the peloton. Already, the race was speeding up in preparation for the intermediate sprint, and there were riders who had been doing the bulk of the work for their teams peeling off, exhausted. There were some as well, Maggie suspected, who had done little work at all but who were finding their conditioning was not sufficient for the unexpected rigors of this race. Rigors that weren't purely physical.

She rode on, pushing herself so that she could rejoin Nicholas in the peloton and guide him through the upcoming sprint. When she had slowed at the American team car to load up with the bottles Tammy the soigneur handed to her through the window, Lydia had reminded her that the approach to the sprint point was complicated, being in the middle of the town of Cadiz and featuring a ninety-degree turn just three hundred yards before the line. The sprint trains would be well in control of the peloton by that point, flying, and Maggie intended to have Nicholas well back from the front in case there were crashes going into that final bend.

She needn't have worried. Though she saw nothing of the sprint, she could hear the excited calls of riders telling one another to move up or to move aside. She heard Lydia and David calling encouragement to the sprint train over the radio and, wonder of wonders, she even heard cheers. The people of Cadiz had come out to see the race pass through their little town.

Maggie barely registered the passage through the village, concentrating on navigating its streets and finding her way back out onto the open road. The sprinters and their lead outs drifted back into the peloton, excitedly chattering about what apparently been a very close sprint.

Then Michael was right there beside her. "I think I got it!" he said. "I think I pipped that tall woman from California right on the line!"

Lydia's voice came, "They're saying they're going to a photograph to determine who took it. Camerastats are feeding data to the race director now."

Then, a few minutes later, a loud whoop in her ear. "Michael Hammersmith first!" said Lydia.

All the Americans cheered, and the woman from California rode up beside Michael and gave him a grudging pat on the back. "Hope you saved something for the *real* finish, rookie," she said. "I won't be holding back when we get to the Obelisk."

Michael took this in good humor, and told the woman he would be showing her a clean pair of wheels at the line next time, meaning he meant to beat by her a bike length or more. The woman smirked and drifted back over to her own teammates.

The Obelisk was still hours away. With no more water crossings, the race settled into the pattern it would have shown from the beginning had it been run anywhere besides the Commonwealth. A couple of miles past the intermediate sprint, two riders—one of them the rider from Mexico who had spoken to Maggie, the other a Cuban man with the build of a climber—attacked the front of the peloton to form the day's escape. No team manager directed a chase, and they were soon lost from view, if temporarily.

"We can give them a bit of a leash," said Lydia. "Let them settle in about three minutes ahead. We'll start the chase at Hopkinsville if nobody else does."

But it was the Californians who began ramping up the pace at the army town of Hopkinsville, where the race was saluted in passing by the armored division headquartered there. There was another, far different crowd on the eastern edge of the town. Behind a chain-link fence running along the left side of the road, line upon line of silent onlookers in wheelchairs were parked in the spacious green lawns of an enormous brick hospital.

"Who are they?" Nicholas asked Maggie.

"Viewers at Home," she replied. "Or rather, Viewers at Home who rejected cable but couldn't come fully back to the world. My father told us that some fairly high percentage of people's minds are destroyed by the link, but that the federal government and the cable company collude to keep the real number quiet. Is there no cable where you're from?"

Nicholas shrugged. "There are no Viewers who reject cable where I'm from. Or anyplace else I've visited. These people, they're like those riders at the river, after they were . . . taken."

Maggie glanced over at the patients before they disappeared behind them. There *was* a similarity. But her father had never made a connection between cable and the Voluntary State. And as he was someone who saw hidden connections behind everything, that seemed to Maggie to mean there couldn't be one.

The catch was quick in coming, the peloton reeling in the escapees at the exact moment a gasp went up from the collected riders.

The Obelisk had come into view on the eastern horizon.

"Sprint train to the front," said Lydia, and Michael's three lead-out riders guided him up the right side of the road. Other teams were massing their sprinters as well, and the speed was going up quickly.

Not so quickly that the ubiquitous camerastats could not keep up, of course, and now these crowded in more closely than ever. It appeared as though each of the principal sprinters had drawn their own personal camera, and one flew alongside Michael, so close that Maggie imagined that her brother could lash out and hit it with his fist. She wouldn't have been surprised to see him do just that, in fact.

But no, Michael was concentrating. He cared little about the thanks the other riders had given him for getting them safely across the Cumberland, but he cared very much indeed about proving himself on the open road. He'd already done that, taking the Cadiz sprint over the more experienced riders, but now he was hungry for something else altogether. Michael wanted his first professional win, and Maggie wanted it for him as well. She wished that she could have been leading him out with the others, but contented herself with slotting in behind him, Nicholas on her wheel.

So there on the road that was once called the Jefferson Davis Highway, with a crosswind threatening to split the peloton and the noise of the derailleurs and the wheels combining into their high hum, Maggie was placed so that when the camera spoke to her brother, she heard it too.

"Michael," it sang.

Michael cursed. "Hardly the time for an interview!" he shouted, practically spitting the words out.

The Obelisk loomed, and the first lead outs began drifting back, work done, and the speed went higher.

At this point, Maggie should have drifted back into the peloton with Nicholas, letting the sprinters have their dangerous sport. But she had recognized the voice of the camera. She had *remembered* it.

She had dreamed it. She had heard it say, "Oh my daughter." It was the voice of a river and of a woman both. It was the voice of what claimed to be their mother, and now it was calling to Michael as they fast approached the finish line of the race.

"You must listen to me, my son," said the camera in the lilting sing-song voice from Maggie's dream. "You and your sister have a great task ahead of you."

Michael didn't answer. He rose out of the saddle and gave a tremendous dig, pulling away from Maggie for all that she rode as hard as she could. She heard Nicholas cry out something from behind. She would be in trouble tonight for leaving him to fend for himself, but that thought vanished as soon as it crossed her mind.

This was her team, but Michael was her brother.

The camerastat still flew beside Michael, if anything even closer than it had been before. A rider drifted back, and Maggie saw with a start that it was Samantha, Michael's final lead out. The sprint had started.

Why am I up here? Maggie asked herself, and heard her answer from the camera, which said, "Your father is in danger, and he will not listen to me. If—"

But the camera did not continue speaking, because Michael lashed out. He leaned against it, sitting back in his saddle and punching wildly to the right, even throwing his helmeted head at the flying thing. He clipped it with his right fist, and wobbled wildly, and Maggie, right on his wheel, pulled hard to the left, and then he was down, and then *she* was flying, as Michael's violent riding brought down the whole front of the peloton in an enormous crash.

Chapter Seven

Maggie had been holding her breath the whole time Tammy stitched up the gash on her elbow. When the soiegneur tied off the thread, she let it out, resisting the urge to punctuate the exhalation with something from Michael's repertoire of curses.

Tammy took up a spray can and shook it, and said, "This will feel cold," before aiming a stream of frigid analgesic over Maggie's elbow. This time, Maggie *did* curse.

"She speaks!" said Tammy, not unfriendly. "I was thinking you'd damaged your voice in that crash in addition to the cut on your elbow. And the gash on your knee. And the sprained wrist."

Maggie didn't need to be reminded of this laundry list of injuries. Her entire body ached, but she wouldn't complain. There were other riders injured far more badly than she, two of whom had been forced to retire from the race with broken bones. The American team itself was intact, but in addition to she and Michael, Samantha had gone down in the crash, so fully half the squad would be sporting bandages and splints on the next day's stage.

"Okay, now it's massage time," said Tammy, rubbing desanitizer into her hands. "Hop up on the table. I'll work around your wounds, don't worry."

"Michael's still outside," said Maggie. "Shouldn't you see to his cuts first?"

Michael had landed heavily on one side and had what the cyclists called road rash, deep scrapes, from his ankle to his shoulder. He also had a deep cut over one eyebrow and had been holding a wad of cotton against it for well over an hour, the whole time since the peloton had limped across the finish line.

Tammy said, "Uh, Lydia wants me to let him stew for a little while. I'm supposed to get everybody seen to before him. And before you, too, for that matter. I'm afraid you guys are a little bit on the outs with our directors at the moment."

With their directors and everyone else involved in the race.

Only a few riders had made it around the crash that Michael had precipitated. Maggie had heard that the stage had been taken by a rider from the Cherokee Nation team, a squad that didn't even have a pure sprinter but had just happened to be riding on the left side of the road and taken advantage of the carnage.

The rules stated that in the event of crashes so close to the finish line, that riders involved would be given the same finishing time as the winner, so the overall standings weren't affected. Practically the entire peloton was tied for first or within a second or two on the general classification. Except for Michael.

He had been relegated to last place, even though he limped over the line carrying his unridable machine before several others. A penalty of thirty seconds had been assessed against him, so on what was to have been his day of glory, he found himself the *lanterne rouge*, the rider in dead last.

As well as being the most despised rider on the race. Other riders, even other team directors, had not been shy in making their feelings known, and Maggie couldn't exactly blame them. As Tammy began kneading the deep tissues of her legs, Maggie thought of the curses that had been voiced, the angry looks thrown their direction. Even the Mexican woman who had invited Maggie to join their team had given Michael a long, cool look, and this was to say nothing of the members of their own team.

Samantha in particular, who was badly banged up, had positively seethed at the twins. "What was that? What the *hell* was that? I know you're rookies, but I also know you can organize a sprint because we *just won one.* That camerastat was nowhere near enough you for you to go off your line!" She'd turned on Maggie then. "And you! What the hell were you doing up there anyway? Did you forget about our GC man? Did you know that Nicholas had to *jump* his bike over two downed riders to avoid crashing himself?"

She hadn't waited for answers, but simply stalked off to the team bus for her turn on the massage table. Lydia had been standing nearby, watching silently. Meanwhile, David and the team mechanic could be heard cursing loudly at the work they had to do to repair the racing machines. The race would start the next day at the scheduled time, despite all.

"That's it," Tammy said on finishing. "Um, I'm supposed to tell you to go see Lydia now. And you can send Michael in on your way out."

Outside the soigneur's tent, Michael was sitting on the ground, still in his shredded racing kit, legs splayed out in front of him. He held the bloody wad of cloth over his right eyebrow and when he saw Maggie began the obviously painful process of standing. Maggie held out her hand, but he waved her off.

"When are we going to talk about it?" she asked him.

Michael shook his head, if gingerly. "What's to be said that hasn't been already? I screwed up. I went off my line and fell and nearly took out every rider in the race."

Maggie said, "You know that's not what I mean. I mean that camera. What it was saying. Who was *doing* the saying."

"I couldn't hear what it was saying over the noise of the race," Michael said. "I just thought it was flying too close and let my temper get the better of me."

Maggie looked at him for a moment. Then she balled up her fist and hit him solidly above his unwounded eye, and then Michael was sprawled on the ground again.

Maggie stepped over her brother and put one bare foot on his chest, holding him down.

"What the hell, Maggie?"

She looked around and saw that no one was nearby. She had protected Michael as much as she could, but maybe it was time to stop. The voice had been unmistakably the same one from her dream.

Maggie leaned over, putting more weight onto his chest, and said, "No. Not this time. *Something* has been trying to contact us, something that's obviously from Tennessee and something that obviously wants us to think it's our mother. Now it's tracked us here and now *you've* jeopardized everything we've ever worked for because you're afraid to find out what it is. Go get sewn up, and then find me at our tent. I have to go make excuses for you to Lydia, but we *are* going to talk about this."

With that, she walked away.

▷▷▷

Lydia was at the table on the team bus, looking at a map of the next day's stage. She motioned for Maggie to sit down across from her, barely looking up.

She let Maggie sit in uncomfortable silence for a few long moments, then pulled a sheet of paper out from beneath the map.

"Injury report from the race director," she said. "Shall I read it to you?"

Maggie said nothing.

Lydia slid the paper across the table. "Why don't you read it to me?"

"I already read it," said Maggie. "They've posted it all through the village."

Lydia nodded. "Yes, they have. That and the results, which show that I'm directing the rider in last place, which means with today's times that I'm directing the *team* in last place. How do you think I should feel about that?"

Maggie said, "He knows it was his fault."

"Oh, does he? You mean he knows what everyone else on the race or watching at home knew from the second he threw a punch at a camerastat? You mean he's *aware* that he sent two riders on other teams to the hospital and off the race entirely, and has caused untold difficulty for everybody still here? Every team's mechanics will be up all night repairing bicycles or building up spares for the bikes they can't fix, and more than half—*more than half*—the riders will be trying to sleep with injuries."

Maggie looked at her hands. Any other time, she would have been mortified for Michael, trying desperately to argue in his favor, making excuses for him. But all she could think about was the camerastat and its abbreviated message. *Your father is in danger and he will not listen to me. If—*

If what? What happened if *they* wouldn't listen either and their father really was in danger?

"You're not even listening to me," said Lydia in an exasperated voice. "And I've not even gotten to what *you* did wrong, dragging our GC rider to the front of a sprint, then leaving him to his own devices when you go chasing after your brother. What on earth were you thinking?"

Maggie thought about the letter Lydia had shown her. She thought about having no friends besides her brother, no allies even, with the possible exception of Japheth Sapp. *Should I tell her what really happened?*

"Now," said Lydia. "Why don't you tell me what really happened?"

"What?" said Maggie, startled that her director had echoed her thought so exactly. "What do you mean?"

"The race director says that the feed from the camerastat Michael went after cut out *before* he touched it. And though it's no excuse for what he did, it *was* flying closer to him than it should have been."

She knows so much already, thought Maggie. So she said, "It was talking to him."

Lydia narrowed her eyes. "The camera?"

"Yes. Or something *through* the camera, anyway."

Lydia cursed under her breath. "Was it her?"

Maggie said, "It claimed to be. And it mentioned our father."

"A threat to the race?"

"No, no, it said he was in trouble. I think it wants us to help him."

"'It,'" said Lydia. "Not she? Not her?"

"You saw the riders who were taken at the Tennessee," said Maggie. "Do you think my mother could have survived the Green River any better?"

Lydia frowned. "She was an extraordinary woman. Not just as an athlete. But no, I don't guess so. But the alternative is that that someone, some*thing*, is disguising itself as her. Why?"

Maggie shrugged. "To get us to do its bidding? To recruit us as spies?"

"Cycling spies?" asked Lydia. "What state secrets do you think we come across in our races? And what kind of sabotage could you get up to? No, the key to this is your father, the preaching man." Lydia's eyes widened. "The preaching man who figured out a way to defeat Athena Parthenus's nanomachines in the river."

Maggie said, "You think the Governor of Tennessee knows who my father is? And sees him as a threat?"

Lydia was thinking fast and got up to pace. "She styles herself—it styles itself, whatever—the 'Queen of Reason,' right? And what's left of the federal government and much of the rest of the world are terrified of what she's done in Tennessee, so much so that the country went bankrupt building the Girding Wall, fracturing the union in the process."

Maggie knew all this. She'd grown up hearing her father lecture about the dangers of the Voluntary State and of the federal government both. The idea that her father, for all that he *could* manipulate the waters infected by Tennessee, could be perceived as a danger by what he called the "Great Enemy" seemed . . . unlikely. She loved her father, but as she had grown older, and especially in the years since he'd left them, she'd come to think of him as something of a crank. She tried to think of a way to say this that also conveyed the boundless love and respect she had for the man, and realized that she couldn't fully articulate her complex feelings for him even to herself.

So she said, "What's all this got to do with a bicycle race?"

Lydia's expression showed that she thought Maggie had come to the key question. "I suppose," she said, "that you'd better find out."

When Michael, walking like an arthritic old man and much bandaged, arrived at their tent, Maggie was standing outside watching the sunset. He started to wordlessly move past her, but she took him by the arm and turned him around, guiding him back into the narrow lane between two rows of tents.

"Where are we going?" he asked irritably.

"Away from the village," Maggie said. "Somewhere we won't be overheard."

He didn't reply, but when he shrugged out of her grasp, he nevertheless walked alongside her.

Soon, they realized that the best place for privacy was the place they least wanted to go. The base of the Obelisk.

The twins walked around the monument so that they stood in the shadows opposite the race camp. There were benches of poured concrete set on the grounds nearby, and they settled down on one of them, Michael letting out a soft gasp of pain when he did so.

"Anything broken?" Maggie asked.

"My pride," he said.

"That seems unlikely," she answered. "But listen. I don't blame you for the crash. I mean, you caused it, but anyone would have done what you did."

"They can't know!" Michael said. "Not a word of this to anyone!"

Maggie took her brother's hand. "It's too late, Michael. I told Japheth Sapp about the phone calls. And I told Lydia Treekiller about what happened at the sprint today."

She anticipated the anger and recrimination to come, but when he looked sharply up at her, he didn't speak, and was in fact then looking *past* her, and standing and trying to shove her behind him. She turned around and saw what had he had seen.

A half-dozen greasy-haired men in gray wool uniforms, carrying rifles and grinning broadly, were walking toward them from the trees.

"Get to the camp," Michael whispered urgently. "Find help."

But one of the men lazily brought his rifle up, pointing it in their direction, and said, "Nah, better you don't go anywhere."

Maggie moved to stand shoulder to shoulder with her brother, thinking that they must look ridiculous, covered with bandages, standing up to six armed men. But she said, "We don't want any trouble. We're with the race and are just out for a walk."

Another man grinned broadly, then spat a stream of tobacco-stained juice on the ground before turning to his fellows. "Hear that, boys? They're with the race. Hell, I guess we'd never have figured that out on our own, would we?"

Michael tensed, and Maggie put her hand on his arm.

The spitter must have been the leader, because it was him who walked up, separating himself from the others, strutting. "Don't really give much of a damn about bicycle racing," he said. "But we surely would like to know how you know Japheth Sapp."

Chapter Eight

When the Reenactors made a ragged circle around them on the bench, Maggie whispered, "Don't do anything stupid, Michael."

The leader spat again and said, "That's right, Mikey. Nothing stupid."

Michael bristled. He hated any and all diminutives of his name. Their parents had never called him anything but Michael.

The Reenactor who had first aimed at them laughed roughly. "He's going to do something stupid, look at him. He ain't going to be able to help himself."

"Michael!" Maggie whispered again, pleading with him.

The leader walked within a few feet of them, close enough that they could smell his unwashed body. "Nah, Mikey ain't stupid. Mikey don't want his sister to get shot, now, does he?"

"People from the race will be looking for us," said Michael, and Maggie breathed a sigh of relief. "They'll be here any minute."

The leader laughed. "Hear that, boys? Bicyclists is gonna come kick our asses, I guess."

"What do you want with us?" Maggie asked.

"I done told you, little girl. You were telling Mikey here about some conversation you'd had with Japheth Sapp. That's a name we know. That's a name we don't care too much for."

"He's just a neighbor of ours from back home, away east," said Maggie. "We've only ever even seen him once."

"Well, that don't sound too neighborly now, does it?" The man ran a hand through his lank, greasy hair, then pulled out a folding pocketknife and began to ostentatiously clean his fingernails with it.

"See, once upon a time, we offered your neighbor the hospitality of our camp, and that didn't turn out too good for anybody. A man died that night. A good man."

A Reenactor the twins hadn't seen before rounded the Obelisk. "There's people moving around over there, sir," he said, nodding back toward the race village. "Looks like something's up."

"Well now," said the leader, "Maybe Mikey was right about folks coming to look for him after all."

Maggie tried to hold her brother down, but he stood despite her efforts. "It's Michael, you ignorant redneck. My name is Michael Hammersmith."

Anticipating a blow at best and a gunshot at worst, Maggie stood next to him. But neither came.

Instead, the leader had backed away a step and was clumsily folding up his knife to tuck away in his pocket. The man who had pointed his gun at them had paled, and said, "They must be his kids, the one that was with Sapp, he said he had children!"

"Look, we don't want any trouble," said the leader. "We're just camping out here on the grounds like y'all are. No need for any entanglements."

Entanglements, thought Maggie. *What does that mean? What's going on?* "Do you mean that you've met our father? How recently?"

Their father had been headed deeper into the hills, not to the flatlands. Why would he have been here?

The Reenactors were melting into the darkness, calling to one another in some kind of battle cant that saw them splitting off in many different directions. When only the leader remained in sight, he paused, nodded at the twins, and saluted. "Your father is known everywhere he travels," the leader said.

Then he was gone.

Before either Maggie or Michael could speak, the bright white light of an electrically powered lantern flooded the area. Shielding their eyes against the glare, the twins could just make out the helmeted form of the race director, flanked by a pair of the red-clad referees they'd seen aback motorcycles during the day's racing. One of these held the lantern, and the other approached.

"Director says it's best you get back to camp," she said in an up-east accent. "He's made an agreement with the Reenactors to divide the grounds for the night, and you two are right up on the edge of the border."

Maggie looked at the director's helmet, blazoned with the features of an owl over its smooth faceguard. She repeated to herself, "Right up on the edge . . ." Then Michael took her hand and led her back to their tent.

"Why did you tell her?" Michael asked softly, returning to their conversation before the Reenactors had interrupted.

"What if Dad does need our help?" Maggie replied.

She didn't expect him to answer, and so she wasn't disappointed when he didn't.

The second stage of the race was set to be another hard, fast run across flat country, beginning at noon. The first order of business though, was breakfast.

The whole team gathered in an open-sided canvas shelter around portable tables groaning beneath the weight of the thousands of calories they would take onboard. Muesli and other cereals, rice, fish, lean beef, and liters of fresh water, thick coffee, and electrolyte fluid were spread out, with each rider filling their plates more than once. They would expend a tremendous amount of energy over the course of the day, so, slim as they were, they ate huge quantities of food, concentrating on carbohydrates.

"How about passing the soy milk, Crash?" asked Jordan, who was sporting a bandage above her right eye. Her tone was jovial.

Maggie saw that the glass pitcher, condensation beading on its sides, was sitting directly in front of Michael. He did not respond, and Maggie didn't think he'd even heard the jibe. For all that he was surrounded by his teammates, Michael was breakfasting alone with his misery.

Maggie thought of an old joke of her father's.

"There's no such thing," she said to Jordan.

A quizzical expression crossed the green-haired woman's face and she shook her head in confusion. "No such thing as what?"

"Soy milk," Maggie said, and kicked her brother under the table to be sure he was listening.

All the riders were paying attention now, and Samantha pointed at the pitcher. "That's soy milk right there."

"That's soy *beverage*," said Maggie, and she was so thankful when Michael spoke up, finishing for her.

"Beans don't lactate," he said, his voice deepening slightly in unconscious imitation of their father.

Telly laughed softly, and it spread around the table, all of the riders nodding at the small witticism, with only David shaking his head in confusion. "I do not follow that," he said. "Beans?"

They all laughed louder, and when Michael joined in, Maggie breathed a long sigh of relief. He may not have been completely forgiven for the disaster of the previous day, but he was still part of the team.

And he was still her brother.

So after breakfast, when the team was warming up with their bicycles mounted on stationary trainers lined up alongside the team bus, Maggie took advantage of the fact that the two of them were at the end of the line, and that Samantha, to her right, was listening to music on headphones so loud that Maggie could almost understand the lyrics.

"I need to know," she said quietly, "I *deserve* to know if yesterday was the first time she's reached out to you other than the phone calls."

Michael had the resistance on the trainer set too high for a warm-up. A bead of sweat tracked down off his forehead and dripped off the end of his nose. He waited so long to answer that Maggie thought he was ignoring her, but then he said, "It's not her."

She nodded. "*It*, then. Was that the first time *it* has reached out to you?"

David worked his way down the line of cyclists, checking their machines and sharing a few quiet words with each of them. He smiled when he reached Maggie, leaning in to read the wattage measurement on the computer mounted on her handlebars. "Good," he said, "That's good."

But when he saw Michael, he frowned. "What is this? Are you trying to exhaust yourself before the race?" He leaned down and made an adjustment where the rear wheel of Michael's bicycle was meshed with the training unit. Michael's pedaling rate suddenly increased as the resistance in his pedals dropped away. He'd been pushing himself hard.

David shook his head, then snapped his fingers in front of Michael's face. Annoyance showing, Michael looked up at the Frenchman.

"Many years ago I rode the Strade Bianche in Tuscany. Do you know this race?"

Michael nodded and looked over at Maggie, his expression telling her that he wanted her to do the talking. She opened her mouth, hesitated, then closed it and looked down at her front wheel.

After a bare moment, Michael said, "Yes. Our mother placed third there once. Strade Bianche means 'white gravel roads.' A race for hard riders, it says in her old magazines."

"A race for the mad," said David. "It is run over sections of that white gravel instead of good smooth pavement. My bike handling, it was . . . not up to the challenge."

Michael didn't reply, so Maggie said, "You crashed?"

David pulled down the collar of his knit shirt, revealing an ugly scar running across his right collarbone. "*Spectaculairment*," he said. "And I took down a dozen other riders with me, including my team captain, who was riding for a repeat win in the race."

Michael blinked sweat out of his eyes. "But racing is racing and the whole peloton forgot about it and forgave you, right?"

David smirked at Michael's bristly tone, and said, "No. Well, yes, actually, but that is not the point of this story. The point of this story is that *I* forgave *myself.* My mistake, well, it was not quite so stupid as yours, but it *was* a mistake and it ended the race for me and for many others. You are lucky to be riding today. You all are. In this crazy place, anyone is lucky to be riding on *any* day. Remember that. And don't exhaust yourself before today's stage." With that, he strode away.

Michael reached back and amped up the resistance on his trainer again.

Maggie looked over and saw that the other four riders were all looking at the pair of them quite frankly. So she said nothing more.

The racing was aggressive from the start, but tightly controlled. Numerous escapes went away, only to be brought back in by the high speed of the peloton. Jordan, detailed to be the go-between ferrying bottles up from the follow car to her teammates, spread Michael's new nickname of "Crash" through the whole race, and Maggie heard her father's joke about soy milk being told in a half-dozen languages over the course of the day.

Stage Two ran for 110 miles from the Obelisk and through the towns of Elkton and Russellville and Auburn before the race rolled through the lands of the Amish, and the peloton was all together, speeding through flat farmland, when the first sign of them came.

Maggie was riding behind and to one side of Telly, who was pacing Nicholas. The team's GC rider had not suffered as many hurts in the previous day's crash as other riders, but he had yet to speak to Michael despite the general feeling of forgiveness on the race. He seemed, as he had the first day and as Maggie supposed someone riding for the overall win must, supremely concentrated. So it surprised her when he changed position on his machine, moving his hands from the drops to the top of his handlebar, and pulled off his gold-lensed riding glasses. These he threaded into the air vents in his helmet and he put a hand out to Telly's shoulder, indicating that the older rider should look sharp because Nicholas was no longer watching the road, but the sky.

"The camerastats are all pulling up and away," he said, and some of the riders around him followed his gaze up and out.

"Mind the road, now," Telly said in a clear voice, and the racers all began playing the neat trick of splitting their attention between riding in close formation at high speed and watching the dozens of flying cameras peel away to either side of the road, gaining altitude as they went.

"What's going on? Is it another river crossing?" Nicholas asked, and Maggie realized he was talking to her. There had been no mention of an interruption in cable coverage at the morning meeting or at the sign-in, and Maggie supposed he was depending on her local expertise. She started to say she didn't know when she heard Michael speaking into her right ear, his voice barely discernable above the spinning of the flywheels and the hissing of the tires on asphalt.

"Amish," he said. "No cable allowed."

And Maggie remembered, then, what their father had taught them about the Amish.

"Only river today is the Barren, at Bowling Green," she reminded the others. "And the machines of Tennessee are short-lived and have little power in that water." The reasons for the die-off of the invisibly small invaders from the Voluntary State in the Barren were mysterious, but thought to be related to the general miasmic nature of the river, which supported no fish or insects. No wildlife drank from it, and even plants struggled to thrive on its banks. The federally supported university at Bowling Green, the campus of which they would be racing through soon enough, was given over to the study of the river and its effects.

But the Barren was a test for later in the day, at the 59 mile marker according to the short-handed stage description David had taped to her top tube. The Frenchman either hadn't known to mark the Amish holdings in his notes for the riders or hadn't thought the scant three or four miles notable in any way.

"So if not a river, what then?" asked Nicholas. His tone was businesslike, but not unfriendly.

"We'll be riding through farmlands held by the Amish," said Maggie. "They don't allow anything to do with cable television or the Viewers at Home on their lands."

This seemed to satisfy Nicholas, who nodded and said, "We've people like that in Oklahoma."

"They're a . . . a membership, I guess you'd say," said Maggie. "They're great builders and farmers."

And then the road was on Amish lands for sure, as the fields became even tidier. Orchards, pastures, gardens, and croplands of every sort were spread out and the road swept left to arrow due east between two long rows of people, who waved as the racers passed, but did not cheer.

And then there was a stranger thing, because two girls on the right-hand side of the road, gawky teenagers, had clambered atop the stone fence and unfurled a quilt that had been made into a banner. It was pieced so that flags of America and Kentucky were at the corners, and sober letters were spelled out, reading, "We support Team USA. We support the Hammersmiths."

"You've fans," said a trade-team rider from behind Maggie.

He must have been speaking to Michael, because her brother answered. "Not fans enough to use an exclamation point on their sign," he said.

Maggie was about to protest his meanspiritedness when the girls suddenly reversed the quilt, showing that a different message was spelled out on its back.

"And he that curseth his father, or his mother, shall surely be put to death. Exodus 21:17."

"Michael!" she said, and he gave her a curt nod. He'd seen it, too. Then they were through the raceside crowd and back on the flat, open road, Maggie trying to use her body and her bike to communicate with her brother, to tell him to drop back from the pack so they could talk about the Amish and their message.

Who can it have been from? We haven't cursed our parents, have we? Could the Reenactors have spread word of the two of us being in the race? They had clearly been familiar with Brother Theodore. That seemed more likely than that whatever it was from Tennessee was trying to contact them through an Amish quilt.

Michael was willfully ignoring her, though, going so far as to try to strike up a conversation with a woman riding at his other shoulder who swiftly proved to speak no English or Spanish. That or swiftly proved that she had no interest in speaking to Michael. For all that their team had forgiven him, there were still riders in the pack who brusquely maneuvered away from him when he came close, or threw him angry looks.

It would be a long day, Maggie realized, and not just because they were riding almost 110 miles, wind at their backs but on false flats the whole route, steadily climbing a gradient invisible to the eye but taxing to the legs. At least there was one tiny little climb to look forward to, according to the race bible. When they reached the city of Bowling Green they would all experience the short, sharp shock of the hill the university there dominated, its old buildings spreading down the flanks of the only significant terrain feature for miles around.

Only significant feature except for the Barren River, which shouldn't prove nearly so much a challenge as the rivers of the day before, being a slack and lifeless thing, not only free of any influence of the Voluntary State, but also devoid of any life at all. No fish swam its dark waters.

The day stretched out with a break establishing itself shortly after the troubling encounter with the Amish. This annoyed Maggie somewhat, because the three riders out front would soak up all the climbing points, pitifully few as they were, for the collegiate hill in Bowling Green. She looked down at the abbreviated cue sheet taped to her top tube, and hazarded a guess that the breakaway riders would be caught by the bunch roughly at the halfway point between the small city of Glasgow and the finishing line in the village of Edmonton. Maggie had visited both places on long rides out from the house above the

Green River, though rarely. She and Michael tended to ride east on their training rides, into hillier terrain.

Michael managed to keep himself apart from her in the pack for the next hour, and Maggie eventually gave up on the idea of talking to him during the race. She would corner him tonight at the race village. They *had* to determine what was going on, and no amount of ignoring the problem would make it go away. Not that Michael was really ignoring it. She knew him so well, knew that he was turning everything that had happened over and over in his mind, from the telephone landing on the road in front of them to the camerastat's message to everything else. The problem was that he wouldn't be trying to find an answer, he would be trying to find an escape.

Maggie had always thought that Michael was more like their father than he realized.

The radio crackled and Lydia's voice came through. "We're still in good shape for the general classification. But wouldn't it be nice to win the climber's jersey, too?"

Maggie didn't immediately make sense of her director's question, but then Telly and Jordan launched themselves out of the pack, speeding ahead up the road and raising multilingual curses from the rest of the peloton.

"What are they doing?" Maggie said to herself, but Nicholas heard her and laughed.

"They're chasing down the break," he said. "So that you can get the climbing points in Bowling Green."

And then, surprising her and throwing tactics to the wind, the Dual Champion of Oklahoma and of the Cherokee Nation rode past her and went to help his teammates.

The university at Bowling Green was the Commonwealth's only remaining institution of higher learning, and in her rare daydreams about what her life would be like after cycling, Maggie had sometimes imagined herself a student there. But as she rode past the gasping riders from the earlier breakaway at the foot of the school's hill, she took a precious second to glance around. A second was enough to see that she could never have thrived there.

The university was the province of the Owls of the Bluegrass, scholar-savants like the race director who foreswore individuality in favor of heightened expertise in their dual missions of preserving knowledge of the past and combatting the designs of Athena Parthenus. The slopes of the hill were aswarm with Owls.

One or two—students, Maggie imagined, though their helmets and robes made everyone in the teeming crowd more or less identical—attempted to run alongside her as she launched herself ahead of the thinned peloton and began flying up the hill. She left the runners and the racers alike behind. And climbed.

A great disappointment of Maggie's life was that she had never had—perhaps *would* never have—the opportunity to ride up one of the great passes of Europe, the finest and most challenging climbs in cycling. She had read about them, dreamed about them, ever since she discovered her talent for riding bicycles up steeply pitched pavement. Now, on this little climb that wouldn't even be rated if there had been anything else like a hill on the day's stage, she recited the beautiful names of those beautiful mountains across the sea, *sotto voce*, timed to her pedal strokes. "*Alpe d'Huez, Col du Galibier, Col de Madeleine. Passo del Stelvio, Passo di Gavia, Colle de Finestre. Sierra de la Pandera, Pico de Veleta, Alto de L'Angliru.*"

The most difficult climbs in Kentucky were in the mountains to the east, but those were low, old mountains compared to the Alps and the Dolomites and the Pyrenees. Maggie knew she had the physical skills of a great climber, and believed she had the heart. But she had never truly been tested, and doing well in this race was an opportunity, an *invitation* to those legendary climbs abroad. She spun the pedals faster, still breathing easily. She was determined not only to do well, not only to excel, but to *electrify*.

Maggie was so attuned to her own body that she knew another cyclist had latched onto her wheel not by seeing or hearing him, but by feeling the shadow he cast across her back. She spared a glance back and saw a grimacing Quebecois rider grinding a large gear. Down the slope, the rest of the pack was making their way up, apparently content to let this lone rider challenge her for the first-place points on offer at the top.

She considered what to do. There was no time on this short climb to play games, to ease up and force the other racer to pass her so that she might herself gain the tactically superior position immediately behind the leader on the road.

No time at all, she thought, as she noticed the barriers alongside the road, and the sign marking the one hundred meters to go mark.

She clicked her gears up. She stood up on her pedals. And she rode away from her rival.

Maggie smiled at the hooting, wordless cheers from the Owls of the Bluegrass gathered at the hillcrest. She forced herself to remember that this was not the stage finish, that she had many long miles to race before the day was done, but here was some glory. She spotted the team's soigneur, Tammy, holding out a bottle at the roadside and grinning broadly.

She expected the girl to shout encouragement or congratulations, but instead, Tammy said, "Look at the statue! Look what's written on it!"

Taking the bottle, Maggie looked over at the bronze image of a man in scholarly dress. She'd seen it before on her previous trips to Bowling Green, but had paid it little mind beyond noting that the figure depicted wore no owl helmet. This time, though, she read the words engraved in the limestone pediment. *The Spirit Makes the Master.*

Maggie took a swig of water, settled herself onto the saddle, and began the descent. *I suppose it does,* she thought.

The crossing of the Barren River was sedate, dead waters stirred to a semblance of life by the simple expedients of watersheds and topography and gravity. Nothing of Kentucky or Tennessee either one lived there, so the race, regrouped after the shock of the climb, passed over it on an old poured concrete bridge at the edge of the city. Then it was into the rolling terrain of the Pennyroyal region, the kind of riding Maggie and Michael knew best, the route skirting the dangers of Mammoth Cave and staying south of the Green on a long east-bound approach to the finish in Edmonton.

No more escapes went away, and this time the sprint finish was a picture-perfect thing of colorful lead-out trains jockeying for position and cranking the speed up higher and higher. Michael won by half a bike length.

Chapter Nine

"This race is too short for any more playing about. If we are to make a run for the general classification, it must be today."

It was the next morning, and Lydia was thumbing through the stage bible for the day's long trek northward to the Kentucky River.

Michael, stretched out on one of the couches and taking more than his share of room, pointed to the green jersey he now wore as leader of the race's points competition. Then he nodded at Maggie, in the white jersey with red polka dots that marked her as the Queen of the Mountains, leader of the climbing competition. "We have two of the three jerseys. Shouldn't we race to protect them?"

David Bonheur rolled his eyes. "You think a stage win and that jersey wins you back into our good graces? Easy as that?"

Michael pursed his lips as if in thought, and Maggie winced at the old sure signal that he was about to erupt in some tirade of sarcastic barbs.

"It wasn't easy," said Nicholas, unexpectedly. "And he *is* back in our good graces, or at least in mine. Both of the twins road extraordinarily well yesterday, and we should be realistic about our chances. A stage win and two jerseys are nothing to sniff at, and Maggie has a real shot at the time trial tomorrow."

Lydia looked at her nephew thoughtfully, then said, "And so do you. As you do for the overall win. We have a legitimate chance of winning all three competitions, not to mention the time trial and perhaps the last day into Mayfield, which should suit the sprinters again."

Then almost everyone started talking at once, Michael grinning broadly in contrast to David's scowl, the other riders babbling about their chances. Only Nicholas kept quiet, studying the map spread across the table. Only Maggie heard his question.

"This river here, the Kentucky. It's the worst of them?"

Maggie looked at the spot on the map where Nicholas had rested his finger. The bright yellow line of the route map crossed the river in a place she'd heard of.

"High Bridge," she said, thinking. "High Bridge is held by the Shakers of Pleasant Hill."

By the time she had finished the sentence, the cross-talk had stopped and everyone heard her last few words.

"Shakers?" asked Jordan. "Those are like the Amish? Except they"— and she made a wild flailing gesture with both hands—"dance? Right?"

Maggie shook her head. "Not like the Amish at all. Well, they're churched, but the Amish reject technology where the Shakers seek to make their communities as heavenly as possible, so they adopt— maybe I should say *adapt*—every advantage available to them. They're masters of technology. Perfecters of it."

She realized everyone was looking at her, and she blushed.

"At least that's what my father taught me."

Lydia held up the race bible. "Your father apparently taught them as well. The Shakers, I mean. It says here that our crossing will be an easy one because the Shakers at this High Bridge . . . Well, it says 'they are continuously praying and singing above the river.' They now keep a twenty-mile stretch clear of Tennessee's influence. We stay at their village tonight and caravan across in the morning for the start of the time trial in Lexington."

Nicholas looked from one twin to another. "I have heard of your mother's great accomplishments all my life," he said. "But your father's exploits amaze me as well. He must be the greatest defender of your Commonwealth against Athena Parthenus."

Michael's face had darkened, and he shook his head and shrugged, clearly uncomfortable with the unexpected turn of the conversation.

Maggie shook her head, too, but replied. "He doesn't want to defeat her," she said. "He wants to redeem her."

There was a knock at the door and a muffled voice called, "Line them up!"

It was time to race.

For two days, they had ridden east, but now they turned north through the Pennyroyal region of Kentucky, aimed for the heart of the Commonwealth, the more gently rolling hills of the Bluegrass, where the Horselords reigned. These were roads the twins knew well.

At Greensburg, in Green County, they crossed the Green River. It was a near the beginning of the race, and no riders had escaped up the road, so the peloton let the American team ride to the front so the twins could sing them across.

Maggie won the day's only climb, over a knob near the village of Gravel Switch. Michael took second in the sprint at the Civil War town of Perryville, gaining more points and solidifying his hold on the green jersey. And the race was all together as they approached the day's finish on the palisades high above the Kentucky River.

US 68 passed through the quiet town of Danville, given over completely to the Viewers at Home, and then reached northeast straight into Pleasant Hill, the holding of the Shakers. Even above the noise of a peloton winding up for a sprint finish, the racers heard the Shakers long before they saw them.

They were singing:

> "*Welcome here, welcome here,*
> *all be alive and be of good cheer.*
> *Welcome here, welcome here,*
> *all be alive and be of good cheer.*"

The race finished on a long straight stretch in front of the Shaker house of worship. This time his leadout was perfect, and Michael's hands were in the air when he crossed the finish line in first.

Deep in the peloton, shepherding Nicholas, Maggie threw up her on hands in victory when she saw that her twin had won again. But then she started and had to correct a drift off line when she saw something that Michael couldn't have. On a large screen beside the road, showing the feeds that the Viewers at Home consumed, Michael's victory was being repeated in slow motion. He was better than a bike's length ahead of the Mexican rider who came second. And impossibly, standing in the road next to him, holding her hands up in supplication, was the wavering, transparent image of their mother.

"Did you see that?" Maggie asked Nicholas as they coasted across the line.

"Yes!" he answered. "Fantastic! He's really found his sprint. We'll keep the points jersey for sure, now!"

"No, I meant . . ." She let her voice trail off. Nobody in the crowd of Shakers and people affiliated with the race seemed to be looking at the screen, which now showed an aerial shot of the village and the surrounding farmland. Nobody she could see wore an expression that indicated they'd seen something impossible or shocking. In fact, the only person not looking up the road at the excited scrum around Michael was the race director, who seemed to be looking directly at her. Though of course, behind the fixed features of his owl mask, it was impossible to tell whether he wore any expression at all.

Maggie and Nicholas slowly picked their way toward the bus, frequently stopping when Shakers, race officials, riders from other teams, and others dashed in front of them. The finish of a stage was always a madhouse. As they neared their destination, they saw Michael climbing aboard the bus—he would be massaged first today.

"I guess we have a little time to kill," said Nicholas. "We should take a cool-down spin."

He was talking about riding even more, but now it would be at a slower pace, designed to slowly bring their muscles and cardiovascular systems down to a resting rate, with no bothersome camerastats following them. Usually such a ride was only necessary after a much more strenuous effort than the two of them had made, sitting tucked in the peloton all day as they had been.

"Back down the race route?" Maggie asked absentmindedly. She was trying to decide if she had imagined what she had seen on the screen.

"No," said Nicholas. "I saw a road leading down to a landing on the route map. I want to go down to the river."

The way he said it, the precise force with which he hit each word, almost as if he were sounding notes, made Maggie realize he was quoting an old hymn.

"To pray?" she asked him, finishing the line.

Nicholas smiled, but shook his head. "I'm not, what's the word you use? Churched? I'm not a churched person. But this might be the only opportunity I have to stand right beside one of these invasive rivers instead of speed across one."

Maggie said, "It's dangerous. They probably have it blocked off."

"If they won't let us approach it, then it won't be dangerous, now will it? And besides, I have you to protect me."

Which was true enough, but Maggie still worried over the ghostly image of her mother, which was, if anything, gaining clarity in her mind's eye. What had she been trying to communicate, raising her hands to the heavens like that?

Then she realized she had a reason to go to the river of her own.

"Okay," she told Nicholas. "But I probably *will* pray."

The road down to Shaker Landing was narrow and shaded and steep. It reminded Maggie of the Ginnie Hill, and the telephone call, which had come, she realized with a start, less than a week before. So much more time than that had seemed to pass. So many miles *had* passed.

The road was damp from a rainfall that the race had managed to miss, so she and Nicholas were careful, feathering their brakes as they

let gravity take them down the road cut into the side of the towering palisades that bound this stretch of the Kentucky River. Halfway
down, they came upon a pair of Shaker women standing at a wooden
gate across the road, but the women had opened the gate as they
approached and then wordlessly waved them through.

"It's like someone told them to expect us," said Nicholas.

Maggie wondered. The reenactors at the Obelisk and the people
with the quilt at South Union had all seemingly had encounters with
her father or Japheth Sapp or some of her father's friends, and recently.
But it had been *three years* since their father had left on his mission trip,
and his direction had been opposite that of the race's start.

The road leveled out onto a long, wide shelf that had clearly been
constructed by human hands. Poplars and other water-loving trees
crowded the road, and then, after a hard turn right, the road plunged
straight into the green waters of the Kentucky River.

They came to a halt. There was nobody in sight, either along the
road, in the woodland tangle on the opposite bank two hundred yards
away, or, of course, on the river itself. There was no sound other than
the lapping water, not even birdsong. The air was still and heavy.

"It just looks like a river," said Nicholas, so quietly that he was
almost whispering.

Maggie thought of what her father had taught her. "The Kentucky
was the first of the Commonwealth's rivers to be invaded. Athena sent
two of her Commodores across the border to Beattyville to pour part
of her essence into the confluence of streams that mark the source."

"When?" asked Nicholas. "I thought the Girding Wall kept the
Commodores at bay. Though I saw the wreck of one in Oklahoma
once, where the Federals left it after a battle."

Maggie had only seen drawings of the towering Commodores
and was glad of that. She answered Nicholas. "A long time ago. I don't
know for sure. Before either of us was born, certainly."

They clipped out of their pedals, then swung off their machines.
Maggie leaned over and undid the fasteners on her shoes then kicked
them to one side before peeling off her socks. The grass beside the

old pavement of the road had been cut short, and was cool on her tired feet. She took off her helmet.

Nicholas clacked around on the road, still in his hard-soled racing shoes. He looked at everything—the trees and the sky, the opposite bank, the ramp down into the water, the water itself. Especially that. His gaze kept returning to the Kentucky River.

"What do you see?" Maggie asked him.

He shrugged. "Water. Just water."

Maggie sang, *"Everywhere we look there's water, water."*

The river sang, *"Dondequiera que miremos hay agua, agua."*

Nicholas strode closer to the riverside, picking his way carefully down the concrete ramp that led right into the water. Maggie joined him, and when he stepped close enough to actually lean out over the green water, she placed a warning hand on the small of his back.

"We don't know how powerful the Shaker singing is," she said. "There could be, I don't know, scouts in the water. Remnants."

"I want to see my reflection in it," he replied.

This struck Maggie as an odd thing to say, but she realized that the oddness was probably a product of the prejudices and fears instilled in her by a lifetime on the Green. And then she realized that she, too, wanted to see her features in the water.

"Well," she said, stepping in front of Nicholas. "Let me go first, in case I have to sing it down."

She unconsciously held one hand behind her for balance and was surprised when Nicholas took it in his own. She looked back over her shoulder and he shrugged. "For safety," he said.

Maggie leaned out and looked down. She saw her features, softer than she imagined since she looked at Michael more often than she looked at mirrors. Her hair was matted and sweat-slicked. She leaned out farther, and a drop of sweat from her forehead fell.

She watched it all the way, accelerating at nine point eight meters per second per second, the salty water of her body falling into the unknowable water of the Kentucky.

"Dondequiera que miremos hay agua, agua."

The drop that fell into the river consisted mainly of water, but also had detectable mineral content. Sodium, potassium, magnesium, and calcium—along with several exogenous organic compounds encoded with Maggie's DNA—were present in trace amounts. It would take a sophisticated machine to analyze the drop, and to identify a particular human individual from its makeup.

The Kentucky River was a very sophisticated machine.

"Dondequiera que miremos hay agua, agua."

"What's happening?" Nicholas shouted. "What's that noise?"

Because the river was *thrumming*. Concentric rings that spread hugely and impossibly out from where her sweat had made contact with the water's surface sounded deep, ringing notes as they grew into waves washing on both shores. Maggie leaped back, barely keeping clear of the tumultuous river.

"Go!" she yelled. "We've got to get away!"

But it was far too late for that.

An arcing column of green water grew up from the center of the river, somehow keeping its cohesion as it reached out and over the pair of them, plunging down onto the road and spreading, spreading, spreading until Maggie and Nicholas stood beneath a dome of sunlit water.

The wall of the dome was full of motion but did not move. Maggie saw that there were currents in the dome, that the water was flowing. Then she saw that features were appearing where she looked, on the dome's riverward side. Features she recognized.

A woman made all of green river water stepped out of the wall.

She said, "Oh my daughter, oh my beautiful daughter."

Maggie opened her mouth, but before she could scream, a stream of water flew out from the woman's palm. It flowed into Maggie's mouth and nose and ears. Before she could close her eyes, the green water was there, holding her lids open. A globe formed around her head, and Maggie felt herself lifted up until her she was dangling with her toes just above the ground.

Nicholas tackled the river woman, or tried to. When he dived against her, he fell *through* her, and then bounced hard off the watery dome. Through the water and her own panic, Maggie saw him rolling on his back, scratching at the mask of water that now covered his features.

"Don't hurt him!" she shouted, but the sound was muted by the water filling her mouth and throat.

Why am I not drowning? she wondered, and an answer came into her mind.

You are not drowning because the water in the sphere holding you up is hyperoxygenated. Your lungs will work a little harder, but you will not asphyxiate. Your body will remember what it is like to be enveloped in water, as you once were inside me.

Maggie was still staring wild-eyed at Nicholas, who now lay still while she struggled yet.

The boy is well. He is simply unconscious.

Maggie tried to speak again, but was frustrated in the attempt. So she *thought* instead. *What are you? Why are you doing this? Why are you pretending to be my mother?*

The flowing features of the river woman softened, and water flowed from water then as tears fell from her eyes.

I am not pretending to be your mother, Maggie. I am remembering to be. And it is very hard. The Kentucky is not my river, and Athena will sooner or later discover that I have cut her leash.

Maggie thought, *You're dead. You drowned many years ago.*

The river woman who looked so much like her nodded at Maggie. *I drowned, yes, but I did not die. Not all who are taken by the Voluntary State's northern waters are completely destroyed. Some of us are absorbed to greater and lesser degrees. My body is gone, but my consciousness, my mind, were taken by the waters and held apart.*

Maggie tried to make sense of that. *The rivers are . . . are purgatory? Your soul has been kept from its reward?*

A theological explanation is as good as any, replied the river woman. *You are certainly your father's daughter in that, though he would caution you against particulars and parallels. If he could. If he could.*

What does that mean? Where is my father? Have you done something to him?

Wait, said the river woman. *Someone comes.*

And then Maggie was laying on the ground, coughing up water. The upland side of the dome suddenly exploded inward and the entire structure collapsed, water falling like a torrential rain. The dome was breached, Maggie saw, by a speeding bicycle.

And Michael was there.

Chapter Ten

Lydia had cleared the rest of the team and the staff out of the bus, and now sat silently at the end of the table while Michael railed and cursed.

Maggie and Nicholas, their cycling kits still damp from river water, sat on a narrow couch, watching Michael pace back and forth, the two of them not daring to say anything.

"The rivers have taken *six people* on this race," he said, repeating himself for a third or fourth time. "And you would have been the seventh if the Shakers hadn't told me where you'd gone!" He had yet to mention Nicholas, or even look at him.

"You know better than anyone, you *should* know, the dangers of the waterways, especially the Kentucky! You were *engulfed* by the waters! If the race director or any other Owls find out about this they'll turn you over to the Federals and you'll never be heard from again!"

Maggie was tired of being shouted at, and thought, *Never being heard from again is kind of the family tradition.*

Except it wasn't, of course. Not now. No wonder rivers liked the sound of their voices. Or the part that was their mother did.

"Michael, you've made your points," said Lydia. Seeing Maggie and Nicholas relax somewhat at that, she added sharply, "And they're good ones. What you two did was reckless and foolish. You endangered yourselves and Michael both, and the risk of being ejected from the race or arrested is far from the worst that could have happened. Now . . ." She looked carefully at Maggie. "Are you going to explain yourselves?"

But it was Nicholas who spoke. "It's my fault. I wanted to see the river. I thought it was supposed to be safe through here because of the Shaker influence."

Michael muttered, "*Always* taste it, *always* fear."

"He wouldn't have gone if I hadn't agreed to it," said Maggie, and Lydia gave her a curious look, as if she noticed that Maggie wasn't exactly apologizing.

Michael finally spoke to Nicholas. "What did you think you were going to see? Athena's Commodores wading upstream? Rock monkeys on war barges out of Nashville? The dangers of the waters aren't things *you* see coming."

Nicholas glanced over at Maggie, but she said nothing. So he said, "We *did* see something. So did you, for that matter, you saw that dome, but we saw more than that. We saw your—"

"We saw her," said Maggie. "We saw Mama." And it occurred to Maggie that she hadn't uttered that precise word aloud in at least a decade.

Michael's fury was back in an instant. He looked from Lydia to Nicholas to Maggie and said, "*Still?* You still want to talk about this, and now in front of strangers?"

Maggie said, "Sit down. I'm tired of you looming over me. I'm tired of you denying what's been happening and I am *so damned tired* of you shouting all the time!"

Lydia stood up and signaled for Nicholas to do the same. "We'll leave you two," she said. "You can have the bus for now, but remember, we're leaving in an hour. And Michael." She turned to him. "We're not strangers. We're your team." They left.

Michael said, "You told her."

Maggie pointed to a chair.

Michael hesitated for a moment, but then sat. "Look, I was just . . . *terrified*," he said.

She almost went to comfort him, but . . . *No, not this time.* They were not the only family each other had. They were *not.*

"It . . . *she* said she's escaped Athena Parthenus somehow," she said.

"If she's escaped then why is she sending telephones from Tennessee? If it's really her . . . *how* can it be her if she's . . . she's what I saw down there. All water."

"I don't know, Michael. But she's trying to tell us something so important that she'd risk her freedom and ours in the telling. It has to be about Daddy. I think we should listen to her. And I think I have a plan of how we can, safely."

Michael looked up at her, fear and curiosity as plain on his face as it was in Maggie's heart. "How?"

"First," said Maggie, "I have to ride my bicycle faster than I've ever ridden."

The race caravan crossed High Bridge that evening, Maggie riding with the other Team America cyclists in the team bus. Shakers lined either side of the centuries-old iron span, singing down to the river hundreds of feet below.

And then they were north of the river, and in the rolling, sparsely forested hills of the Bluegrass, country of the horselords. For twenty miles, the caravan travelled along broad, smooth roads toward Lexington, where the start and finish of the next day's time trial was located, and where they would spend the night in actual beds instead of on cots in tents. The horselords maintained an enormous inn at the center of their capital, built among the towers that housed the city's relatively few Viewers at Home.

It had turned out that the most difficult thing to convince Michael of wasn't Maggie potentially placing herself in danger, or even his own relative lack of participation in what she planned for the next day, but instead he bucked at taking Lydia and Nicholas further into their confidence. He wasn't used to sharing secrets, not even really with Maggie. It had never mattered, because Maggie always knew what he was thinking.

"She already knows most of it," Maggie had said, and told him about the letter Lydia had showed her. "And Nicholas saw more than you did this afternoon. I really believe we can trust them. All of them."

Maggie knew that might be considered naïve, but she saw little choice. She needed to speak to her mother again, and for that she needed time alone by the river, time that could only be won by turning in a truly epic performance in the next day's time trial.

The individual time trial was the only discipline in road cycling where a rider found herself alone on the road for any significant period of time. It was not a race against the other riders, strictly speaking, but a race against the clock. The riders would leave the start house one at time, separated by two or three minutes, and ride over the same course as fast as they possibly could.

"Three minutes isn't much," Michael had said.

"It will be more than that," said Maggie. "It's a course for climbers. I'll be pulling away from the rider who starts behind me."

"What if you catch whoever starts before you before you get to the river?"

"It depends on when and where. If there's time, and I'm strong, I'll just leave her behind, too. Otherwise I'll have to stay just behind her and make sure she's out of sight up the road when I stop on the bank."

They told Lydia and Nicholas privately before dinner that night. Crowded into the room the twins had been given at the inn, the two Oklahomans met the plan with skepticism. They had asked about the camerastats, but Maggie was confident that the limited number available would be following the GC riders starting behind her. She was also convinced they wouldn't be a problem for her, not that day, since her mother had used one to talk to Michael and then there'd been the image of her on the screen.

"At the absolute most you'll have five and half minutes alone by the river before another cyclist comes by," said Nicholas. "And that's if you manage to almost catch your three-minute man on a very challenging course."

"Three-minute *woman*," said Maggie. "I'm immediately behind Mexico's road captain on the GC."

The order the riders would depart depended on their overall place in the general classification, with the last-place rider leaving first and the yellow jersey wearer last. Because of his wins, Michael was relatively high up and would start late in the day.

"Whoever it is," said Lydia, "the timing is exceedingly fine, and you'll need to ride the time trial of your life. Are you up to it?"

Maggie said, "I believe I am," at the same time Michael said, "Of course she is."

Lydia smiled. "If you had your brother's self-confidence you would be among the finest climbers in the world."

Maggie thought about that for a moment, about her confidence in herself, and realized that her director's observation was . . . inexact.

"I don't need confidence," she said. "I have faith."

Michael said, "Our father would remind us of the eldest servant of Abraham right now, of his prayer when Abraham sent him to take a wife to Isaac."

Lydia and Nicholas glanced at one another, and Lydia said, "I don't think either of us know that prayer."

"It's the one I'll pray on the start ramp tomorrow," said Maggie. "O Lord, send me good speed this day."

The Owl held his hand up in front of Maggie's face, fingers spread. He spoke in French, the traditional language of competitive road cycling.

"*Cinq,*" he said, and Maggie made a microscopic adjustment to the position of her hands on the handlebar drops.

"*Quatre,*" he said, folding his thumb across his palm. Maggie gave a shake to her thighs, nervous energy expressing.

"*Trois,*" said the Owl, holding up three fingers now, and Maggie looked again at the stage directions taped to the top tube of the twitchy, unfamiliar time-trialing bicycle the team had provided. Out of the start house and turn left, so many hundred yards and turn right, a short hill, another left, and then a lengthy rolling ride out of the city to the steeply pitched roads along the river where most of the time trial would take place.

"*Deux.*" Two fingers, and Maggie inhaled mightily, began leaning forward. She felt Lydia, who was standing directly behind her and holding her upright in the start house, begin to loosen her hold on the seat post.

"*Un,*" and there was one finger now, held parallel to the ground, directly in front of her eyes, and Maggie's heart beat three times before the Owl said, "Commencez!" and pulled his hand away, leaving her path down the ramp of the start house unobstructed.

She stood on the pedals, forcing all of her weight and strength into a down stroke on the right and pulling up slightly with her left hand to maintain her line. Lydia shouted something behind her but whatever it was lost in the roar of the crowd gathered in the plaza at the center of Lexington. Thousands of people had gathered, the most people Maggie had ever seen in one place in her life, by far, far out-numbering the crowds they'd seen at Bowling Green and Pleasant Hill.

Maggie begin building up speed, but immediately had to bleed some off for a sharp left turn around a stone pillar topped, incongru-ously, with a statue of a traveller mounted on a camel. David Bon-heur, who had gone over the course with all the riders in the morning meeting, had said it was a good sign, meant to bring luck to travelers. On she flew.

Through the grid of city streets with their towers, then out a broad boulevard lined with trees and enormous houses, building speed, always building speed, headed for the river and the sketchy descents and tor-tuous climbs the race's designers had scheduled in a clear attempt to make this the day the general classification would blow apart. Today was the day the race's real leaders would establish themselves, as sprint-ers like Michael would struggle and fall down the overall placings and time-trial specialists and climbers like Maggie and Nicholas would form a select group minutes ahead of the bulk of the riders.

That was the state of the race. That was the supposed point of the extraordinary effort Maggie found herself putting forth. That was the furthest thing from her mind.

Time. She needed to build up time ahead of the rider starting behind her and avoid coming to the river in sight of the woman ahead of her on the road. She needed time alone to break every rule her father had ever set down, to break actual laws enacted by the Com-monwealth and by the Federals. She needed time to speak to her mother, and *this* time, she would have answers.

She was doing it. She knew instinctively that she was riding well, was riding *extraordinarily* well. She could feel it in the way she carved out the turns, leaning almost recklessly into them and then standing and coming back up to speed on the straightaways. She could feel it when she sped down the narrow roads that led to the river, trusting to skills that had taken years to develop so that she could ride faster, faster down the hills than anyone else would dare. And she could espe-cially feel it in the climbs.

She had picked out her spot. She knew exactly where she would come to a stop and, while incidentally losing any chance of taking a win on the day's stage, attempt to make contact with the river woman. It was a few miles ahead. It was three more descents. It was two more climbs.

When the road turned upward, Maggie could not help but smile. She remembered what Lydia had said about her possibly being among the best climbers in the world and her own thoughts about confidence and faith, and she thought to herself that it was neither of those things that was propelling her up the hillsides at astonishing speeds. It wasn't confidence or faith or strength or skill, none of those things alone at least. More than anything, it was *glory.*

Maggie *gloried* in climbing hills on her bicycle. She gloried in the pain and the suffering that led to the joy of summiting. She gloried in excelling at something that most people, even most fellow cyclists, shuddered at even attempting.

She danced, always on the ascents, she danced on the pedals.

Maggie saw the jersey of the Mexican rider disappear around a river-bottom curve up ahead and realized that she had timed everything perfectly. The rider ahead of her would be struggling up the final climb of the day before turning back to Lexington, while the riders behind her, she was confident, were long minutes away, left behind by the finest riding Maggie had ever done.

She had no time to think about any of that, though, as she clicked out of the pedals and leaned her bicycle against a tree at the roadside. The river was a dozen yards away, and Maggie cursed at the tangle of brush and vines that choked that little distance. It would take valuable time to get to the muddy bank, time she—

A pillar of green water rose out of the river's slow running surface, refining itself into a woman who strode directly *through* the undergrowth toward Maggie.

Today, the river woman was more distinct. Maggie saw that she wore a cyclist's kit, even to the point of holding a helmet under one arm.

I watched you through the camerastats, Maggie heard in her mind. *I've turned them away from here for now.*

"You watched me race?"

You are better than I ever was. You are extraordinary.

Time.

"Thank you," said Maggie, her voice almost failing her, wanting to protest, fighting back tears, cursing time. "We only have a moment. I need you to tell me whatever it is you've been trying to tell us. Why have you risked so much for all of us to contact Michael and me?"

The river woman, her mother or some part of her mother, stretched out her hand, and again, Maggie found herself engulfed in water that somehow sustained her instead of killed her. She started to protest, but then an image came into her mind and she came as close to gasping as she could with her mouth and lungs full of water.

She saw a man.

She saw the chains trailing from his wrists and ankles as he struggled away from her, saw him stumbling, saw him gaining his feet and moving painfully slowly toward a wide brown river, the largest river Maggie had ever seen.

The man turned, but he needn't have for Maggie to recognize her father. In her mind, Maggie saw Brother Theodore Hammersmith, a prophet of the Lord, rushing to drown himself in the muddy waters of the Ohio.

Chapter Eleven

The inn in Lexington was large enough that each team had been given a private dining room. Team America's was furnished with a long low oak table, and one entire wall was a limestone fireplace set with kindled split wood but unlit this warm evening. The six riders were relaxing around the table after an enormous meal, idly listening to David Bonheur talk over the events of the day.

"Were there disappointments? Yes. Maggie, you started out much too strong and didn't manage a top ten, which we were hoping for."

The team heartily booed the Frenchman, and the usually quiet Telly even tossed a half-eaten roll at the assistant director. David raised his hands in mock defense, letting his stern visage crack into an enormous smile. "Okay, okay," he said. "I cannot think of a better day for any team at a race of this size."

Maggie looked down at the polka dot jersey she had kept by a single point over her closest rival, rewards of her fast start and grim ride home after the riverbank encounter. Beside her, Michael was resplendent in green, as there had been no change in the points competition for the sprinters. And then of course there was Nicholas, decked out now in the yellow jersey of the race leader, his by dint of winning the day's stage by just over a full minute. The race was not tracking a separate teams competition, like many races did, but Maggie knew that David had calculated the summed times for each of the squads and that if there had been such a contest, they would have been leading it as well. They were thoroughly dominating the race.

Samantha, sitting across the table from Maggie, caught her attention. "What's up with you two, anyway?" asked the tall woman. "This is your first national race and you're both in leaders jerseys, and here you sit all glum. I told Jordan I expected Michael to be down in the bar dancing with the local girls!" ·

"Or picking fights with the other sprinters, eh, Crash?" added Jordan.

Michael's smile was thin. He was obviously as distracted as Maggie by what she had told him in the scant minutes they'd managed alone in their room after the race. They hadn't had time to talk about what the vision she'd had of their father meant, or what the river woman's last obscure words meant, either—*He won't listen to me. This is coming.*

The door opened and Lydia Treekiller entered, looking distracted, worrying at some twisted bit of black in one fist. She had been at a meeting of all the team directors, planning the next day's crossing of the Licking River, the only serious challenge on the route. The room quieted, but instead of taking a seat, Lydia waved at the twins. "You two, there's a man here to see you. He's waiting for you outside your room."

Maggie and Michael exchanged worried looks, and it was obvious to Maggie that her brother had no more idea who the visitor might be than she did. But then Lydia opened her fist, revealing what she held there. A crow's feather.

When the twins made it to their room on the second floor, they found Japheth Sapp crouched in the dark hallway, back to the wall and sitting on his heels. His broad-brimmed hat was sitting on the floor beside him.

He rose in one smooth motion and nodded at them. "I understand congratulations are in order. Y'all are all the talk down at home."

"Let's go inside," said Maggie, nodding at Michael to lead the way into their room. Once inside, she and Japheth each took a seat on one of the beds, while Michael leaned against the wall beside the window.

"What's happened?" Michael asked. "Why are you here?"

Maggie started to protest her brother's rudeness, but Japheth held up a peaceable hand. "As to your first question, I've got the same one for you two. Which more or less answers your second one. I came to find out what's been found out. And to tell you a little bit of something I've learned since I last saw you."

Michael said, "This is getting ridiculous. You might as well have come with Lydia into the dining room downstairs since so many people know so much of what's happening. We might as well tell the whole team. We might as well tell that Owl who's running this race."

Japheth said, "That Owl is kin to me, as it happens, and he always knows more than what he's letting on. I'd advise you to treat him as an ally, if an unwitting one. He is no friend of the Federals and is a great enemy of Tennessee."

"What's that got to do with anything?" asked Michael.

"What it's got to do with anything, young man," replied Japheth, "is everything. The Federals and the Voluntary State are the two obstacles you'll have to overcome if you're to help rescue your father."

Maggie and Michael spoke at once, but Michael quickly quieted, deferring. "How do you know anything about that?" she asked.

"I don't, not precisely," said Japheth. "But I know that *you* know. Or I'm guessing you do, but it's an educated guess. A man came to me two nights ago, a man your father and I had placed among the Reenactors in the west to keep an eye on them. He judged it important enough to leave his post and run himself ragged over a hundred miles to find me and tell me about what happened at the Obelisk."

"The wreck?" asked Michael. "What about it?"

Maggie was more interested in learning how and why her father and Japheth Sapp had either the desire or the means to be placing spies anywhere, much less among Reenactors, but Japheth answered Michael before she could speak.

"Not the wreck. The *contact*. The latest of many attempts your mother—if that's what she is—has made to reach out to you two and to others over the last year or so."

"It's her," said Maggie quietly. "I believe that—I *know* that now."

Japheth Sapp's hard features softened a bit. "You know, I didn't. I thought your father was right, that it was an assault on him, an attack. But now I think it's her, too."

"Wait a minute," said Michael. "What others are you talking about? Who has . . . that woman contacted besides us?"

Maggie said, "Lydia Treekiller for one," and told Japheth about the letter in a few words.

Japheth reached inside his long coat and pulled out a bundle of papers tied with string.

"When these come," he said, "Mr. Pelly always brings them out to the lake himself instead of trusting them to one of his daughters, blind as he is."

Maggie reached out for the packet of letters, but Michael snatched them from Japheth's had first. He quickly scanned the top one, not bothering to untie the string, then handed them all over to Maggie. "It's her writing," he said. "But that could be faked. Anything can be faked."

Her brother often wore the cloak of cynicism. But she knew inside his faith was strong. She knew him in the way only a twin could, better than he knew himself. He wanted to believe. He was afraid to.

That she understood too.

Maggie set the bundle on the bed beside her. "What is the substance of these, Mr. Sapp?"

"Oh, there's little to surprise you in there. She mainly asks me to look after the two of you, and to give you any help you need when the time comes for you to go and rescue your father."

"Rescue him?" asked Michael. "Rescue him from what?"

"From the chains that bind him," said Maggie simply. "That's what she showed me in the vision, isn't it?"

Japheth Sapp shook his head. "You'd have to tell me what vision you're talking about."

Maggie explained, telling him about the visitations she'd had with the river woman both at Shaker's Landing and earlier that afternoon during the time trial. The only detail she left out was Nicholas's presence on the first occasion. She saw Michael staring at her curiously during her recitation.

"The Federals and the Voluntary State," said Japheth. "The chains and the Ohio River. Everything points to your father's incarceration at the internment camp near Mayfield, just upriver from where your race finishes tomorrow. He must be planning an escape. A *sort* of escape."

"Impossible," said Michael. "He would never contemplate suicide."

Maggie started to say that going into a river polluted by Athena's machines was not suicide, but Michael spoke on and over her.

"And he would never give himself up to the Voluntary State, either. He's spent our whole lives preaching against it."

"Not just preaching," said Japheth. "Working. *Working* against it. Your father is one of the deadliest enemies Athena has in the Commonwealth, for all that he refuses to work with the Federals or any other authority. That's almost certainly why they took him. He didn't lie to you, he really was headed into the mountains on a mission trip. But he had more than one mission, and I'm certain that it was his most recent successes against Tennessee that caused the Federals to finally take him. They want to know what he knows."

"Why doesn't he just tell them?" asked Maggie.

Japheth looked troubled. "I think he might have, once. Now, though . . ."

The twins looked at one another.

"What do you mean? You know something more that you're not telling us, don't you?" demanded Michael.

The older man hesitated for a moment and then said, "It's this. I've seen him. I've seen your father as recently as three days ago. From a distance, anyway."

"In the prison?" asked Maggie while Michael cursed.

"Yes. We've had it under surveillance for months now, but it took a long time for us to identify your father. He's . . . different now."

"How do you mean?" asked Maggie, putting what she hoped was a calming hand on her brother's shoulder.

"This is why I'm here. Your father is too important to our movement to lose, but all our efforts to reach him have come to nothing. We've smuggled prisoners out of that camp before, and even smuggled people *in*, but he won't listen to anyone besides the creature that the Federals have him tending."

"What kind of creature?" demanded Michael. "What do you mean he won't listen to anyone?"

"Japheth," said Maggie. "Tell it plain. And tell *all* of it."

Japheth nodded. "This encampment is a holding facility built by the Federals originally to contain and study agents and artifacts of the Voluntary State. Over time, they also started housing other prisoners there, the people they describe as rebels. Friends of your father's and mine, to be direct. There's nothing in it of rehabilitation, obviously, or even punishment, really. It's just a place to stick people, people and *things*, that trouble them."

"But something's changed," said Maggie. "Or else you wouldn't be here tonight. Else you wouldn't have flown us to Paducah in the first place."

"We believe the Federals are going to remove your father and several others from the facility tomorrow night and take them out of the Commonwealth altogether. Probably back east someplace. Someplace inaccessible to us, at any rate."

"A *creature*," growled Michael.

"Yes, I was getting to that. The Federals have captured one of Athena's larger pets and interred it in a large pit in the camp. Your father lives in a tent next to the pit and feeds the thing, spends his days shoveling coal over the side and, I think, talking to it."

"Coal?" asked Maggie, incredulous. "You mean it's a coal mole? Those things are *real?*"

"As real as the telephones or the sky bears or the Commodores themselves, yes. It's how she powers her state, sending those things wriggling along the ore lines in the mountains, eating up the coal and storing the energy in it in their bodies somehow. The Federals believe they're killed outright when they return to Tennessee. 'Harvested' is the word they use."

"But you said our father talks to this thing? They're intelligent?" asked Maggie.

"Yes. Well, for some definition of intelligence. This one, at least, speaks, though whether it developed that capacity before or after it was captured I cannot say. It's been there for years, much longer than your father has, and has had other tenders before him, though none lasted even half so long as he has at the job."

"They were transferred out?" asked Maggie.

Japheth shook his head. "From what we've been told by the other people who've been interred there, the tenders eventually, well, go mad. They either leap into the pit and are killed by the acidic mucous that coats the coal mole or they're shot attempting to climb the walls."

"It drives them crazy?" asked Michael.

"Any sustained contact with the creatures of the Voluntary State is dangerous, as you well know, Michael," said Japheth. "It's a tribute to your father's strength of mind that he's lasted this long. It's probably another reason the Federals are taking him away. To figure out how he's managed that."

"Wait," said Maggie. "You said they're taking him tomorrow. Why are you sitting here? Why don't you go and rescue him?"

"We tried, this week. He won't come with us. I'm sitting here, Maggie, because I think the only chance we have of rescuing him is if you and your brother go into the encampment and coax him out. I think you're the only people in the world who he still has any loyalty to."

Maggie didn't realize she was crying until Michael reached over and wiped tears from her cheeks with his thumb. Sometimes she wondered if he knew her better than she knew herself too.

"So he's not . . . he's not *himself* anymore?" she asked.

"I wouldn't say that," said Japheth. "Not yet. I'd say he's lost. And I think you two can help him find his way back. I think that's what your mother has been trying to get you to do."

"You think our mother—whatever she's become—wants us to be killed?" Michael said, surprisingly quietly.

"What? No, of course not—" Japheth began to say, but Michael spoke on and over him.

"But that's what you're asking of us, isn't it? You want to set up some kind of raid or something with God only knows what kind of commando squad you've put together and have Maggie and me, what? Sneak in during the confusion and bring Dad out? Bring out a crazy man guarded by some kind of giant slug from the Voluntary State? Not to mention all the Federal guards and whatever other kind of monsters out of Tennessee are roaming the grounds?"

Japheth opened his mouth, closed it, rubbed his hand over his chin, and looked down at the floor. "Well, that's a perhaps uncharitable but remarkably cogent description of what I'm asking of you, actually. But I wouldn't ask it if I thought you would be killed or captured. If your father will respond to you, then I think it will work."

"'If,'" said Maggie, and stood up. She walked over to the window and looked out on the square of central Lexington, filled with the buses and team cars and support vehicles for the great bicycle race that she'd completely forgotten about in the last few moments. "Our mother, the river woman, she said he won't listen to her either. That's why she's come to us."

"There's risk," said Japheth. "But I swear to you I wouldn't ask this if I didn't think you could get him out of there."

"How do you see this working?" asked Michael, and Maggie threw him a sharp look.

"More or less just like you said," said Japheth, turning to face him. "We'll launch a raid in force along the eastern and southern approaches to the prison camp. I'll give you the equipment you need to get over the walls from the west. You make your way to the pit and your father's tent while the guards and, probably, most of the prisoners are making for the walls, and you talk him out."

"Tomorrow night?"

Japheth shook his head. "Shortly after noon, midway through a guard shift and before the prisoner-transport boat docks outside the north wall. That usually happens around sunset this time of year."

Maggie was startled to see her brother nodding, turning the plan over in his head, coming around to being in agreement.

"What about the race?" she asked.

Both men looked at her in confusion for the barest moment, before Michael said, "That's a good point. Are the Federals maintaining watch on all this? With this many people on the move, so many of them foreigners, coming so close to their prison . . ."

"I must admit I hadn't thought of that," said Japheth. "My plan was for you two to leave with me here tonight. But maybe it makes more sense for you to take the start tomorrow, and then join us at a rendezvous point along the route. Wait, let's look at a map." He pulled one out of his voluminous coat and unrolled it across the bed where Maggie had been sitting.

"Yes," he said, pointing at a juncture forty miles south of the finish line on the Ohio. "If you turn right here while the race keeps going, you can join us . . . here," and he jabbed his finger down at another place. "How much trouble will it be for you to get away?"

Michael pursed his lips, considering. "If one of us fakes a mechanical and the other hangs back, maybe."

"'How much trouble?'" Maggie quoted Japheth. "It will only cost us everything. Everything we've worked for over most of our lives and that both of our parents would want for us."

"Maggie," said Michael, but then trailed off. This was a reversal of what either of them would have predicted of the other only days, only hours, before.

"We're talking about saving your father's life," said Japheth. "Surely that's more important than a bicycle race."

"You're talking about us risking *our* lives to save a man who may already be gone for all intents and purposes, even if he *is* sane," countered Maggie.

"You're right," said Michael. "You're right. We shouldn't do this. *We* shouldn't. I'll go alone."

It was the worst thing he could have said. It *hurt*.

Maggie walked over to the door. "When have you ever done anything alone?" she asked, and left.

Chapter Twelve

They were back on the roads of the Commonwealth of Kentucky, racing hard.

For Maggie, the last half day had passed like a fever dream, as a series of images and conversations and actions that didn't *stick*. A night's sleep, breakfast and the morning meeting, the roll-out, none of it seemed to matter now that she was where she was, in the saddle, climbing a long low hill, piloting her team's general classification leader through the peloton.

Michael was tucked in at the rear of the peloton, keeping to himself except when the race moved through a feed zone and he happened to be the one who picked up the musettes filled with sandwiches and energy drinks for distribution to the rest of the team. When he rode up alongside her to hand over her lunch, he gave Maggie an unreadable look, then drifted backward again. They were a dozen hilly miles, less than a half hour of riding, from the point Japheth Sapp had told them to split off from the race.

To *abandon.*

Maggie had often thought that word had a peculiar weight, even independent of its particular meaning in the world of bicycle racing. She remembered looking it up quite recently in the big multi-volume dictionary in her father's study at home. A verb and a noun both, abandon, though the meanings were quite different depending on the part of speech. To give up as an action, the act of giving in as a noun. *He will abandon the race with wild abandon,* she thought.

But when he *did* leave, Michael went quietly.

"Where is your brother?"

Lydia's voice crackled over the team radio, not addressing Maggie directly as she had no need to since nobody else on the team, or indeed, in the race, had a sibling present.

Not that I do either, now, thought Maggie. What if he didn't make it back? He hadn't even told her good-bye.

"Maggie?" Nicholas said. "Lydia is calling for you."

Maggie glanced over at her team leader, dressed in yellow from head to toe today, even down to the earpieces on his sunglasses.

"I heard her," she said. "I'm just trying to figure out how to answer her."

Nicholas stopped pedaling, raising a curse from the rider behind him. The whole peloton slowed, adjusting, maneuvering, in response to the GC leader's sitting up.

"What do you mean? What's happened?"

Maggie responded to Nicholas and to his aunt at the same time, reaching up to hold in the transmitter taped under her jersey. "Michael abandoned," she said.

She expected a stream of questions at the least and possibly even of invective. But the only thing that came over the radio was the crackling noise of a transmitter being thumbed on, then off.

After a moment, she heard Lydia's voice again. "Maggie, I've turned off the team broadcast. You are the only one who can hear me now. I need you to tell me, are you going to go after him?"

Maggie reminded herself of how much Lydia knew, and of how much she didn't. The woman had obviously intuited that something was up, probably something dangerous, and she was putting the facts of the twins' situation ahead of the race.

"I hadn't planned on it," she answered after a moment.

"Well," said Lydia, "make your decision soon. I still want to win this race whatever the hell your crow friend is planning on unleashing on the Federals, and if you leave, I need to adjust where the others are riding."

Maggie felt a brief surge of anger. *She's concerned about a bicycle race when so much is on the line?* Then she laughed softly to herself. *Just like I was,* she thought.

She was about to fail her team. She might be about to fail her family.

She remembered her mother's long-ago words: We have to take risks. You can't be afraid of falling. You will fall.

"You'd better signal Telly to come take my place," she said.

"Acknowledged," was the one-word response.

Maggie started to ease up her pace, moved her hands into the drops where she could reach the brakes. Nicholas was still right beside her.

"Do you want me to come with you?" he asked.

She looked over at him. He'd taken off his sunglasses and threaded them through the airvents on his helmet. His expression was unexpectedly serene, as if he'd reached a difficult decision and made peace with it.

Maggie doubted the expression was mirrored on her own face.

"I want you to win the Race Across Kentucky," she said, and began the delicate process of negotiating her way to the edge of the fast-moving peloton. The road was still rising.

Maggie coasted to a stop and watched the race leave her behind.

Then she turned, clipped back into her pedals, and rode the other way.

There was an abandoned windblown barn at the crossroads Japheth Sapp had marked as their rendezvous, and as there was no one in sight outside it, Maggie pushed her way through the hanging curtain of dead vines that covered its open door. Inside, she found Michael's bicycle leaning against one of the support posts.

The dirt floor of the barn was much disturbed, with the footprints of many boot-shod people all around, and also the distinctive crosshatched tread of one pair of cycling shoes. Shoes which Maggie found in a stall beside Michael's neatly folded cycling kit.

She wondered if her brother was now dressed as a soldier, or as one of Japheth's brother Crows. For the first time she could remember, she had no idea how Michael was doing.

There was nothing for her to change into, so when she left, riding north toward the internment camp, Maggie was still dressed as a bicycle racer.

The Ohio River was the largest body of water Maggie had ever seen. It dwarfed the Green and the Kentucky and all the other Commonwealth waterways she had helped the race negotiate over the past few days. Looking down into its floodplain from a forested hilltop, Maggie could see another state of the Union on its far shore, something else she'd never seen.

But she had little time or attention for those new things, because something else new, something terrible, took up a great swath of the territory between her and the river. A square complex, completely fenced in with high cement walls topped with barbed wire, was spread out before her.

The camp was all grays, cinder-block towers at the four corners guarding cinder-block buildings in regular rows on the inside. There was no sign of green within, not a tree or even a blade of grass visible from where she stood. Gravel covered the alleys between the buildings, except for a rectangular patch near the center, where bare earth dotted with mounds of coal gave way to an enormous pit. A pit with a tent pitched to one side. At this distance, it was impossible to make out the features of the man who stood beside the tent, but it was not impossible for Maggie to recognize his stance. It was impossible for her to not recognize her father.

He was standing with his back to the pit, looking toward the inland gate, which hung half off its hinges and was swarming with men dressed in black, battling desperately with other men dressed in gray.

Japheth Sapp's "distraction" had begun.

Where is Michael? Maggie thought desperately.

Then she realized that even if she spotted him from this distance, there would be nothing she could do to help him. So she rode on, down the hill, toward the battle at the gates.

And curved away, realizing there was no way through.

She flew along a perimeter road, taking sharp turns at high speed, the wall of the prison at her right and a tangle of underbrush at her left. She was headed north, looking for a way, *any* way, inside, when the road suddenly angled down, ending in a ramp leading into the swirling brown waters of the Ohio.

She hesitated for a moment, considered pulling both break levers, hard. But then she sped up, riding forward, faster and faster, until she plunged headlong into the water.

Everywhere we look, there's water, water.

Maggie laughed, blowing some of the soap bubbles piled high in her chubby hands into her mother's face. "Bath!" she shouted.

"Yes, bath!" said her mother, laughing too. "Or, *bañera.* Say that, little one?"

"*Bañera!*" shouted Maggie, and splashed her fists down into the warm water, causing little waves to roll out and over the lip of the cast-iron tub set beneath the poplar tree outside the kitchen door. A hen had been pecking in the dirt beside the tub and let out an indignant squawk. Maggie laughed even more when the bird flapped away.

"Time to wash your hair, now, little one. Ready to go under? Can you hold your breath?"

"Yes!" said Maggie, and ducked down even as her mother gently put one hand atop her head and guided her down beneath the surface.

And held her there.

"What's happening?"

"You are drowning. But I am going to save you."

"I'm in the river?"

"You are within me. Where you began."

"Why are you doing this?"

"To save you. So you can save him."

"Why haven't *you* saved him?"

"I tried and failed. Only you can save us all."

Maggie rose up out of the Ohio on a fountain of roiling water. It carried her upstream and onto a concrete dock extending from another gate. Tendrils of water darted out and pushed the gate open.

She looked behind to see if the river woman, her mother, was visible, but the fountain subsided as she watched, leaving her only with the echo of those last words in her mind. *Save us all?*

There was a tremendous crashing noise from the south, from the inland gate, Maggie guessed. It reminded her to hurry.

Inside the walls, concrete-block buildings—Maggie supposed they were barracks of some kind—were laid out in neat rows. Despite the calamitous noise from across the complex, there was no one in sight. Japheth's plan seemed to be working as a diversion, at least.

She thought back to her view of the complex from the hilltop, remembering the open pit near the center. *It should be just ahead.*

"Notification has been *sent.*"

The words came in an overwhelming chorus as Maggie rounded a corner, coming face-to-face with a building different than the rest. This one was nothing but a cage with a low roof, packed with dozens and dozens of dull-plumed telephones. They were jammed in so tightly that the ones on the edge were forced against the iron bars. Their glassy eyes all fixed on Maggie as they repeated their warning, losing the unison of it though, until it became an incoherent babble.

She hurried on.

And heard other words she had heard before.

Her father's voice was raised, and pitched in the sing-song cadence it always took on when he was quoting.

"'And it came to pass, that, as I made my journey, and was come nigh unto Damascus about noon, suddenly there shone from heaven a great light round about me.'"

A deep, mellifluous voice rose up from the pit her father was facing.

"At noontime, at the latitude of Damascus, would that not be the sun? Perhaps it was coming out from behind a cloud, thus accounting for the suddenness."

"Hush mole, I'm teaching."

"Daddy," Maggie said.

He turned, and took a sudden step backward, taking him danger-ously close to the edge of the pit.

If she didn't know the way he stood and moved so well, if she hadn't heard his voice, she might not have recognized him. His short red beard was now a long shock of pure white. His eyes . . . His blue eyes were the green of river water.

"Maggie!"

The shout did not come from her father, but from Michael, who was running down the gravel lane toward them, black-feathered cloak flying behind him.

"Who—" their father began, but stumbled over his own feet and went down hard on his hands and knees.

Maggie rushed toward him, reaching his side simultaneously with Michael.

"You're dead," said their father, staring up at Maggie. "You've gone to your reward."

"No!" said Michael. "This isn't your wife, this is your daughter. And she *shouldn't* be here!"

This close to the edge of the pit, Maggie nearly staggered under an overwhelming kerosene scent. An orange glow lit the bottom of the trench, but she turned away from it without looking, the wonders of the Voluntary State holding no appeal for her at the best of times. The deep voice rolled up again, though. "These are your children! She told you they would come!"

"Maggie? Michael?" said their father. He seemed bewildered, those wrong-colored eyes darting back and forth as he looked from one to the other and back again.

"We've got to get him out of here, now!" said Michael. "Japheth and the others are barely holding the gate."

Eyes the color of river water . . .

"We're too late," said Maggie, voicing the realization even as she had it.

"What? What do you mean?" asked Michael, frantic.

"The Federals, they gave him up," said Maggie. "He couldn't fight it either."

"These are the words of the Psalmist," said their father, struggling to his feet. "'Turn again our captivity, O Lord, as the streams in the south.' Notification has been *sent*."

A horrified expression came to Michael's face, though whether it was on hearing Maggie's words or their father's, Maggie could not say. For once, she had no idea how Michael felt. Only how she did.

"He's *infected?*" Michael asked.

The coal mole spoke again. "Our captors have tested him in many ways. He has sought to protect himself by constructing an exaggerated simulacrum of his own personality. He is an odd creature, now, this man. He is . . . bifurcated."

Maggie's thoughts raced. She remembered the vision of her father immersing himself in the Ohio of her imagination, and wondered if it had meant something else altogether from what she had decided it meant.

"There has to be a way to get him back," Michael said.

Maggie shook her head. "No, Michael. We can't get our father back. But we might be able to save him."

"What's that supposed to mean?" Michael said, his voice breaking.

"He just told us," Maggie said. "Didn't you, Daddy? Whether you meant to or not. There's only one way out of this captivity."

There was a loud chattering noise from the front gate, and the sounds of screams.

"Your friends will retreat soon, I think," said the coal mole.

"Come on, help me," Maggie said, taking her father by one arm and indicating that Michael should take the other. "I came in from the river gate, and there are no guards."

"How did you even get there?" asked Michael, as they hustled their father away from the pit.

"I had help," said Maggie.

When they reached the dock, the river woman was standing on the rippling surface at its end, a statue of flowing water, simultaneously in motion and unmoving.

Theodore Hammersmith, his gait grudging to begin with, came to a halt. He tore away from Maggie's hand and pointed. "Shake off that visage, demon. You are not my wife, but an apostate of hell."

Michael was staring, too, and Maggie realized this was the first time he had actually seen the river woman.

"My family," said the woman in the water. "Oh, my family."

"That's not her," said Michael, sounding his old complaint. "It can't be her."

"It's what she's become," said Maggie. "It's *who* she's become."

"A demon, like he says. Athena's creature."

"No," said Maggie. "She's escaped. And Daddy can, too."

"You want him to die?" Michael implored.

"I want him to be born again," said Maggie, and took her father's arm once more. "Daddy, that is no demon. That is Maria Galdeana, your loving wife. You have to go and be with her now."

Tears swam in his eyes, and Maggie thought for a moment that behind those tears she saw a hint of blue. But then he blinked, and they were green again.

"Is this the River Jordan?" he asked. "Have I come to the Holy Land at last?"

Maggie was crying, too. "It's the Ohio River, and Kentucky isn't the Holy Land. It's a between place, a border state, and you're going to a between place, too."

Unexpectedly, he smiled, and for a moment, despite the patriarchal beard and the lines around his wrong-colored eyes, he looked like the man who had raised them. "Neither at the right hand, nor the left, then," he said.

He walked to the edge of the dock and held out both hands. His wife took them in hers, and water flowed over him. He was lifted up.

"Will you come, too?" asked their mother.

Michael looked aghast, but Maggie only shook her head. "No," she said. "We have a race to finish."

At the barn, Maggie stood awkwardly astride Michael's bicycle and asked her brother once more, "You won't come with me?"

Michael, in his cloak of black feathers like all the other women and men in Japheth's band, smiled sadly. "I abandoned the race, Maggie. I'm going to carry on his work. You weren't the only one who had dreams . . . but mine were different. They were about crows, about *me* with the crows. No going back for me."

No going back for any of us, thought Maggie.

She clipped her shoes onto the pedals and stood up, balanced for a moment like a track racer waiting for the start gun. Poised at the end of something, or the beginning.

Michael waved his hand back and forth, mimicking the motion of a race director signaling that the stage had begun. And, though it hurt to leave him, she rode away.

Her radio had apparently shorted out when she was immersed in the river, or else it had been so long since everyone else finished that there was nothing being broadcast, either on the general race channel or the team's.

She passed no stragglers on the road. No spectators lined the route. No camerastats buzzed around her. She had no idea what sort of welcome would await her, if the team would even allow her to return. But when she crossed the finish line, one race official was still stationed there to mark her time.

His voice muffled by his owl helmet, the race director said, "Congratulations. You have done remarkably well."

Maggie said, "I finished last."

The owl shrugged. "You finished. Lydia and your teammates will be very glad to see you." He pointed toward the team busses.

Maggie started to ride that way, but then hesitated. "Did Nicholas win?" she asked.

"Win?" asked the owl. "Oh. The bicycle race. Yes." He turned away.

Lydia Treekiller stood up from the camp chair outside the bus where she'd obviously been waiting. There were raucous sounds coming from all the team's encampments, but none of the parties were louder than the one Team America was apparently throwing.

"We started without you," said Lydia.

"You finished without me, too," said Maggie.

"No," said Lydia. "The team isn't finished until the last one of us crosses the line. Are we finished now or is Michael still coming in?" She looked down at the machine Maggie had just dismounted. "On your bicycle, for some reason?"

"No," said Maggie. "Michael has gone home." Wherever that was for him, now. "I suppose I'll be heading home myself."

The thought of her well-loved house, it wasn't the comfort she expected. How could it feel like home, with only her and her memories to live in it?

Lydia shook her head. "No time for that, I'm afraid. I just got word from the UCI. We've been selected to participate in a race in Spain and we have to leave first thing in the morning."

Maggie said, "I thought . . ." But choked on the next word.

"I'm looking forward to see how you do on those climbs in the Pyrenees," said Lydia. "Now those are a place to prove yourself a Queen of the Mountains."

Maggie didn't know what to say.

"Come on," said Lydia. "Let's get some champagne."

So they left Michael's bicycle there, leaning against the side of the bus, and went to join the rest of the team.

These are the ways that Maggie came to love the world.

Maggie loved bicycles, those extraordinary conveyances that turned her effort and her will into speed and motion. She loved the way they looked, the elegance and strength of their lines, and as much as she loved racing them, she loved them more for themselves. Maggie was not a philosopher, but if one had told her she loved bicycles because they were democratic machines, she would not have disagreed.

And oh, how Maggie loved mountains. The high passes and cols of Europe became her usual workplace, yes, but there were mountain roads to climb in Colorado, where she came to make her home, and in Colombia and the other Andean states of South America where she loved to train at altitude. Once, years after she had retired, then come out of retirement to race again, and then took Lydia's place leading Team America, she even rode in a dirigible over the ice-cloaked mountains of Antarctica, and though she never rode up them, she loved those mountains, too.

Maggie loved her team, changing as it was, because Maggie came to be a great lover of people of purpose and good will. She found, as she grew older, that her antogonists were rarely her enemies, and was thankful that she lived a life where that was possible.

Maggie loved her brother, oh, how fiercely she loved him, though she rarely heard from him and even more rarely saw him once he took up with Japheth Sapp and the band of people who did everything they could to protect the very world they were rebelling against. Wherever she went, and she went many places, she carried a crow's feather.

And though she never again received a telephone call from the Voluntary State, or a letter from beyond the grave, or even a mysterious dream, Maggie loved the rivers of the Bluegrass. "Everwhere we look there's water, water," she would sing when she went there.

And every time the waters ran clear.

Publication History

"The Contrary Gardener," *Eclipse Online*, October 2012.

"Another Word For Map is Faith," *The Magazine of Fantasy & Science Fiction*, August 2006.

"The Jack of Coins," tor.com, May 2013.

"The Unveiling," *Asimov's Science Fiction*, January 2015.

"Nowhere Fast," *Steampunk! An Anthology of Fantastically Rich and Strange Stories*, 2011.

"Two Figures in a Landscape Between Storms," *Twenty Epics*, 2006.

"Gather," *The Del Rey Book of Science Fiction & Fantasy*, 2008.

"The Force Acting on the Displaced Body," *Trampoline*, 2003.

"The Voluntary State," *SciFiction*, May 2004.

"The Border State" is published here for the first time.

Acknowledgments

The stories in this book were all developed and improved by their original editors, to whom I owe a great debt. They are Ellen Datlow, Gavin J. Grant, Susan Marie Groppi, Kelly Link, David Moles, Jonathan Strahan, Gordon Van Gelder, and Sheila Williams. Gavin and Kelly also edited this collection as a whole, and published it, for which I offer thanks.

As a writer, and as a person, I have benefited enormously from my association with several workshops. I first learned to take myself seriously as an artist and to think carefully about the crafting of stories at the Clarion West Workshop in Seattle in 1996. I completed my formal training as a writer under the tutelage of Derek Nikitas at the Bluegrass Writers Studio of Eastern Kentucky University. Most of all, though, I here acknowledge the sincere thanks I owe to those many colleagues who read and critiqued most of these stories at the annual Sycamore Hill Writers Workshop, now guided by my best unbeaten brother, Richard Butner.

Finally, all who read these stories should know that almost none of them would have been even begun, much less been finished and published, if it weren't for the essential, indispensable contributions to my art and to my life made by my wife, Gwenda Bond. Whatever I have accomplished as a storyteller in the 21st century, I could not, would not, have done without her.

About the Author

Christopher Rowe has published a couple of dozen short stories, and been a finalist for the Hugo, Nebula, World Fantasy, and Theodore Sturgeon Awards. His work has been frequently reprinted, translated into a half-dozen languages around the world, praised by the *New York Times Book Review*, and long-listed in the *Best American Short Stories*. He holds an MFA from the Bluegrass Writer's Studio. Christopher and his wife Gwenda Bond co-write the Supernormal Sleuthing Series for children, and reside in a hundred-year-old house in Lexington, Kentucky.